STRANGE ANGELS

Lili St. Crow was born in New Mexico and fell in love with writing when she was ten years old. She now lives in Vancouver, Washington, with her husband, three children and a hous[illegible] *trange Angels* is her first YA novel.

LILI ST. CROW

Quercus

First published in 2009 by the Penguin Group
Penguin Young Readers Group
345 Hudson Street, New York, New York 10014, USA

First published in Great Britain in 2009 by

Quercus
21 Bloomsbury Square
London
WC1A 2NS

A CIP catalogue reference for this book is available from the British Library

ISBN 978 1 84916 125 1

10 9 8 7 6 5 4 3 2 1

Printed and bound in Great Britain by Clays Ltd, St Ives plc.

For Gates, who caught the line when I threw it.

A *fronte praecipitium, a tergo lupi.*

PROLOGUE

I didn't tell Dad about Granmama's white owl. I know I should have.

There's that space between sleep and dreaming where things—not quite dreams, not fully fledged precognition, but weird little blends of both—sometimes get in. Your eyes open, slow and dreamy, when the sense of *someone looking* rises through the cotton-wool fog of being warm and tired.

That's when I saw it.

The owl ruffled itself up on my windowsill drenched in moonglow, each pale feather sharp and clear under icy light. I hadn't bothered to pull the cheap blinds down or hang up the curtains. Why bother, when we—Dad and me—only spend a few months in any town?

I blinked at the yellow-eyed bird. Instead of the comfort that means Gran is thinking about me—and don't ask how I know the dead think of the living; I've seen too much *not* to know—I felt a sharp annoyance, like a glass splinter under the surface of my brain.

The owl's beak was black, and its feathers had ghostly spots like cobwebs, shadows against snowy down. It stared into my sleepy eyes for what seemed like eternity, ruffling just a bit, puffing up the way Gran always used to when she thought anyone was messing with me.

Not again. Go away.

It usually only showed up when something interesting or really foul was about to happen. Dad had never seen it, or at least I didn't think so. But he could tell when I had, and it would make him reach for a weapon until I managed to open my mouth and say whether we were going to meet an old friend—or find ourselves in deep shit.

The night Gran died the owl had sat inside the window while she took her last few shallow, sipping breaths, but I don't think the nurses or the doctor saw it. They would have said something. By that point I knew enough to keep my mouth shut, at least. I just sat there and held Gran's hand until she drained away; then I sat in the hall while they did things to her empty body and wheeled it off. I curled up inside myself when the doctor or the social worker tried to talk to me, and just kept repeating that my dad would know, that he was on his way—even though I had no clue *where* he was, really. He'd been gone a good three months, off ridding the world of nasty things while I watched Gran slide downhill.

Of course, that morning Dad showed up, haggard and unshaven, his shoulder bandaged and his face bruised. He had all the ID, signed all the papers, and answered all the questions. Everything turned out okay, but sometimes I dream about that night, wondering if I'm going to get left behind again in some fluorescent-lit corridor smelling of Lysol and cold pain.

I don't like thinking about that. I settled further into the pillow, watching the owl's fluffing, each feather edged with cold moonlight.

My eyes drifted closed. Warm darkness swallowed me, and when the alarm clock went off it was morning, weak winter sunshine spilling through the window and making a square on the brown carpet. I'd thrashed out of the covers and was about to freeze my ass off. Dad hadn't turned the heater up.

It took a good twenty minutes in the shower before I felt anything *close* to awake. *Or* human. By the time I stamped down the stairs, I was already pissed off and getting worse. My favorite jeans weren't clean and I had a zit the size of Mount Pinatubo on my temple under a hank of dishwater brown hair. I opted for a gray T-shirt and a red hoodie, a pair of combat boots and no makeup.

Why bother, right? I wasn't going to be here long enough for anyone to care.

My bag smacked the floor. Last night's dishes still crouched in the sink. Dad was at the kitchen table, his shoulders hunched over the tray as he loaded clips, each bullet making a little clicking sound. "Hi, sweetheart."

I snorted, snagging the orange juice and opening the carton, taking a long cold draft. I wiped my mouth and belched musically.

"Ladylike." His bloodshot blue eyes didn't rise from the clip, and I knew what that meant.

"Going out tonight?" That's what I said. What I meant was, *without me?*

Click. Click. He set the full clip aside and started on the next. The bullets glinted, silver-coated. He must have been up all night with that, making them and loading them. "I won't be in for dinner. Order a pizza or something."

Which meant he was going somewhere more-dangerous, not just kinda-dangerous. And that he didn't need me to zero the target. So he must've gotten some kind of intel. He'd been gone every night this week, always reappearing in time for dinner smelling of cigarette smoke and danger. In other towns he'd mostly take me with him; people either didn't care about a teenage girl drinking a Coke in a bar, or we went places where Dad was reasonably sure he could stop any trouble with an ice-cold military stare or a drawled word.

But in this town he hadn't taken me anywhere. So if he'd gotten intel, it was on his own.

How? Probably the old-fashioned way. He likes that better, I guess. "I could come along."

"Dru." Just the one word, a warning in his tone. Mom's silver locket glittered at his throat, winking in the morning light.

"You might need me. I can carry the ammo." *And tell you when something invisible's in the corner, looking at you.* I heard the stubborn whine in my voice and belched again to cover it, a nice sonorous one that all but rattled the window looking out onto the scrubby backyard with its dilapidated swing set. There was a box of dishes sitting in front of the cabinets next to the stove; I suppressed the urge to kick at it. Mom's cookie jar—the one shaped like a fat grinning black-and-white cow—was next to the sink, the first thing unpacked in every new house. I always put it in the bathroom box with the toilet paper and shampoo; that's always the last in and first one out.

I've gotten kind of used to packing and unpacking, you could say. And trying to find toilet paper after a thirty-six-hour drive is no fun.

"Not this time, Dru." He looked up at me, though, the bristles of his cropped hair glittering blond under fluorescent light. "I'll be home late. Don't wait up."

I was about to protest, but his mouth had turned into a thin, hard line and the bottle sitting on the table warned me. Jim Beam. It had been almost full last night when I went to bed, and the dregs of amber liquid in it glowed warmer than his hair. Dad was pale blond, almost a towhead, even if his stubble was brown and gold.

I've got a washed-out version of Mom's curls and a better copy of Dad's blue eyes. The rest of me, I guess, is up for grabs. Except maybe Gran's nose, but she could have just been trying to make me feel better. I'm no prize. Most girls go through a gawky stage, but I'm beginning to think mine will be a lifelong thing.

It doesn't bother me too much. Better to be strong than pretty and useless. I'll take a plain girl with her head screwed on right over a cheerleader any day.

So I just leaned down and scooped up my messenger bag, the strap scraping against my fingerless wool gloves. They're scratchy but they're warm, and if you slip small stuff under the cuff, it's damn near invisible. "Okay."

"You should have some breakfast." *Click*. Another bullet slid into the clip. His eyes dropped back down to it, like it was the most important thing in the world.

Eat something? When he was about to go out and deal with bad news alone? Was he *kidding*?

My stomach turned over hard. "I'll miss the bus. Do you want some eggs?"

I don't know why I offered. He liked them sunny-side up, but neither Mom or me could ever get them done right. I've been breaking yolks all my life, even when he tried to teach me the right way to gently jiggle with a spatula to get them out of the pan. Mom would just laugh on Sunday mornings and tell him scrambled or over-hard was what he was going to get, and he'd come up behind her and put his arms around her waist and nuzzle her long, curling chestnut hair. I would always yell, *Ewwww! No kissing!*

And they would both laugh.

That was Before. A thousand years ago. When I was little.

Dad shook his head a little. "No thanks, kiddo. You have money?"

I spotted his billfold on the counter and scooped it up. "I'm taking twenty."

"Take another twenty, just in case." *Click. Click.* "How's school going?"

Just fine, Dad. Just freaking dandy. Two weeks in a new town is enough to make me all sorts of friends. "Okay."

I took two twenties out of his billfold, rubbing the plastic sleeve over Mom's picture with my thumb like I always did. There was a shiny space on the sleeve right over her wide, bright smile. Her chestnut hair was as wildly curly as mine, but pulled back into a loose ponytail, blonde-streaked ringlets falling into her heart-shaped face. She was beautiful. You could see why Dad fell for her in that picture. You could almost smell her perfume.

"Just okay?" *Click.*

"It's fine. It's stupid. Same old stuff." I toed the linoleum and set his billfold down. "I'm going."

Click. He didn't look up. "Okay. I love you." He was wearing his Marines sweatshirt and the pair of blue sweats he always worked out in, with the hole in the knee. I stared at the top of his head while he finished the clip, set it aside, and picked up a fresh one. I could almost feel the noise of each bullet being slid home in my own fingers.

My throat had turned to stone. "'Kay. Whatever. Bye." *Don't get killed.* I stamped out of the kitchen and down the hall, one of the stacked boxes barking me in the shin. I still hadn't unpacked the living room yet. Why bother? I'd just have to box it all up in another couple months.

I slammed the front door, too, and pulled my hood up, shoving my hair back. I hadn't bothered with much beyond dragging a comb through it. Mom's curls had been loose pretty ringlets, but mine were pure frizz. The Midwest podunk humidity made it worse; it was a wet blanket of cold that immediately turned my breath into a white cloud and nipped at my elbows and knees.

The rental was on a long, ruler-straight block of similar houses, all dozing under watery sunlight managing to fight its way through overcast. The air tasted like iron and I shivered. We'd been in Florida before this, always sticky, sweaty, sultry heat against the skin like oil. We'd cleared out four poltergeists in Pensacola and a haunting apparition of a woman even Dad could see in some dead-end town north of Miami, and there was a creepy woman with cottonmouths and copperheads in glass cages who sold Dad the silver he needed to take care of something else. I hadn't had to go to school there—we were so busy staying mobile, moving from one hotel to the next, so whatever Dad needed the silver for couldn't get a lock on us.

Now it was the Dakotas, and snow up to our knees. Great.

Our yard was the only one with weeds and tall grass. We had a picket fence, too, but the paint was flaking and peeling off and parts of it were missing, like a gap-toothed smile. Still, the porch was sturdy and the house was even sturdier. Dad didn't believe in renting crappy bungalows. He said it was a bad way to raise a kid.

I walked away with my head down and my hands stuffed in my pockets.

I never saw Dad alive again.

CHAPTER 1

"Miss Anderson?" Mrs. Bletchley's voice droned through my name.

I'd propped my cheek on my fist and was staring out the window at the cold wasteland of a baseball field, waiting for the chimes to sound. Foley High School didn't believe in bells. Instead, a sound like a cell phone ringing would echo through the room when it was time to go run on the treadmill in another classroom.

The pencil in my hand rested against blank paper, and I brought my gaze around slowly, sudden silence in the room meaning all eyes were on me.

I hate that.

Bletchley was round-faced, white-haired, and plump. The other teachers probably thought she was a kind, harmless soul. She had small dark hazel eyes behind steel-rimmed glasses and carnelian lipstick feathering off the edge of her lips. Her hands, when they weren't clasping a yardstick like a cane, were constantly picking at the bottom edge of her lumpy cardigan. She alternated between three sweaters: primrose, blue with knitted roses, and a bilious yellow one with a Peter Pan collar. Today it was the yellow.

She looked like a weasel getting ready to steal its next chicken. The kids called her Mad Dog behind her back, and she could smell weakness.

There are two species of teacher—the soft and the hard. Soft teachers might genuinely want to help, or they might have been broken in. They're usually nervous and afraid of kids, especially high school boys. The hard teachers are another thing entirely. They're like sharks—machines made for eating, with a finely tuned sense for blood in the water.

"Were we *paying attention*, Miss Anderson?" You could have stropped a knife on Bletchley's tone. A tide of whispers ran through the room. Bletch had picked her target for the next thirty minutes, and it was me.

I just *love* being the new girl.

I really shouldn't have even opened my mouth. Hard teachers are like bullies. If you don't react, pretty soon they think you're stupid and they leave you alone.

The half-Asian goth kid in front of me shifted in his seat. He was tall and skinny, with a mop of wavy dark hair. The back of his neck was visible as he bent down in his seat, the collar of the black coat he never took off sticking up at the corners but folded down in back. I stared at his nape under the dark curls.

What the hell, might as well. "Fort Sumter," I said.

Silence. Bletchley's eyes narrowed behind her steel-rimmed glasses, and I'd opened my mouth. So I jumped in with both feet.

"You asked where the first shots of the Civil War were fired. It was Fort Sumter. April 12 to April 13 of 1861." I delivered the words in a flat, bored monotone, and the whispers turned into the particular type of silent laughter a hard teacher hates most.

Who knew sophomore American History could be so fun?

Bletch eyed me for a moment. I wasn't quite a known quantity yet, so I might actually get away with it. The goth kid in front of me squirmed again in his seat, making it creak.

The teacher visibly decided to pick on someone else, with a look that promised me trouble later. "Thank you, Miss Anderson." Her pause lengthened as she tapped meditatively on the desk with her yardstick. Her ankles were swelling out of her oxfords, despite the heavy dark nylon socks she wore under a long waddling denim skirt. They looked like circulation socks—the kind they give diabetics.

Gran used to wear those when her ankles pained her. My skin chilled as I slumped in the hard plastic seat, not daring to look out the window again. Bletch might just as easily circle back to me. I hadn't told Dad about the owl on my windowsill. Was he still home?

The unsteady, sinking feeling in my stomach got worse. I stared at the boy's neck in front of me, but he shifted again, tugging at the corners of his collar with nervous fingers.

Don't move, I wanted to whisper. *She's looking for her next victim.* If I'd been all there in the classroom instead of worrying about Dad, I might have done something like smacking him on the back of the head to save him, since I didn't give a good goddamn if I was sent to the office or signed up for detention or whatever.

The axe fell. "Mr. Graves." Bletch's eyes lit up.

The kid in front of me stiffened, his shoulders going tense.

Blood in the water. I tried not to feel guilty.

"I certainly hope you're taking notes. Since Miss Anderson has answered the question about the *start*, perhaps you can tell us about the *causes* of the Civil War?" Her eyebrows went up, and the predatory gleam in her eyes reminded me of cottonmouths in glass aquariums, staring lidless before they opened their mouths and made that awful ratcheting sound. The thumps of snakes hitting the glass echoed in my head, along with the smell of red beans and rice, body odor, and incense.

We were a long way away from Florida. The proprietor of that little occult store had given me the genuine willies, what with her filmy eyes and the shifting mass of stuff trailing behind her—a cloud of disturbance regular people wouldn't see, but would feel like a cold draft. She'd given me a long, measuring look before Dad snapped his fingers and informed her that she was talking to *him*, thank you very much, ma'am.

I should have told him about the owl. The sudden certainty was chilling, and my fingers turned numb, prickling with cold.

"Um. Causes of the Civil War. Uhhh . . ." The kid in front of me stumbled, and Bletch had him. She spent the rest of the class period picking on him, even though he eventually came up with the right answers—when she let him get a word in edgewise. By the time the chimes rang for the end of the round, even the back of his neck was red. I felt bad about it, but I didn't let it slow me down.

The halls were the usual crush, jocks snapping like sharks, cheerleaders simpering, and the rest of us just trying to get by. A contingent of stoners clustered around a locker, and I'm sure I saw a brown paper bag change hands. I glanced back—nope, no teachers in sight. A girl from art class looked right past my tentative wave and swished away, her backpack sagging dispiritedly from one shoulder.

I hate being the new girl.

The cafeteria was a surf-roar of noise and the smell of floor wax and industrial food. I had some change for the bank of pay phones between the caf and Death Alley leading down to the office, so I plugged it in and dialed the number written in my Yoda notebook—the last in a string of similar numbers scrawled in pencil or blue pen. The phone had been on when we moved in, listed under the last tenant's name, and it was easier just paying the bill for a while. I couldn't be expected to memorize every goddamn phone number. Or at least, that's what I'd told Dad when he ragged me for having them written down.

He told me to watch my mouth and stopped bugging me about it. Domestic harmony, thy name is Anderson.

The handset rang in my ear. Once. Three times. Five.

He wasn't home, or he was working out, not picking up. I thought about skipping the rest of the day, but he'd be pissed off and I'd just get another lecture about the value of education. If I dared to point out that education wasn't everything and high school wouldn't teach me how to exorcise a room or put down a zombie, I'd just get *another* lecture about how I was supposed to be normal.

Just because he hunted things out of fairy tales didn't mean I had any right to skip school. Oh no. Even if he was pretty blind without me, since only the maternal side of his family was the one gifted with what Gran always called "the touch."

Some touch. I haven't figured out if it meant "crazy" or just "spooky." The jury, you could say, is still out on that one.

Dad never seemed sad or unhappy about missing out on the woo-woo train. Then again, Gran never did stand for much of what she called "moping," and I couldn't imagine her being any different when Dad was a kid. Weird as it is to think about him being gawky and adolescent—but I've seen the pictures.

Gran was big on pictures.

I hung up after fifteen rings and stood staring at the phone, chewing on a hangnail. It hurt like hell, and there was a healing scrape on my left-hand knuckles from the heavy bag. Other girls don't have fathers who yell at them to work through the pain, to hit harder, to *get in there and kill it kill it kill it!* Other girls never filled thermoses with holy water or handed ammo through a window while their fathers held off skittering things like giant mutant cockroaches. That had been Baton Rouge, and that had been *bad*. I'd had to drive Dad to the hospital and lie about how he got the chunk taken out of his calf.

Sometimes it was hard to tell where the lying to the normal world ended and the bullshit posturing necessary in the Real World began. There's so much paramilitary hanging out under the edge of the Real World that the macho bull snorting reaches epic proportions.

The phone just kept ringing.

"Screw it," I said under my breath, under the surf-roar of noise echoing from the cafeteria. I didn't even get my fifty cents back; the machine ate it.

For a second I stood there, just looking at the phone like it might suddenly give me a good idea. It smelled like damp wool and wet concrete in here, as well as formaldehyde carpet and the exhalation of two thousand kids. Not to mention sweaty stocking feet and food pried from underneath Ronald McDonald's bumpers. School smell. It's the same pretty much everywhere in the U.S., with only slight regional differences in the foot-sweat and served-roadkill departments.

The crowd noise from the caf hurt my ears and made my head ache like one of Mom's migraines. I was hungry, but the thought of going in there and elbowing through the line, then finding a place to sit where I wouldn't be required to look at anyone or share a table with some jackass kids just seemed like too much hassle.

If I went home and Dad was there, I'd get The Lecture. If I

went home and he *wasn't* there, I'd just wait and worry. If I went through geometry and art class this afternoon I'd go bazonko nuts, even though art class was generally the most enjoyable part of the day. And forget about the waste of time they called "civics class." I'd seen more real-life civics on afternoon CNN. That is, if you define *civics* as "blowhards with expensive hair."

None of these classes taught you anything *real*. I'd rather be with Dad on stakeout or doing what he called "intel runs"—going to occult shops or bars, places where people who knew about the Real World, the dark world, got together and spoke in whispers between shots.

Like the tea shop where Dad's old buddy August hangs out in New York, where you step up to get into the bar's dark gloom—and you step up *again* to get out. Or the bar in Seattle where the proprietor has tusks growing out of his lower jaw and a warty broad face that looks like something that lives under a bridge and eats goats. Or the nightclub in Pensacola where all the flashing strobes of light look like screaming faces when they hit the floor. And that country store out on a back road near Port Arthur, where the woman sitting in her rocker on the front porch will have what you need in a paper bag sitting right next to her, while the dust streaks and twinkles on the window, even at night. There are places like that all over—where you can buy things that shouldn't or don't strictly exist.

If you're willing to pay. Sometimes in money. Most times in *information*. And other times in something less tangible. Favors. Memories.

Even souls.

Maybe I could do some recon of my own, find Dad a good place to plug in. The watering holes for the Real World are hidden from the normal world, but they always stick out like a sore thumb to me. I think it's because Gran always had me play "what's on the table"—

that game where you shut your eyes and try to remember everything she'd set out for lunch or dinner, canning or quilting.

That sounded better than putting up with the same bullshit everyone my age has to put up with. So I turned and went the other way, toward the doors that would lead out to the soccer fields and baseball diamond. I could cut across the fields and maybe slip out through the greenbelt—Foley was one of those schools with an open campus, a rarity anymore. I had that extra twenty, enough to sit in a café or coffee shop where nobody would bother me before I put on my serious face and started following the tickle of intuition.

The cold outside was like a slap to already-stinging cheeks. It still smelled like iron, the way a penny tastes when you suck on it. I walked with my head down, my boots crunching frozen weeds, my nose immediately running.

What a choice. Skip school and freeze your ass off, or go back inside the building where it's warm and get bored literally to death.

"Hey! Hey, you!"

I ignored the voice, swiping at my nose with the sleeve of my sweatshirt jacket. Footsteps crunched behind me. I didn't hunch my shoulders—that's a dead giveaway that you've heard someone. If it was a teacher, I was going to have to come up with a reason why I was out here, and I began to think about exercising my creative lying muscle.

They should have a class for that. Who would teach it? I wonder if it would grade on a curve.

"Hey! Anderson!" The voice was too young to belong to a teacher. And it was male.

Shit. Just my luck. The bullies don't usually mess with me, but you never know. I set my heel down in the gravel and whirled, my head coming up and my hair falling in my eyes despite being mostly stuffed under my hood.

It was the half-Asian goth kid from American History class.

He was too tall, and the long black coat flapped as he skidded to a stop. He'd pushed his collar up again, and the cold made his cheeks and nose cherry red under his mop of dyed-black hair. He wheezed for a second, his narrow chest heaving under a Black Sabbath T-shirt, and peered at me through strings of hair. His eyes were an odd pale green, but his hair managed to keep them from doing more than peeping out every once in a while. In a few years he'd probably be a real looker, with those contrasting eyes and the thick wavy dark hair.

Right now, though, he was in that funny in-between stage where every part of a guy's body looks like it was pulled out of a different parts catalog. Poor kid.

I waited. Finally, he got his breath back. "You want a cigarette?"

"No." *Jesus, no.* He had the type of baby face most guys would curse at in the mirror, at war with its own nose and cheekbones. The kind of face some half-breeds get stuck with if they don't draw the pretty card. It made him look about twelve, except he was so *tall*. The hair was maybe an attempt to look like he really was "sixteen, honest." He had nice boots, steel-toed combat numbers laced up to his knees. To top it all off, an inverted crucifix dangled from a silver chain, against his bony sternum.

I backed up another step and took another look at him. Nope. Nothing of the Real World on this kid. I didn't *think* so, but it's better to check. Better to check twice and be relieved than only check once and get your ass blown off, Dad says.

Dad. Is he gone already? It's still daylight, he's probably okay. I didn't like the way my chest was getting tight.

The kid dug in a pocket and fished out a crumpled pack of Winstons, the corners of his eyes crinkling. At least he hadn't drawn the really slit-eyed card a lot of half-breeds have to play, where they look like they're squinting to beat Clint Eastwood the whole time. "You want one?" he asked again.

What the hell? I stared at the crucifix. Did he have any idea what that *meant?* Or how quickly it could get him in a lot of trouble, in some places?

Probably not. That's why the Real World is the Real World: because the normal world thinks it's the only game going.

"No thanks." *I want a cup of coffee and a club sandwich. I want to sit down someplace and draw. I want to find some place where the sunlight doesn't get in and I don't feel like a total alien. Leave me the hell alone. I should have told Dad about the owl.* My conscience pricked me. "Sorry about Bletchley."

He shrugged, a quick birdlike movement. All of him was birdlike, from his beak of a nose at war with his caramel-skinned baby face to the restless way his fingers moved. He tapped a cigarette out of the pack and produced a silver Zippo, lit the cancer stick, exhaled a cloud of smoke, and promptly went into a coughing fit.

Jesus. Here I was freezing my ass off with Cool Goth Boy. Some days were so much worse than others it wasn't funny. "It's okay," he said when he could talk again. "She's a bitch. She does that all the time."

Glad to know I didn't interrupt anything. I stood there with no real idea of what to say. I settled for a shrug of my own. "See you."

"Are you skipping?" He fell into step beside me, ignoring the fact that I was *walking away*. "Off to a good start."

Leave me alone. "I don't want to deal with it today."

"Okay. I know a place to go. You shoot pool?" He managed not to choke himself on another drag of cigarette smoke. "I'm Graves."

When did I invite you along? "I know." I looked back down at my boots, marking off time. "Dru." *And don't you dare ask what it's short for.*

"Dru." He repeated it. "You're new. Couple of weeks, right? Welcome to Foley."

State the goddamn obvious and bring out your suburban Welcome Wagon. I couldn't see any way to ditch him just yet, so I just made a noise of assent. We crossed the soccer field in weird tandem, him shortening his stride out of respect for my lack of grasshopper legs. I sized him up as we walked. I'd give myself better odds in a fight, I decided. He didn't look very tough.

Still, I was walking into the woods with a kid I didn't know. I stole quick little glances at his hands and decided he might be okay. At least I could kick his ass if he tried anything, and the greenbelt wasn't very big.

He tried again. "Where you from?"

A planet far, far away. Where nightmares are real. "Florida." The question always came up, sooner or later. Sometimes, mostly when I was younger, I lied. Most of the time I just pretended like I'd always lived in the last place we'd come from.

People don't really want to know anything about you. They just want you to fit into their little predetermined slots. They decide what you are in the first two seconds, and they only get nervous or upset if you don't live up to their snap judgments. That's one way the normal world's like the Real—it all depends on what people *think* you are. Figure that out, play to what they expect, and it's clear sailing.

"Yeah, you sounded a bit down-South. Big change for you, huh? It's going to snow." He announced it like I should be grateful to him for telling me. The strap of my bag dug into my shoulder.

I tried not to bristle. *I do not sound Southern. I sound like Gran a little bit, but that's all.* "Thanks for the warning." I didn't bother disguising the sarcasm.

"Hey, no problem. First one's free."

When I glanced up at him, he was smiling under his hair. It almost threatened to eat his nose, that hair. The proud, bony nose was putting up a good fight, though, and he looked miserably cold. He didn't even have any gloves.

For a second I toyed with the idea of telling him something. *Hi. I'm Dru Anderson. My father went way-out wack after my mom died and now he travels around hunting things that go bump in the night, killing things you only find in fairy tales and ghost stories. I help him out when I can, but most of the time I'm deadweight, even though I can tell you where anything inhuman in this town is likely to hang out. I'm skipping school because I won't be here in another three months. None of it goddamn well matters.*

Instead, I found myself almost smiling back. "You should wear some gloves."

He peered at me, shaking his hair away. His eyes turned out to be green with threads of brown and gold, thickly fringed with dark lashes, change-color eyes. Boys always get the best eyelashes; it's like some kind of cosmic law. And half-breed kids get some kind of extra help there from genetics, too. Once he grew into that nose and his face thinned out a bit, the girls would like him a lot. Maybe it would even go to his head.

"Ruins the image," he said. Silver glittered in his left ear, an earring I couldn't quite make out.

"You'll goddamn well freeze to death." We reached the end of the soccer field and he took the lead, going to the right along a dusty footpath. Bare branches interlaced above us, and the dry smell of fallen leaves tickled my nose with dust. The brick pile of the school behind us would soon be out of sight, and that made me happier than I'd been all day.

Graves snorted, tossed his hair back as he took another drag. The smoke hung in a feathered shape for a moment as he exhaled, but I blinked to clear my eyes. "Hey, we've got to suffer for beauty. Chicks don't go for guys with gloves."

I'll bet chicks don't go for you at all, out here in Stepford Podunk. "How would you know?" I stepped over a tree root, my bag bumping my hip.

"I know." He shot me a look over his shoulder, his hair almost swallowing his grin, too. "You never said if you liked shooting pool."

"I don't." I felt a little guilty again. He was trying to be nice. There was one in every school—some guy who thought his chances were better with new girls. "But I'll beat your ass at it, okay?"

I decided I could wait to find the local paranormal hangout. Dad would probably give me another version of The Lecture if I went looking for it alone. There was that one time in Dallas when he found me trading shots of Coke with a pointy-eared goggle-eyed gremlin and about had a cow—

"Fine." He didn't even sound insulted. "If you can, *Dru*."

I thought about telling him Dad had taught me to shoot pool when we were low on cash, and decided not to. Maybe if I embarrassed the kid he'd leave me alone.

CHAPTER 2

I got home a little after five, riding the jolting, bumping bus all the way from downtown. Graves had wanted me to hang around and shoot a few more games, but the place—an all-ages pool club with a jukebox and indoor basketball and tennis courts—was loud and full of funky smells, as well as being jammed with kids who should have been in school themselves. So I bailed and had to figure out the bus. I'm used to figuring out the public transportation in just about any part of America, and this place actually had a good system.

Dad's truck was gone, but he'd left the light on in the kitchen and a fifty-dollar bill next to a note. *Don't wait up. Order pizza. Homework before TV, kiddo, and do your katas. Love you. Dad.*

Other dads actually sat at the dinner table. Mine left me a fifty and a reminder to do my goddamn katas.

I was cold anyway, so I dropped my bag in the kitchen and bashed my way out into the garage, the big broken-spring door rattling as the wind teased at it. The heavy bag creaked, swaying a little, but I shucked my coat and shivered in the middle of the concrete floor instead.

Dad liked karate, and he was big enough that it was a good choice for him. But I'm built rangy, like my mom, except she had nice chestworks and a pretty curve to her hips. I'm just angles except for the breasticles, which are more trouble than they're worth, especially when it comes to boys. I don't have the kind of muscle mass you need to meet a punch with direct force.

So for me, it's tai chi and what Dad called "The Basic Dirty-Fightin'" when he was sober and "Six Great Ways to Bounce an Asshole" when he'd had a few Beams. I like tai chi—I like the slow way each movement flows into the next and the breathing smooths everything out. It's still hard work, because your knees always have to be a little unlocked, and after a while it really murders your quads and hamstrings, but it's nice.

Push-pull. Part the horse's mane. Catch the swallow's tail. Warmed up and loosened, and feeling a little better, I finally inhaled and exhaled, as close to at peace as I guess you can ever get. The outside world rushed in as soon as I opened my eyes, and I began worrying about Dad again before I even opened the door to the kitchen and stamped through, making a lot of noise I really didn't have to.

It's the only way to fill up an empty house.

I dug through the fridge and eventually settled on a bowl of Cheerios. I'd scarfed a greasy slice of pizza at the pool hall, and the thought of more half-cardboard cheese didn't appeal to me, even with pepperoni. So I wolfed the cereal, spiked a glass of Coke with some of Dad's Jim Beam, and wandered up to my room to lie on the bed and look at the light on the ceiling. Every room is different, and the way outside light reflects up onto the spackle stuff smeared on most ceilings is unique. I could probably describe pretty much every place we've ever lived in terms of ceiling light.

The worst part about Dad being out on hunting runs was the way whatever house we were in got really creepy around dusk. Night is when most of the stuff in the Real World comes out to play—and by *play* you can mean "have a little fun," "go grocery shopping because sunlight burns like acid," or "make unwary people disappear, yum yum." Take your pick.

I pulled Mom's red-and-white quilt around me, snug as a bug in a rug, and sipped at the Coke until my taste buds burned off a little—I'd made it about half and half, and began to get a warm glow after a while. My clock blinked its little red eyes, and darkness gathered deeper and deeper in the corners. The wind made the glassed-in screen door on the enclosed back porch rattle.

When we lived in apartments, I would play the game of listening to the sounds in the building as everyone came home, and imagining stories for all of them. Most apartment buildings aren't quiet if you're really listening. After a while the noises begin to seem like family, and you catch the rhythm of each separate life in your building working together to make the melody called home. One place we lived, the guy next door played the cello after dinner every night. That was nice to listen to, even if the *other* guy down the hall beat his wife once a month when rent came due.

Houses are different. They creak to themselves, muttering, when night comes around. An empty house around dusk starts to talk, no matter how newly built it is. I used to play music to cover it up, but after a while the thought that I wouldn't be able to hear if anything was sneaking around the hallways got to me.

When you can see apparitions and poltergeists in living, solid color, that sort of thinking usually does start getting to you.

So I mostly listened and waited on nights when Dad was "out." Night gets kind of strange when you're waiting for someone to come home. I've seen shit on TV you wouldn't believe, stuff that only happens when you're alone and nobody can verify the sighting. Once Dad found me curled up on the floor of the mobile home we were renting in Byronville, clutching a baseball bat and sound asleep while a *Twilight Zone* rerun blared out of the television. I'd eaten a TV dinner and my hair had gotten into the empty tray. After that he made me promise to go to bed and not wait up, but that just meant that I fell asleep sitting up in bed and thinking about all the ways things could go wrong.

Things can go very, very wrong. They go wrong all the time in the normal world, and the Real World just means they go wrong with teeth and claws, quicker than your average bear. August called it "the Situation." Dad called it "gone south." Juan-Raoul de la Hoya-Smith called it "*mala* goddamn *suerte, chingada.*"

I didn't know what Dad was after this time. He hadn't said anything on the way from Florida. That was a little unusual—normally he had me looking through the boxes of old leather-bound books he picked up here and there, searching for odd bits of information. Or helping him make bullets and sharpen the knives, bouncing ideas off me or quizzing me on tactics. I'm probably the only sixteen-year-old girl in a three-hundred-mile radius who knows how to distinguish a poltergeist from an actual ghost (hint: If you can disrupt it with nitric acid, or if it throws new crap at you every time, it's a poltergeist), or how to tell if a medium's real or faking it (poke 'em with a true-iron needle). I know the six signs of a good occult store (Number One is the proprietor bolts the door before talking about Real Business) and the four things you never do when you're in a bar with other people who know about the darker side of the world (don't look weak). I know how to access public information and talk my way around clerks in courthouses (a smile and the right clothing work wonders). I also know how to hack into newspaper files, police reports, and some kinds of government databases (primary rule: Don't get caught. Duh).

Hey, even if you've got great intuition you can't just walk up to people and ask them about the resident exorcist or the last unsolved murder that was committed during the new moon. You *also* can't ask them about the haunted houses that serve as nodes or the local werwulfen hangout—where the burgers aren't just rare, they're raw. And served in big bloody piles.

Sometimes you have to go digging to find the pattern behind events that to other people just look like random bad luck.

Get information and you'll find a pattern, Gran said. *Find the pattern and you have your prey,* Dad said.

He also said, *Don't let the backwoods woo-woo take the place of logic.* He said that a lot.

I wondered where he was and took another gulp of Coke and Beam. My CD player was across the room, the concrete-block-and-plywood bookcase empty except for my clothes. There was another pile of clothes and my CD case in front of the closet, and other than my mattresses and the nightstand, that was about it. The lap of luxury at Casa Anderson. I'd stopped putting up posters or hauling my books upstairs. It wasn't worth it and Dad didn't care as long as the laundry got done. To my everlasting relief, he'd also stopped with the starch a few years back. The military made him big on spray starch, but I point-blank refused to touch the stuff after a while. He finally gave up doing it himself, and I manfully restrained myself from pointing out that the world didn't explode when he did.

And they say maturity is just for adults.

The house was empty. It started talking, groans and squeaks as the wind outside rose. Everywhere you go, the air changes around dusk. Sometimes it's soft and sweet, or whistling just enough to make you feel happy to be inside and snuggled up.

When something bad is coming, it's different. Like a moan, only with big glass teeth.

Tonight the wind had that sound. I hoped Dad would be home soon. Once I finished my drink I fished in my bag for a pencil and paper and started to draw. The long curved lines turned into a frilly iris, one of Gran's favorite flowers. I got into it, shading the different textures of the petals, imagining the colors—vibrant purple, snowy white, the green of the stem. I'd drawn a lot of irises, especially after Mom died and Gran got me paper and a pencil to keep me busy while she worked in her cabin.

When I think of right after Mom died and Dad disappeared for the first time, the smell of paper and the sound of Gran scrubbing something—she was always cleaning—mixes together with the feeling of a pencil in my hand. She was always washing the floors with hawthorn water or wiping down the windows, in between the other tons of work that had to happen to keep the cabin running right. Like collecting eggs or feeding the pigs or splitting wood. I still can't pass a house without looking for the best place to put a woodpile, and I always spin the eggs once clockwise on the counter before breaking them.

Somehow she found time to keep the place clean as a whistle and rinsed down with all sorts of floor and window washes—hawthorn, mountain ash, true rowan, sometimes yarrow or lavender. Bundles of wild garlic and onions strung up everywhere, and Gran working on her spinning wheel late at night, the thump and whirr getting into my chest as I cried myself to sleep, missing Dad, wanting my mommy, terrified and lonely and not understanding.

What does a five-year-old understand about "dead"? Or "forever"? Or even about "be back in a while"?

Full night fell. The clock blinked on and on. I got up to go to the bathroom a couple times, taking the quilt with me. Once I went downstairs for another Coke and Beam. Dad would give me another Lecture—probably the one about Responsible Choices and Adulthood, and how I wasn't close to either yet—if he ever guessed I drank while he was out. But since he put the stuff away at a pretty steady rate himself, I don't think he ever twigged.

I went on to drawing simple shapes—the lamp on my nightstand, the bookshelves, the closet doors. Then I sketched the pile of laundry in front of the closet, taking care to shade everything just so. The clock kept blinking. I finished the second glass of Jimmy Beam lightly misted with Coke and fell asleep with the pencil still in my fingers, a jagged line sliding down the pad of paper in my lap, opened to a fresh page.

When I woke up in the morning, Dad still wasn't there.

INTERMEZZO

He walked down *a long corridor, picking his way carefully in booted feet. The concrete was crazed with broken lines and slick with fat rivulets and lakes of something best not to name; he stepped over them like a kid stepping over sidewalk cracks, break your mother's back.*

A buzzing had started in my head. I wanted to open my mouth, tell him not to go down that hall, that Something Invisible was looking at him. But the hall was so long, and it was so hard to think through the hornets in my head. They were having a fine old time building condos inside my skull, and the buzzing spread through my bones as if I'd stepped on a live wire.

I didn't use to have these buzzing dreams often. Lately they've been once a month or so, usually just before I start my period, cramps and weird sleeping going hand in hand. But this one wasn't the usual buzzing dream, where I am flying over rooftops, or even the worst dream of all that ends with me in close darkness, surrounded by stuffed animals.

No. This dream was hyper-colored. I could see every hair on his head, the fine lines of lavender in his blue irises, the nap of his favorite green Army jacket, every line and crease on his polished combat boots. The gun gleamed dully in his hand, held loosely, professionally.

There were fluorescent lights overhead, their buzz echoing the idiot noise in my head. That's why I couldn't speak, you know—that sound just destroys anything you might say, like static on the television screen will eat whatever you're thinking for hours at a time. You can just sit and stare. Like some brain-sucking thing has, well, sucked your brain.

Time slowed down, getting all stretchy and elastic. Each step took a century, and by the time the door came into view—just a plain steel door, with those fluorescents noising overhead—the hornets weren't just crawling through my bones and brain but touching my skin with fleshy little prickling feet.

There was something behind that door, something that smelled of iron and cold darkness, a freezing shiver up the spine. It was like the feeling I got in that broken-down house on the outskirts of Chattanooga, my first job with Dad, right before a poltergeist started throwing little shards of glass hard enough to bury them in rotten drywall with little sounds like puckering lips.

Or like that small podunk in South Carolina where the local voodoo king sent the zombies around because Dad was cutting into his business by breaking the hexes the king had been throwing at people who got in his way—or who wouldn't give him what he wanted. I'd had to use every scrap of anti-hexing Gran taught me and a few things from our books to break through some of those old, nasty curses, and Dad had lost some serious blood fighting off the zombies. That had been bad.

This feeling was worse. Much, much worse.

Don't go in there, *I wanted to say.* There's something in there. Don't do it.

He walked down the hall, and the buzzing got so bad it shook everything out of me, the dream running like colored ink on wet paper, and as it receded I struggled to say something, anything, to warn him.

He didn't even look up. He just kept walking toward that door, and the dream closed down like a camera lens, darkness eating through its edges.

I was still trying to scream when Dad reached out his free hand slowly, like a sleepwalker, and turned the knob. And the darkness behind it laughed and laughed and laughed. . . .

CHAPTER 3

I came awake all at once, with a jolt like five shots of espresso hitting my bloodstream at full speed. The pencil had snapped in my fist, and I was clutching the two broken pieces. My head felt like a bowling ball being cracked by a giant's fingers, and I moaned and blinked. Gray light coming in through the window was empty, sterile, and infinite.

The house was a still, cold cave.

I pushed myself up, head throbbing and ribs aching. I'd fallen asleep and slid over to the side, my back against the wall and my artist's pad digging into my stomach. I rubbed what felt like a half-ton of sand out of my eyes and listened for the heater, for the sound of breathing, for the creaks of Dad moving around.

Nothing. And my alarm clock was turned off. I vaguely remembered something noisy happening earlier and me fumbling for it, almost spearing my palm with the broken pencil.

I rolled up out of my mattresses and shuffled barefoot into the hall. The quilt wrapped around my shoulders wouldn't keep me warm enough. I made my way down to the other bedroom at the end of the hall, the one next to the stairs.

The door was open but the blinds were down. I peered in. Dad's cot was there, and his metal footlocker. A wooden box sat by the door, Dad's private box; I didn't lift the lid. The cot was neatly made, and I thought it hadn't been slept in. You could always bounce a quarter off Dad's cot, though, even five minutes after he got up.

No problem. He's downstairs; he fell asleep over the table again. Or he's in the living room with the TV on mute, bandaging himself up. Go down and look. You'll see. He's there.

My heart knew otherwise. It pounded inside my ribcage, each pulse accompanied by a sick squeeze of pain inside my skull and a flip-flop of my stomach. I made it down the stairs like an old woman, holding on to the icy banister.

Silence like the heavy quilt wrapped around my shoulders.

There were boxes in the living room, and my orange beanbag chair. Dad's camping chair sat at its usual precise angle to the television. The red eye of the cable box blinked, and I could almost hear it flicking on and off, it was so quiet.

Dad wasn't in the kitchen. Dirty dishes still piled in the sink, and the house was *cold*. I shuffled out into the hall and punched the buttons to turn the heater on.

The heat pump soughed into life with a *wump*. It was so loud in the stillness I jumped, pulling Mom's sunrise quilt closer around my shoulders. Then I walked slow dream–like down the hall and to the front door, unlocking both deadbolts and yanking it open.

The cold hit me like a hammer, stinging my eyes and robbing the breath from my lungs. The front yard lay under a sheet of white, bits of the broken picket fence buried under mounds of heavy wet snow. The driveway was a pristine carpet.

Dad's truck was nowhere in sight. The entire neighborhood dozed under its cold, thick blanket.

I think that's when I knew. I shut the door, locked both deadbolts, and went up the stairs at a stumbling run, my head pounding and my entire body jolted by each footstep. I banged down the hall and into the bathroom, where I slammed the door and started heaving over the toilet. I didn't produce anything but bile, even though I retched so hard tears squirted hot out of my burning eyes. I stopped long enough to cry, my forehead against the cool white porcelain of the toilet, and then I had to pee so bad I nearly wet myself. While I was sitting on the toilet I had to retch again, so I bent over and tried my best to swallow whatever came up.

I don't know how long it lasted. By the time it was over I could only think about one thing at a time.

He might come back, I told myself. *What if he got stuck in the snow? It happens. He got stuck somewhere. Or something.*

Except there wasn't enough snow for him to get stuck in. The truck was heavy, and it had chains in a box under the passenger's seat. Dad was too cautious to let something like weather get in the way of an operation. Or in the way of coming back to get me.

Then he called and you missed it because you were passed out.

That couldn't be it either. He wouldn't call; he would just come home. If he got fatigued or the mission went sideways, he would come and collect me and we'd blow town. It had happened before. Since he'd picked me up from the hospital when Gran died, he'd always come back for me. It was like sunrise, or the tide.

So something's happened to him.

I rested my forehead on my knees, staring at my jeans rucked around my ankles. My underwear was white cotton, startling against the dark blue denim.

The practical part of me that got the laundry done and kept track of the boxes spoke up, in its calm, cool whisper. *Did you hear me, Dru? Something's happened to him.*

"I know," I whispered. It was the only sound other than the heater's sighing. My heartbeat and my whisper were loud as thunder. My mouth tasted foul.

So something's happened to him. Maybe he'll come home.

Maybe he would. The best thing to do was wait. I was *supposed* to wait for him. If it had gone sideways, he would come get me and we'd pack and leave town ASAP. It was standard operating procedure. The old SOP, to be done ASAP, all CYA and BYOB. All the little paramilitary letters lined up in a row, a private language none of the kids at school had to know.

What if he doesn't? Answer me that, Dru. What if he doesn't?

That was what I was trying not to think. He'd always come home before, sometimes at dawn. He'd *never* been completely gone overnight, or left in the morning without leaving me a note. He called to check in. It was just what he did.

My forehead was fever-hot. So were my cheeks. My hair hung down in curling strings, dark brown with threads of gold, darker and stringier than Mom's. I felt greasy all over, and the zit on my temple hurt along with the rest of me. My stomach rumbled. I was hungry.

I decided to get up. I couldn't crouch on the toilet forever. Dad would come home; he *would*. I'd wait for him.

In the meantime, I'd take a shower. I'd clean up the house so I had something to do, and so when he came home he wouldn't have to look at a mess. That would make everything all right. He might be wounded or tired when he came home, so I'd get out the first aid kit and make sure everything was ready for whatever had happened to him.

Yeah. Do that, Dru. That'll make everything just about okay. Just ducky.

I wiped and stood up, stepped out of my jeans and panties, and dragged Mom's quilt back into my bedroom. I grabbed fresh clothes and went back to the bathroom to clean myself up.

First a shower, then I'd clean up the kitchen. After that, the living room. I'd get out the first aid kit and restock it.

Yeah. That was what I'd do.

So I did it.

CHAPTER 4

It started snowing again late in the afternoon, big wet spinning flakes from a sky like smooth-beaten iron. I went outside to look at the driveway, shivering in Dad's green Army sweater. I didn't have much in the way of winter clothes; pretty much all my wardrobe was summer stuff since we'd spent so much time below the Mason-Dixon. We'd been down south for at least two years, between the Carolinas, Baton Rouge, Chattanooga, Atlanta, and Florida. If I tanned at all instead of burning, I might have looked even weirder up here with the goddamn polar bears.

I tilted my head back and looked up into infinity. Snow whirled out of the half-darkness, each flake bigger than a quarter and very wet. They stuck to my hair, still damp from the shower. Dad's sweater was way too big for me, and I had the cuffs turned down so they covered my fists, clenching and releasing. I had to take a deep breath to uncurl my hands before I trudged back inside.

I'd already done three loads of laundry and cleaned up the kitchen. The heater was going; it was nice and warm. I was organizing the boxes in the living room, unpacking some and arranging things. I'd already gone through some of the ammo cache and organized the clips according to the guns they were for. Dad would be oiling the rifles soon—it was about that time of the month. Taking care of your gear is essential, especially when you're after things that may or may not be able to mess with complex machinery and electronics. That's why Dad didn't carry a cell phone, they were like magnets for poltergeists and other things.

I tried not to think about it.

My stomach growled and I felt weird, like my head was full of rushing noise. I drank four glasses of tap water through the afternoon, sucking them down in between whatever I was doing, and that helped with everything except the roaring tornado between my ears.

Snowy light came through the windows; the blinds were pulled up. I could see a stretch of the front yard and the clogged street. Some cars had struggled by during the afternoon, none of them fishtailing, all of them wearing snow chains and rattling into their own driveways down the street.

None of them was Dad. I checked every time I heard the clattercrunch of chains or the sound of an engine. They all trundled past to their warm garages, ignoring our lonely house out at the end of the lane. Dad had picked this house because it was solid, but also because it stood apart from the others—which is more of a rarity than you'd think in the Midwest, since they have all that prairie space to shut out.

I was on my knees putting the last clips in the box when I heard something tapping in the kitchen.

Tip-tap. Tip-tap. Taptaptap.

My skin chilled, gooseflesh rising hard and fast on my arms. My head jerked up, hair falling in my eyes. It wasn't frizzing today, for once. Go figure—the day I stay home from school I have good hair.

What the hell is that? It wasn't the screen door on the enclosed porch back there rattling; I already knew that sound.

The gooseflesh didn't go away, little nuggets of ice under my skin.

Tap. Tap. Like little rubber-covered sticks drumming hard against a windowpane. My mouth had gone dry and my fingers were numb. Then I got the taste of oranges and salt in my mouth, and I knew something bad was about to happen. Gran called it an "arrah"; it was only later I found out she meant "aura." Like before a migraine, or the envelope of light Gran always said you could see around people if you had enough of the touch.

With me it was always oranges, and salt. Not real oranges, either. I can't explain it better—it's like wax oranges, maybe.

Oh shit. Shit.

The strangest thing of all was how calm I was. The light was failing—even if snow bounced back streetlight shine, it was getting darker. I always expect creepiness around dusk, and I had the howlin' heebie-jeebies anyway.

I got up, my legs turning to wood and shaking like an earthquake had hit. Then I scooped Dad's spare bowie knife off the top of a half-unpacked box. The living room looked like a bomb had hit it; I realized I'd just been unpacking half a box and wandering on to the next. The taste of oranges got stronger, and the tapping came again, a creaking, scratching sound, like small nails against a window.

I held the knife the way Dad taught me, flat along the forearm with the hilt clasped in my hand. That way you can hit someone in the face with the pommel and you can get your triceps and lats—some of the stronger muscles in your body, especially if you do triceps dips or lat pulldowns—into the action. And if you slash up you have your biceps getting busy too, plus you can keep better control of the knife.

Go quiet, Dru. It was Dad's voice in my head, now. A soft whisper, like he was teaching me how to concentrate on a target. *Go quiet and take cover on that side of the hall. It's coming from the kitchen. Do it like I taught you.*

I edged down the hall, cursing the boxes set along the side I should have been taking cover against. The kitchen light was on, sending a rectangle of golden glow into the hall and covering the foot of the stairs. The heater clicked off, and the tapping sped up.

Taptaptaptap. Pause. *Taptaptap. Taptap.*

My heart lodged in my throat, a chunk of beating meat. The big muscles in my thighs trembled like I'd just finished running a hard mile and a half. I slid slow and easy down the hall, little bits of the kitchen coming into view.

The thing they don't tell you about in situations like these—and by "they" I mean horror movies, which are generally better training for this sort of thing than you'd think—is how your field of vision constricts, everything getting narrower and narrower. You can't see enough, and peripheral vision plays tricks on you. The eyes flick around frantically, trying to take everything in and failing miserably. I stepped in front of the stairs and saw the sink, the stove, a slice of the kitchen table.

The window over the sink was empty, full of snowlight. I let out a soft breath through my mouth, as quiet as possible. My heart pounded in my ears like a drum solo in a pair of headphones. The taste of wax oranges got stronger, turned thick and cloying. Rotting in my mouth.

Tap. Taptaptaptaptap. The tattoo of skritching sounds grew stronger, almost frantic.

I stepped into the kitchen.

The back door was set to one side of the counters, Dad's chair at the table with its back to the wall holding the pantry. When he sat down he could see the back door and the entry to the hall, keeping his back to the safest quadrant. The door itself was a prosaic little number, a latticed glass window on top and a flimsy wooden panel with a deadbolt and a chain probably stronger than the door itself on bottom.

My gorge rose hot and thick, fighting with my heart for control of my throat. I choked and almost dropped the knife. I could see it clearly through the squares of double-paned glass, darkening because the enclosed porch was getting dim and dark, light bleeding out of the sky as the snow whirled down.

There was a zombie at my back door. Its eyes swung up, and they were blue, the whites already clouding with the egg rot of death. Its jaw was a mess of meat and frozen blood; something had eaten half its face. Its fingertips, already worn down to bony nubs, scraped against the window. Flesh hung in strips from its hand, and my stomach turned over *hard.* Black mist rose at the corners of my vision, and the funny rushing sound in my head sounded like a jet plane taking off.

I'd know that zombie anywhere. Even if he was dead and mangled, his eyes were the same. Blue as winter ice, fringed with pale lashes.

The zombie's gaze locked with mine. It cocked its head like it had just heard a faraway noise.

I let out a dry barking sound and my back hit the wall next to the hallway, smacking my hip against a stack of boxes.

Dad bunched up his rotting fist, the meat chewed away from fingerbones by something I didn't want to imagine or even *think* about, and punched his way through the window.

CHAPTER 5

I would have stood there forever, staring in dreamy terror at the thing that used to be my father as it battered itself against the back door—if it hadn't been for the phone. It rang shrilly under the sound of snapping wood, and something about that garbled screech jolted me into action. I screamed, a high, girly cry of fear, and dropped the knife. The chime of it hitting linoleum was lost in the groaning noise of breakage as the zombie forced its way through the back door, staring at me. Zombies do that—if something catches their attention they turn blindly toward it and don't stop until they've torn it to bits.

Unless, of course, whoever *made* the zombie had given it a target. Then they don't pay much attention to anything except shambling around in the darkest corners they can find, instinctively avoiding notice as they work their way toward their objective. Not too smart, zombies—but they're determined. *Way* determined.

I should know, I'd watched Dad kill more than a few. Zombies are like cockroaches—you never see them until there's too many of them, and they hang on hard to whatever semblance of life bad contamination or dark magic's given them.

I scrambled back into the hall and bolted for the living room. Each step took a lifetime. My boots slipped on the carpet; I banged into a box and screamed again, diving around the corner and into the living room as the zombie let out a weird bellow. They don't talk, the reanimated. Instead, they let out a whistling groaning noise like a cow in terrible pain, air forced through dead frozen vocal cords. Usually when someone hears that sound, it's the *last* thing they hear, because zombies are eerily quick when they have their next snack in sight.

That's another thing about them. You can bring something resembling life back to a dead body once the soul's gone, sure. But whatever you stick in there always ends up *hungry*.

The nine-millimeter was under the arm of Dad's camp chair in a Velcro holster. I hit the ground hard and scrabbled for it, moving too fast to bother scrambling upright, my feet tangling over each other as I heard light shuffling footsteps and the crunch of broken glass. The zombie blundered into the hall and I heard a god-awful racket—it must have tripped over a box.

My fingers were the size of sausages and clumsy, too. I ripped the cold metal of the gun out of the holster, Velcro tearing free and the chair spinning as I shoved it away. I rolled over onto my back, hearing Dad's voice in my head again.

Easy there, sweetheart. Don't point that thing at anything you don't intend to kill. Always treat a gun like it's loaded.

I *hoped* it was loaded. I knew it *probably* was—Dad wouldn't have a piece on his camp chair if it wasn't. I've been shooting since I was nine and even Gran had a gun in her house and I knew gun safety, didn't I? It was why I was Dad's helper. I knew the right way to handle a firearm and the wrong way, too, and the thing blundered around the corner, fixing me with its terrible rotting eyes that were now unholy, glowing blue. A spark of red revolved far back in the pupils, and I *smelled it*.

Zombies smell worse than anything you can imagine if you haven't been hunting things on the dark side of the world. It's a ripe, gassy odor, like rotting eggs and meat gone bad, crawling blind with maggots. It's roadkill and decayed food and body odor all rolled into one package and tied up with puke.

I screamed again, but all that came out was a whistling sound, because my throat had locked up. I pointed the gun and pulled the trigger.

Click.

Oh shit.

The safety was on. The thing lunged for me, its atonal bellow rolling free of its throat again—

—and it *fell*.

Take the goddamn safety off. I scrabbled with the gun as the zombie splatted onto the carpet. It was covered in snow, wet and running with rot, and it wore Dad's favorite green Army-surplus coat. It had tripped over a box partly blocking the entrance to the living room.

My breath sounded harsh as a crow's caw as the safety clicked off. I lay on my back and pointed the gun.

Dad's eyes met mine. The zombie scrambled to its bare, rotting feet—his *shoes* were gone, where were his boots?—and stretched out its hands, bits of flesh falling and plopping on the carpet. The stink roiled through my nose, filled my head, and I retched as I pulled the trigger.

The first bullet went wide, blowing out part of the living-room wall. I was still screaming and dry-sobbing as the zombie ratcheted forward, falling toward me, its teeth snicking together as its ruined jaw ground shut again and again, practicing the chewing motion that would eat its prey alive. I kept pulling the trigger.

I didn't even hear the shots, though they must have been deafening. All I heard was my own sobs.

It fell on me. Slime splashed and black blood splatted on my face. It burned like acid. It was cold like the snow outside, and it *stank*. Its jaws clicked twice, it shuddered, and a gout of something black and disgusting smashed out of its mouth.

I was still screaming. Couldn't get enough breath, so I was making a high, whining sound. The gun clicked. I was pulling the trigger, but I'd emptied the clip.

The zombie was truly dead. There was a hole in its chest, nicely grouped shots. You have to damage the heart or the thing keeps coming. It's something about the process of making a zombie, the meaning of the heart keeping the whole body going—or so the books say. But I hadn't been thinking about the books. I'd been blindly following training, aiming for the bodyshot like he had taught me.

Don't aim for the head if you've got a choice. Don't pull. Squeeze the trigger, sweetheart. Dad's voice, in my head. With the never-ending refrain repeated so many times, I could have said it in my sleep: *Don't point that thing at something you don't intend to kill.*

I thrashed wildly, smashing the thing on the head with the gun, hammering on it and struggling free of deadweight. Still making that high, whining sound, I crawled fast as I could across the living room until I reached the corner farthest away from the zombie. My left hand got rug burn. My right was full of the empty gun.

I put my back in the corner and heard myself babbling. Weak, incoherent sounds bounced off the empty white walls. I was cold and covered in stinking, burning goo.

The zombie lay facedown. Runnels of filth caved through its rotting skin. The smell was *unbelievable*. It wore Dad's jacket and Dad's jeans. Once you've taken the heart out, a zombie rots real quick. Even the skeleton decomposes into dust.

I started to cry.

The babbling turned into one word, over and over again.

"Daddy? Daddy? *Daddy?*"

He just lay there.

The zombie just lay there.

CHAPTER 6

The mall was open because the snowplows had come out. The main drags were clean and clear. They took winter seriously around here and had everything salted, sanded, scraped, and plowed to within an inch of its life. The buses were still running, too.

Life doesn't stop out on the prairies for a little snow. Canned Muzak still has to play, after all, and if they closed the malls, who would play it?

I stared at the small McDonald's cup. It was full of coffee that had been steaming hot and now just kind of sat there. My eyes burned, full of sand. I'd scrubbed the zombie rot off my skin and thrown some clothes on, shoved all the cash I could find—Dad's billfold was gone, probably tucked into the truck somewhere or, more likely, taken—into my messenger bag and hightailed it out of the house, stopping only to turn the heat off, for some weird reason. The back door was shattered and the smell was incredible, thick as Crisco in the nose.

Did anyone hear the shots? I didn't think so—there had been no sirens, and our house was a pariah, set apart like it had a disease. We heard nothing from our neighbors, and that was the way Dad liked it. The snow would muffle everything, too.

If it had killed me, nobody would even know I was dead. I'd be lying there, and . . .

My brain stopped working, stalled like a choked engine. I shuddered, the plastic chair squeaking. The mall was as brightly lit as Heaven and people were wandering around, shopping like there wasn't a decomposing zombie in my living room. Down on the lower level of the food court a fountain splashed, water rilling musically down squares of Art Deco concrete and sculpted, welded steel.

The Styrofoam cup was a white circle with a brown ellipse inside it, a conical, textured shape. I could draw it. My pad was in my bag, shoved in there with hysterical haste like everything else.

Drawing sounded good, except I couldn't do it with my hands shaking so bad. I shivered again. I couldn't have told you what I was wearing, only that I'd changed clothes after scrubbing the zombie goo off me.

I shot him. I shot Daddy.

I kept bumping up against the memory—Dad's blue eyes with their rotting whites fixed on me, a crimson spark dancing in the depths of the clouded pupil, no longer perfectly circular but fringing at the edges as the tissue died. The gun jolting against my hands. The *smell.*

I realized I was making the sound again, a low whining at the back of my throat under the fountain's wet splishing, and killed it. I couldn't afford to have someone look too closely at me.

I'd just killed my dad.

Hello, Officer? Can you help me? My dad got turned into a

zombie. You know, we've been traveling around getting rid of things that aren't real, and this time they hit back. I really need someplace to stay—but can you make sure I have some holy water or something wherever it is? And some silver-jacketed bullets? That'd be sweet. Yeah, that'd be totally cool. Thanks. And while you're at it, can you tell the guys with the straitjackets that I'm really sane? That would help.

The coffee trembled inside the cup as I touched its rim with two fingers. Soon the mall would start closing down. It was a weeknight. Where would I go? I couldn't get a hotel room with the ID I had on me, unless I tried the bad part of town, and that would cost more cash than I wanted to spend right at the moment. Speaking of cash, I needed to find a way to get more if I ran out, and—

I couldn't even think about planning that far ahead.

I shot my daddy. Jesus Christ, I shot my dad. Tears rose hot and thick in my throat. The awful scratching sound at the back window turned into someone pulling the cheap plastic chair opposite me away from the table and dropping down into it, grinning at me through a mop of curly dark hair.

"*There* you are. Skipping two days in a row. Someone call the cops." Graves set an Orange Julius cup on the table—I'd chosen a place with my back to a wall, jumping nervously anytime someone walked behind me on their way to the restrooms. It was the spot with the best sight lines, and someone had put a fake potted plant behind my chair. Awful kind of them.

I stared at Goth Boy instead of the coffee cup now. The silver earring in his left ear was a dangling skull and crossbones. The faint satisfaction I felt at finally getting a clear look at it was drowned in the panic rising in my throat, thumping behind my heart.

He shook dyed, dead-black hair out of his eyes. They were more green than hazel now, cradled in the slightest of epicanthic folds, and the even caramel of his skin was something to hate him for.

"Hey." The grin faded, spilled out of his face. Today he wore a Kiss T-shirt and the usual black coat, and when he put his long hands on the table I saw he was wearing fingerless black gloves. The inverted crucifix winked at me from its silver chain, and my gorge rose again, pointlessly. "Are you okay?"

I almost laughed. I was *not* okay. I was not anywhere near okay. I was about as far away from okay as it was possible to get. My eyes swiveled back down to the coffee cup.

"Jesus. What happened?" He leaned forward, putting his elbows on the table. I almost flinched.

Don't get too close to me. I just shot my dad.

"Hey. Dru. *Hey*." He snapped his long brown fingers. "Hello. Sitting right here. What happened?"

Oh Christ. The lump in my throat went down, after a short wrestling match. I swallowed convulsively twice and found my voice, weak and watery but still mine. "Fuck off."

His eyebrows shot up. He had actually scraped his hair back behind his ears with both hands, and now he looked very young as he stared back at me. His mouth thinned out, and I thought he was actually going to get up and walk away.

Then he settled back in his chair, arranging his long, gawky limbs as best he could, and picked up his cup. He took a long slurp of whatever was in it, and his eyes turned even more greeny-gold. They caught the fluorescent light and glowed at me.

Graves just sat there like he had all the time in the world.

I finally picked up my coffee cup. It seemed like the thing to do. The crap inside it was ice-cold, but it tasted better than the remainder of the zombie's smell in my mouth. I took a gulp, set the cup down, and grimaced. My face wrinkled up, and I almost spewed cold ash-tasting coffee sludge across the table.

He didn't move.

I listened to the soft strains of canned Muzak, trying to place the song. It was hopeless. Some pop anthem strangled by the gods of commerce. The words curdled in my chest. I couldn't tell anyone what had happened.

Who would believe me? That's why it's the Real World, the night world, and not the normal world. People don't want to know—and the things that eat people or grow fur or tell the future don't *want* people to know. It's a perfect marriage, complete with lies.

Pressure mounted in my throat. I had to say *something*. I leaned forward, resting my elbows on the table too. "I can't go home tonight." The hitch in my voice almost turned into a sob.

His eyebrows drew together. He was perilously close to unibrow; I guess nobody had held him down and administered a good plucking to the caterpillar climbing across his forehead. His earring winked at me.

Graves took another slurp. The unibrow wriggled. Then he pushed the cup away. His knuckles were chapped, I saw. I guess chicks didn't dig hand lotion either, in his book.

"Okay," he said quietly. "Do you have a place to stay?"

I blinked at him. *Oh, no. Christ. Don't try to solve my problems, kid. You have no idea.* "I'll find somewhere." It was the truth. Even if I had to go back to the house. The thought sent a cold chill up my back. Could someone have called the cops? No, they would have caught me in the bathroom—but it was snowing. Maybe the cops couldn't get out to our house in all the snow. But the snow did funny things with sound, and our house was so far away from everyone else's.

The hamster wheel inside my head started up, trying to figure things out from this new angle—and running smack into a wall again.

You're taking this really well, Dru. You just shot your dad. How are you going to explain this to the cops?

Well, technically, with as fast as zombies rotted, there wouldn't be anything other than a broken door and a bullet hole to explain. I could say it was there when we moved in, that my dad worked nights, and that's why he couldn't come to the door—

A dry sob caught me unawares. I folded my arms across my stomach and hunched over. I rested my forehead on the cool, slick material of the table, and it felt good. Almost as good as the cold porcelain of a toilet when you're really, really sick.

My stomach roiled again.

Don't throw up, Dru. Don't you dare throw up on that floor.

Dad's voice echoed in my skull now, the usual mantra while I worked the heavy bag. *Work through it, sweetheart. Come on. One more for Daddy. Do it. Come on, girl, that's not going to cut it! One more for me! Come on!*

"Jesus," Graves whispered. He sounded a lot older than a sophomore now. "How bad is it?"

My teeth chattered. I almost choked on a laugh. *How bad is it? It's so bad you have no idea. That's how bad.* "Just go away," I said to my knees. How had I managed to tie my boots? I didn't even remember getting dressed. I was out in public here at the mall. What was I wearing?

Jeans. I could feel socks. I had my boots on. I plucked at the edge of my T-shirt and saw it was red. I was wearing Dad's spare Army jacket, and there was a heavy weight in the right pocket that had to be something deadly.

Jesus Christ, I'm armed in public. Dad would kill me.

"Dru?" His voice had gotten deeper. "How bad is it? You really can't go home?"

I blinked. I had my gloves on, and someone was talking to me. I uncurled, sitting up. The world fell into place, colors and sounds not running like tinted water over glass. The Orange Julius was across the food court, and its sign suddenly seemed like the most wonderful, brightest beacon of hope in the world.

I smelled french fries, hot grease. I wanted to eat. My stomach growled so loudly I hunched my shoulders, hoping he couldn't hear it.

Graves shifted in his chair again. Then he pushed his paper cup across the table. "Take a drink. Your coffee's cold." Still in that quiet, oddly adult voice. No teenage bluster at all in the words.

I grabbed it, sucked at the straw. The taste of strawberries and fake ice cream exploded against my tongue, cutting through and erasing the stink of reanimated death.

He hauled himself up to his full gawky height, scraping the chair back unmusically against the flooring. "Stay here, okay? Just for a second."

I nodded and took another long swallow. He strode off, using those long grasshopper legs to his advantage. By the time I finished the smoothie he was back, sliding a tray across the table. It was a bacon cheeseburger and fries, with a vanilla milkshake I grabbed at. I wolfed the burger in what seemed like two bites while Graves settled back in his chair, tapping his fingers at the edge of the table. He didn't shuck his coat, but he did take a few fries. He'd even brought packets of ketchup, and the only reason I didn't tear into one was because the thought of the thick red inside made the food back up in my throat.

I slurped the last of the vanilla shake and thought of throwing up. Graves hummed along with the Muzak, tapping at the table's edge. He was offbeat, but it didn't seem to bother him much.

"Thanks," I said finally, shoving my hair back behind my ears. The curls had turned to frizz again.

"No problem." He shrugged, bony shoulders moving. "First one's free. Look, you really can't go home? What happened?"

I shot my dad. But it's okay, he was one of the walking reanimated. The bacon cheeseburger fought for freedom. I put down the revolt with a slight burp that tasted like fake dairy product and slightly-less-fake beef. "You wouldn't believe me if I told you."

"Try me." He leaned forward, resting his elbows on the table. His mouth had pulled in on itself, compressed into a thin line, and his gaze was dead level.

I stared at his right hand, the way the fingers lay against the slickness of the tabletop, the nails bitten down to the quick. His knuckles were still red and chapped, like he'd been outside a lot in the cold. He still had really good skin. A little bit of lotion would probably fix him right up.

I could draw his hand. I bet I could. I'd have to shade it more than I normally do to get all the textures down. "I just can't go home," I heard myself whisper. "Not until tomorrow." *Maybe not even then, either. I don't know.*

Graves was silent for a few moments. His hand was tense against the tabletop, all relaxation spilling out of his fingers. Muzak swelled through horns and synthesizers, echoing through the food court like the noise inside my head. I finally placed the song.

It was, of all things, an inoffensive rendition of AC/DC's "Highway to Hell." Dad liked that sort of music. Every new town we landed in, it was my job to find the oldies station and the classic rock station. I didn't know what Dad would think about one of his favorites having its nuts cut off and played over a mall speaker system.

He's not going to be thinking about anything ever again, Dru. The tears rose again. I snuffled, swallowed hard, and glared at Graves, daring him to say something about me blubbering like a kid.

Finally, he sat back, taking his hand off the table. "Do you have a place to sleep?"

I wish I did. "I'll find somewhere." *A flophouse hotel, or I'll ride the buses all night. Or something.*

More silence between us. I heard a high, cawing laugh, and glanced over at the Orange Julius to see two blonde girls giggling behind their hands. They had a pair of jocks with them, one strapping dark-haired guy I'd seen at school and another who looked like his cousin or brother.

I felt a million miles away from them. Normal goddamn teenagers, acting like idiots in front of a fast-food place. The dark jock put his arms around one of the girls and picked her up. She shrieked with laughter, the sound as bright as new spilled pennies. Her shirt rode up, showing the supple curve of her back. It was snowing outside and there was a zombie dead in my living room, and here this girl was, dressed like a hooker and laughing.

My hand curled into a fist. I took a deep breath.

"I know a place." Graves said it quietly, leaning forward across the table. He braced his thin elbows and rested his chin on his fist. "If you want, you know."

Oh, Jesus. Not now. "Why is it there's always a guy who thinks he can get something out of the new girl?" My fingernails dug into my palm. "Every goddamn town, it's the same thing. Some guy thinks he's God's gift to the displaced."

"I just asked if you wanted a place to sleep." Graves hunched his shoulders defensively. "Jesus."

Then I felt bad. It wasn't his fault I had a dead zombie in my house. The back door was open; the place would be freezing in the morning. I couldn't think about going back until daylight.

Then what will you do, Dru? Dad's voice in my head, as if he was giving me a test. *What's going to happen then? You need a plan. Right now you're running on rabbit.*

Graves was still peering at me, his eyes darker greenish under his curly mass of hair. His earring winked again, a hard clear dart of light.

"Sorry." My throat ached. How loudly had I screamed? Had anyone heard the gunshots? I couldn't stop wondering about it. "It's been a bad day." *You have no idea how bad it's been.*

"No problem." He spread his hands, brushing away the apology. His coat whispered as he shifted in the creaking plastic seat. "So, I'll take you someplace you can sleep tonight. Someplace safe. Okay?"

"How much?" I had some money—usually there was no shortage of cash where Dad was concerned; liquid resources were critical to our type of lifestyle. But if Dad was really, truly gone, I had to take careful stock of what I had and make sure I could get more before I started spending like a maniac.

And his billfold was gone. He might've tucked it in the car. But . . .

"I keep telling you, first one's free." He glanced around the food court. "You want to play some air hockey? Good way to get your mind off stuff."

I don't know how I'm going to get my mind off zombies, kid. But it was something to do. I couldn't just sit here until the mall closed. I'd explode. Or start crying. Or something else guaranteed to draw attention to myself.

"Sure," I heard myself say.

His face lit up. "Cool. You finished?"

I pushed back my chair and felt my back spasm as I hauled

myself upright, wincing and sucking in a sharp breath. I'd probably pulled something, trying to get away from the zombie. "Yeah, I guess. Graves?"

"Huh?" He shook his hair down over his face, but the grin still remained. It made him look a little bit older, cutting lines into his baby face.

"Thanks." The word wasn't adequate, and I searched for something else to say. "Nice gloves."

"Hey, you know." He scooped up the tray and my still-full cup of ice-cold coffee. The unibrow waggled at me, and then he actually, of all things, *winked*. "Chicks dig guys in gloves."

I actually laughed. Call it a miracle.

CHAPTER 7

"You're kidding," I said for the fifth time. "In the *mall*?"

"It's warm and it's safe. It opens up in plenty of time to get to school in the morning." Graves ran his hand back through his hair and checked the hallway. "Come on."

I'd never been behind the scenes in a mall before. They're huge places, and the stores are only half of it. Behind each store and threading through the entire complex were maintenance hallways and office space, just a thin doorway away. Graves loitered in the hall leading to the restrooms until it was clear, produced a thin rectangle of plastic—it looked like a credit card—to slip the lock on one of the doors with the ease of long practice, and motioned me through. He looked over my shoulder when he did, and his face was a lot older than usual, but it smoothed out by the time he pulled the door closed and made sure it was locked.

Muzak filtered into the maintenance hallway only faintly, for which I was unendingly grateful. My right hand ached, both from the kickback of the nine-millimeter and from air hockey. He played a mean game, this beaky little boy, and it was take-no-prisoners time once I beat him in the first two rounds.

I hadn't thought about zombies for five-whole-minute stretches, while lunging over the top of the table. It was easier not to think when you were moving.

Our footsteps echoed on bare concrete. The walls were unpainted, and dust grimed the corners. "How often does anyone come through here?"

"Not very. The maintenance staff is gonna want to go home just like everyone else; if anyone's left after they lock up it'll be a miracle. Even the janitors leave early on days like this." He took a right and led me into a confusing tangle of corridors that all looked the same. It was warm, at least, and I suddenly realized I was exhausted.

I shifted my bag higher on my shoulder, the strap cutting through Dad's jacket and my T-shirt. The wool of my gloves rasped against my hands. "You do this often?"

"When I have to." His shoulders hunched, but he slowed down so I could keep up with him. "We have to stay back here for a little while, until everyone's cleared out. Then it's safe, and we can play."

"Play what? More air hockey?" I just wanted to take my boots off and sit down somewhere. A crying fit sounded good, too. *Really* good. Not to mention a hot shower and some television, while I was at it.

"If you want. Anything *we* want. They've got cameras, but most of 'em don't work. The parent company that owns the mall is too cheap to put in real cameras, so most of 'em are dummies anyway, and the ones that do work don't have any tapes or anything. Come nighttime, this place is a playground. There's shit here you wouldn't *believe*."

I wanted to ask him if *he* had to go home sometime soon.

Decided not to. His home life was his own problem; I had plenty of my own.

Graves turned sharp left, and I found myself in a cavernous space with a huge garage door pulled down, dumpsters lining the walls on the other side. A cardboard-crushing machine telling everyone to *Reduce Reuse Recycle!* with a cheerful cartoon mouse waving under a yellow-painted sun glowered at us. I shivered, hearing the wind pick up outside the big garagelike door. Thin fingers of cold air caressed my face.

It wasn't the low moan of the wind at dusk, but something about it was hungry and ugly just the same. The shivers plucked at the aching muscles of my back, made the rug burn on my left hand prickle.

I kept expecting to hear the tapping again, or the screaming sound of dry tendons working, or a shuffling step.

"You okay?" Graves had turned to face me and stood with his hand on a stack of pallets leaning against the wall. He'd pushed his hair back, tucking some of it behind his ears, and I had to admit he wasn't bad-looking, just babyfaced and beaky. I could see the adult face underneath, in the way his bones held his face up. Even if his eyes stayed muddy instead of greenish.

I'm not going to be okay for a while. I just have to figure out what to do. I swallowed a lump in my throat, my stomach unhappy with the sheer amount of grease in a mall bacon cheeseburger. "Copacetic."

"Okay. You can't tell anyone about this." He hesitated.

I could have told him now wasn't the time for him to be having second thoughts. "I don't have anyone to tell. You're about the only person I know here." *Cut the crap. I'm tired.*

He nodded, chewing at his lower lip, then turned and shimmied sideways behind the cardboard crusher.

You have got *to be kidding me.* I took a deep breath, hitched my bag around so I could squeeze through the narrow slice, and followed.

There was barely enough room for me and none at all for my bag. Still, I struggled through, almost hit my head on something metallic, and whispered a curse. Graves fiddled with the wall and—miraculously—a door opened inward. "They forgot about this once they put the dumpster and stuff down here." His voice echoed and fell flat. There was a click, and warm electric light played over the dirty concrete wall in front of my face. I squirmed around the side of the door frame and almost fell into another hallway. "This used to be an office when it was a loading dock for Macy's. When they did the big remodel two years ago they closed this all up, bricked up the back of the office and stuck all those dumpsters and stuff against the wall. I wondered if you could still get in here, and whaddaya know. Neat, huh?"

I looked around. There was a bathroom off to one side, through a half-open door. The rest of the office looked just like a studio apartment. "How the hell did you get the sleeping bag in here?" I didn't have to work very hard to sound impressed.

He pointed up, a faint blush starting on his cheekbones. Two ceiling tiles were removed, the rest discolored and dirty. The only light came from a naked bulb dangling from an extension cord. "I lofted some stuff up through there. Welcome to Casa Graves, babe."

The sleeping bag lay on a camp cot, and a flimsy plywood bookcase with a Discman and a stack of CDs stood next to a pair of tangled headphones. Jimi Hendrix leered at me from a poster tacked up on the wall. Another poster of a woman's gigantic fake breasts cradling a cold Bud Light bottle stood above a coffeemaker and a hot plate, with a shelf of dishes and packages of Top Ramen stacked neatly underneath. Black T-shirts hung on a folding rack, and a few pairs of jeans were folded up underneath.

It reminded me of Dad's room, always kept military-neat no matter where we landed. No matter what city we were in, I could always find anything in Dad's room in seconds flat.

Dad. The lump in my throat refused to go away. I realized Graves was standing, his hands in his pockets and his shoulders hunched up even further, in the middle of the room next to the cot. His face was a study in disinterest, but I caught the darkening of his eyes and the shadow of hurt around his mouth. He was waiting for me to say something cruel.

I was starting to wonder about this kid.

"It's nice," I managed, around the lump. "It's cozy." It was so warm sweat prickled along my lower back. I slid my bag off my shoulder and felt like an idiot for wondering about his home life. I stripped my gloves off and stuffed them in my left coat pocket, trying not to stare at the breasts-and-Bud poster.

"There isn't a shower." Graves's shoulders dropped down from their hunch, relieved. He stripped off his gloves with two quick movements and tossed them on the bed. They looked like crumpled imposters on its neatness. "But the bathroom works fine, and if I have to I can get a space heater through the roof. It's safe. Nobody remembers it's still here. Close the door, willya?"

I did. The hinges were held on with clumsily attached screws, and I was suddenly sure he'd rehung the door to make it swing inward—after monkeying through above the ceiling tiles. This kid was smart.

I set my bag down near the bookcase and wondered if I should slide out of the green Army coat before I felt the heavy accusing weight in its pocket again. I couldn't remember if I'd shoved a fresh clip in the gun.

Sloppy, sweetheart. Always check your ammo. Dad's voice again. I could almost forget the zombie's howling bellow and the tip-taps of its bony fingers against the glass. The low moaning sound it made, an unmodulated groan. The sound of my own screams drowning out the gun's blunt roar.

I shivered again.

Graves had shrugged out of his coat and tossed it on the cot as well. The entire room smelled like healthy teenage boy, a mix of hair, testosterone, and Speed Stick or Right Guard or one of those deodorants with heavy masculine names. "You can take your coat off. You want some coffee? I've got some Coke, too, but it's not cold. And I've got Doritos, if you're still hungry. Noodles, too."

"No, I'm good." I picked my way over to the bookcase and peered at the paperbacks. He liked horror novels, lots of Stephen King, Richard Matheson, Dean Koontz. But there was also a copy of Sun Tzu's *The Art of War* and a stack of books about the Spanish Civil War, as well as a thick, well-read history of World War II. And—good Lord. There was a whole shelf of romance novels, with pink bodice-ripping covers. Right over the bottom shelf of heavy, thick math textbooks.

This guy was getting more interesting all the time.

"I read a lot," he said behind me, a little unsteadily. "I can't get a TV in here." There were shuffling sounds, and when I looked back over my shoulder, I saw he was making coffee despite his shaking hands. "Sure you don't want a Coke or something?"

He was nervous, blushing, and almost stammering. It was kind of endearing.

"Maybe some coffee," I volunteered, diplomatically. "This is really cool, Graves. It's like your own little world."

"No teachers and no jocks." He made a short snorting noise that tried to be a laugh. "Come on in and sit down. You look tired."

I *felt* tired. But it was weird—I felt safer than I had last night at home. There was no wind moaning at the windows, and I didn't have to wait for the worst—it had already happened. Just having someone else near, talking while he made coffee, was enough to make me feel better.

I folded myself down next to the bookcase and hugged my knees. "You live here?"

A shrug, seen from the back. "Here and other places. Wherever I want." He vanished into the bathroom with the coffeepot. "We can go out the other way once the mall's closed down."

Another way out? Smart, kid. Never have just one escape route. I put my forehead on my jean-clad knees and let out a long breath I hadn't been aware of holding. Trembling spilled through my bones as Graves splashed in the bathroom. He finally came out, and a few minutes later the smell of coffee filled the small studio. It reminded me of Dad—he always needed caffeine in the mornings. I made his coffee the way he taught me, the way they made it in the Marines—strong and bitter enough to eat a silver spoon. Gran had boiled hers in a percolator, and Dad wasn't far behind. I was probably the only kid in three states who knew how to run an old-timey coffee bubbler.

"Hey." Graves had appeared right next to me, crouching down. Strings of wavy hair fell in his face, and he pushed them back with a quick flick of his long fingers. "You okay? You hurt anywhere?"

The question struck me as absurd. I hurt all over, every muscle in my back was tight, my legs ached, my shoulders felt like lead bars, my arms were heavy—and my heart, speared with something dark and terrible, hurt worst of all. My hands shook. Even my *hair* ached, now that I was sitting down, not moving from one thing to the next. I opened my mouth to tell him so, and a dry, barking sob interrupted me halfway.

"Oh shit." He sounded really alarmed, and he dropped down next to me. "Dru? Jesus. Dru?"

I couldn't answer him. Sobs racked me, horrible sounds like I was being strangled because I couldn't keep them back but I tried so hard my teeth locked together, grinding. My jaw creaked, and I couldn't smell the coffee after a while because my nose was full.

Graves put one bony arm around me and didn't say anything while I cried. It was decent of him, and I liked him for it. I was almost sorry I was going to have to blow town and leave him behind.

* * *

He gave me the cot and the sleeping bag, and I passed out clutching my messenger bag to my chest, Dad's coat on the floor next to the bed. When I woke up hours later, Graves was gone. There was a scrawled note attached to the inside of the door with a wad of spearmint gum.

Went to school. I'll bring your homework back. ~~*You should really stop skipping*~~. There was another line, more heavily crossed out, that I couldn't decipher, then: *Stay as long as you want. I'll be back.*

I dug in my bag until I came up with my watch, a waterproof Swiss number Dad had bought in New York when I was twelve. He'd left me with August for about a month while he was up near the Canadian border doing something or another. Even though August was pretty cool and knew more about the Real World than a lot of books, he still wasn't real company, like Dad. And besides, he always made me stay inside while he was out "working." A whole month in

New York and all I knew was one street in Brooklyn.

It was a little after 3 p.m. I'd slept for a long time; my head felt heavy, my mouth sandy and nasty, every muscle stiff and my back hurting like a sonofabitch. I'd definitely pulled something getting away from the zombie.

The thought hurt, but not as much as I thought it would. It was like pinching your toes after they've gone to sleep. Dad was a zombie. Had been a zombie. Whatever.

What am I going to do now? I stood staring blankly at the note on the door for a little while, just breathing and feeling the inside of my head full of cotton wool.

A thought swam through the fuzziness, linking up with the memory of August's close, stuffy apartment. *Contacts. Dad has contacts. I should go find the list and let one of them know.*

We weren't the only ones hunting down ghosts, poltergeists, flickers, bad hexes, chupacabras, gator spirits, bad voodoo, or anything else you care to name. There's a whole underground movement, checking in at occult and Army-Navy surplus stores, passing along information and trading tips on how to best clean out a haunted house or take down a sucker, how to disperse a poltergeist or where the next wave of weird crap moving through a region is coming from.

I shivered at the thought of suckers, gooseflesh rising hard and hot on my arms, spilling down my back. They were bad news, like werwulfen—though wulfen were generally not dangerous to people like Dad, having their own running feud with the suckers to keep them busy.

I shut my eyes. Why hadn't I told Dad about Gran's owl? He might have listened and not gone out that night.

Which made it my fault, in a fuzzy sort of way. And the house was standing open, getting colder and colder, with a hole the size of Texas in the back door and a stain on the living-room carpet, plus a bullet hole in the living-room wall.

What am I going to do?

First things first. I was *starving*. I needed food, and I needed to think. I had to make a list of Things To Do. I'd have to go back to the house during daylight. Daylight was safest. I needed to get the ammo together, and all the weapons. I needed to pack up, and I needed to find Dad's truck.

Our battered blue Ford truck rose up inside my head like a beacon. If I could find the truck, I could make it out of town and figure out what to do next. Gran's house up in the Blue Ridge was still standing solid—we'd been there a few months back, swinging through to check in on it—and mine under the terms of the trust fund she and Dad had set up. I could hide out there. Once I was up in the mountains, I would have a little space to breathe. Nobody would come looking for me there—it took two dirt roads and a piece to even get close, as Gran always said.

Dad deserved a funeral service. There wouldn't be anything left of him but greasy dust and bits of bleached bone, though. Zombies fall apart amazingly quick.

One scorching tear trickled down my cheek, then another. He wasn't going to come stamping in the door yelling, *Dru, honey, get your ass up!* He wasn't going to walk in tired and heavy, lock the door, and ask me what was for dinner. He wasn't ever going to quiz me about sage smudging, hex-breaking, or poltergeist-clearing ever again. Or even leave me a note reminding me to do my katas.

I came back to myself with a jolt and looked down at my watch. It was buckled on my wrist now, my clever little fingers doing the work for me. Thirty minutes had passed while I stood staring at the note on the door. My back ached, every single muscle glued to its neighbors and protesting. I needed some aspirin in the *worst* way.

I had money. I could make it up to the food court—but what if someone saw me behind the mall's scenes? Would I get in trouble I couldn't lie my way out of, or would someone start watching the halls and catch Graves on his way back?

Oh, for God's sake. You've got plenty of problems without worrying about him.

But you don't blow someone else's bolt-hole. It's like a law among hunters. And if Dad was gone, I was the only one left to do the hunting.

That was a scary thought, and one I pushed away as soon as I could.

I stamped back to the bed and dug in my bag. It was deathly quiet down here, but even if I made any noise someone outside wouldn't be able to tell where it was coming from, would they? How often did people scurry down to the dumpsters during the day, anyway? Who used the cardboard crusher?

My artist's pad was a bit worn around the edges from being smashed into my bag all the time. I flipped through it, looking for a clean sheet so I could leave a note for Graves.

The strength went out of my legs, and I sat down hard on the concrete floor, my teeth clicking together as my ass hit.

There was the drawing of the iris I'd been working on, shaded lovingly. Then the doodles of shapes, the closet door, and my nightstand. The pile of laundry. On the next page the pencil had dug into the paper, rasping harshly and shading giant blocks of shadow. I didn't remember drawing this, but I knew I had. Who else could've?

It was the back of a warehouse or another large building butted up against an even larger one, broken windows suggested with slices of pencil shading. There was a busted-down chain-link fence, and in front of the fence was something familiar—a truck crouched like a big cat.

Our truck. I'd know that camper anywhere. My mouth went dry and copper-tasting. My heartbeat thudded in my throat and ears.

I don't remember drawing this. I fell asleep after drawing the laundry—I know I did!

But I'd *dreamed*, hadn't I? A bad dream, about . . . what? Dad, and a door. And something behind the door. The more I looked at the building crouching behind our truck, the more certain I was that something horrible had happened in there, something that ended up with Dad getting turned into a flesh-eating, shambling horror.

The pencil had been broken in my hand, digging in with sharp edges when I woke up. The drawing had obviously been done quickly, using shortcuts I knew about from years of scribbling sketches. It was ridiculous, impossible. Gran would have been proud of me for displaying a new talent, but I wasn't so happy about it at all.

I was still staring at the drawing's heavy, thick strokes when a scratching sound from the wall brought my head up. I dove off the bed and rolled, grabbing the jacket and ending up full-length on the floor, my hand squirming for the gun just like Dad taught me. *Get down first,* then *return fire. Making yourself a target while you fire back is bad business, sweetheart.*

Sanity caught up with me just as the door swung inward. Who else knew I was down here?

Graves hopped through the door and shook his head sharply. He was soaking wet and shivering, water dripping from his curly hair and the hem of his long black coat. His lips were almost blue, his nose bright red and dripping, and his cheeks looked yellow-raw. "It's c-cold as sh-*shit* out there," he stuttered, and blinked owlishly at me as he swept the door closed, a black backpack hanging wetly from one sodden bony shoulder. "And snowing again. I had a hell of a time getting back in here. I brought you something."

I felt ridiculous, lying on the floor, but he didn't seem to notice. He shut the door and stamped, shaking himself like a golden retriever just come up out of a freezing lake. Water flew.

I clicked the safety back on and eased my finger off the trigger. Clambered to my feet, leaving the gun in my coat. "It's snowing again?"

"God, is it ever. You wouldn't believe what I went through to get inside the mall. Here." He dug in his backpack, shaking more water out of his hair. I could see the melting ice sticking to the dark strands. He was *soaked*.

"Jesus." I crossed the small room and tried to take the backpack away from him. "Get out of that coat, your lips are blue. You'd better get into something dry."

"She's already trying to get my clothes off," he announced to the ceiling, refusing to relinquish his bag. "You sound all Southern when you—hang *on* for a second. Jeez, patience is a *virtue*. Slow down, it's for you."

The backpack yielded a smaller paper bag that smelled like meat and fries. I got him out of the coat and was looking around for someplace to hang the heavy dark material when he dropped the pack, pulled his wet shirt off over his head, and shook all over again, splattering me with cold water and bits of ice.

"What did you do, roll in it? Jesus." I rescued the bag of food. "Where did you get this?"

"Place on Marshall that never closes. I worked there one summer. They do good food. Start eating, don't wait for me. You want some coffee?"

He headed off for the bathroom, his shoulder blades like fragile wings under copper-tinted skin. There was a bloom of red across his shoulders from the cold, and he was already unbuttoning his pants. He had nice musculature, a bit scrawny but developed, at odds with his baby-cheeked face.

A flush worked its way up my neck, found my cheeks. I looked quickly away, found a hanger and got his coat hung up where it could drip onto the floor.

He came out of the bathroom with a towel around his waist and another one scrubbing at his hair. I dug in the bag and found three cheesesteak sandwiches and a triple order of curly fries. They smelled *divine*. "Wow. What do I owe you?"

A flash of a grin eased his face. "First one's free, kid. Start eating; you probably haven't had anything all day, have you? They even canceled school, for once. Bletch was madder than a jock with his balls kicked in. It took me a couple hours to get to the place out on Marshall and another—" He broke off, looking down at me with one half of his unibrow cocked. "You'd better eat. I didn't haul it out here for nothing."

At least he was looking a little less like a half-melted Popsicle. "Christ, will you put your clothes on?" Dad walked around shirtless whenever he wanted to and I was sure I wasn't a prude, but still.

"I thought you were trying to get me *out* of my clothes." He snorted his particular sarcastic laugh, half bark and half yip of pain. "Start eating."

"Really, what do I owe you?" *And where do you get your money, kid? Do I care?* There were all sorts of questions about why a kid would live in a mall, but I wasn't so sure I wanted to know. His problems were just that—*his*. I had enough on my hands.

"Told you, first one's free." He actually *winked*, his eyes more brown than green today. He grabbed a shirt and pulled it over his head, took a handful of other clothes while I looked down at the floor, that strange heat swamping my cheeks like water filling up a footprint.

"You bought me dinner the other day, remember?"

"But I *didn't* buy you a Marshall Street Special. I wasn't sure you'd be here, but then I thought you'd probably still be sleeping. You were passed out pretty hard when I left this morning." He dropped down next to me wearing an Iron Maiden T-shirt and dry jeans. The towel landed with a thump near the duffel bag that held his dirty laundry, and he picked up one of the sandwiches. "Hope it's still warm."

My coat was lying on the floor right next to him. It looked innocent, but I knew what was in the pocket. What would he say if he guessed what I'd been about to do?

Just who *was* this kid, anyway? "Why are you doing this?"

His shoulders hunched again. He took a massive bite of cheesy steak sandwich and closed his eyes. The floor was hard and cold, and I wondered where he'd slept last night. I hadn't even thought about it before.

He chewed, his hair hanging in damp black strings over his eyes, and shrugged. "Mrfle."

What the hell does that mean? I decided to let it go. He'd brought me down here, after all, and I wasn't one to throw stones when it came to abnormal living arrangements. "Thank you. I mean, it's been bad. Thanks." The urge to tell him something, anything, rose in my throat.

He swallowed, his Adam's apple bobbing. "Want to talk about it? It's cool if you don't."

What could I tell you that you'd believe? At least when I had Dad I wasn't so lonely.

Dad. I heard that weird bellow again, air forced through a frozen throat. What had the zombie been trying to say? Anything?

Tears prickled my eyes for the thousandth time, hot and hard. The lump congealed in my windpipe. I had to breathe deep. I was starving, and I don't think straight when I'm hungry. "My dad." I unwrapped my sandwich and took a bite.

It was really good, salty and cheesy and full of fat and carbohydrates. The bun was fresh, and it was still warm.

"What about him?" Graves said it carefully, and I could have laughed.

"It's not what you think. He's dead." The word sounded strange in my mouth. A single syllable that didn't belong to my Dad. It belonged somewhere *out there*, and putting it in a sentence with him was wrong, even though I knew it was true.

If he was surprised, he hid it really well. His eyes got really wide and very green. He took another bite, chewed thoughtfully. Snagged a handful of curly fries and stuffed them in his mouth, still watching me. Waiting for the other shoe to drop.

I reached over to the bed and fished my artist's pad out of the tangled mess of the sleeping bag. I opened it to the drawing of Dad's truck. "Do you know where this is?"

He took the paper. His eyes widened briefly, again. He swallowed again, throat working. His earring glittered at me, like a signal. "This is really good."

Duh, I've been drawing since I was five. "Thanks. Do you know where that is?"

"No." He waited, his eyebrows up. His mouth made a little inquisitive movement, and he licked the grease off his fingers.

Shit. "I have to find it. I have to find our truck so I can . . . Well, I have to find it." I took a bite, swallowed it without tasting, and laid down the sixty-four-million-dollar question. "Will you help me? Please?"

"Help you find that building?" He shrugged. "Sure, I guess. It'll take a while with all the snow. The radio said it won't stop for a week. We're in for a regular old whiteout."

I waited for him to ask more questions, but he didn't. Instead, he just ate, watching me between bites. When he finished the first sandwich, he started on the second. I listened to the silence outside the walls, chewing reflexively. It might have been cardboard for all I could taste.

He was halfway done when he stopped chewing and looked at me. "What kind of trouble are you in?"

I don't know yet. I wish I did. If I told you, you'd think I was crazy. "It's pretty bad." That was about all I could say.

"Okay." He shrugged again. "Sounds interesting. We'll start looking tomorrow. But we'll have to do it after school."

My jaw threatened to drop.

His shoulders hunched again. "You think I want to live in the corners like this for the rest of my life? I've got a plan. I'm going to get my GED and go to community college; then I'm going to go to real college. I'm going to be a mathematician. They get paid crap until they get tenure, but after that it's pretty cool. I'm going to be a physics professor."

A *physics professor?* I tried to imagine him as an adult, or as a teacher, and failed. The effort made my brain hurt. He was just so gawky and young. "Everybody's got to have a goal." Odd relief bloomed under my breastbone, filled my entire chest. "You don't skip school?"

"No way. It's a one-way ticket back to foster care if I fly above the radar, you know." The thoughts crossing his face went too quickly for me to even guess at before the wall went back up behind his eyes. "That was my first time, with you." He grinned, a fetching, lopsided smile that he ended up stuffing more curly fries into. "You're a bad influence, Dru."

You have no idea, kid. I was startled into another laugh. The sandwich tasted pretty good after that.

CHAPTER 8

Night came quickly, and when Graves decided it was safe he led me back out through the maze of passages. The mall was deserted, lights turned down low. The fountain on the first floor was shut down too, its surface placid and quiet. Silence wrapped around all the chairs upended on the tables in the food court, tiptoed down the halls, sheathed the stores in darkness. In here, you couldn't hear the wind. We might as well have been on another planet.

Graves leaned over the waist-high barrier and yelled wordlessly into the mezzanine, the sound ricocheting off floor and ceiling, a weirdly distorted echo bouncing back. He surveyed the result with a satisfied air. "See? Pure liberation. You do it."

I let out a shattering war-whoop, the kind I used while sparring with Dad or doing my katas. Graves flinched, but his own yell rose with mine. My cry broke on a laugh, his did the same, and he pushed at me with his bony shoulder, almost toppling me over. I pushed back, and I suppose that's when I started thinking he was a friend instead of just some kid.

The noise died away. "Sometimes I play the games in the arcade by myself," he said meditatively. His eyes glittered in the half-dark. "It's nice having someone else around. You want to play some air hockey?"

I almost shuddered at the thought. "No thanks." My wrist still hurt, along with the rug burn on my left hand. And my back was still unhappy, despite the ancient bottle of Tylenol Graves had stashed in his bathroom. "Can I just walk around?"

"Sure. I'm going to check a few things out. Stay away from Sears, they have a working camera last I looked." He grinned, then whirled on his toes and strode away with a bounce in his step, his long black coat fluttering.

I stood there for a few minutes, my eyes closed. Dad's jacket was heavy and warm. The mall was dark, only the barest of night-lights on in store windows. Grates were pulled down to close the stores off, everything from rolling iron contraptions to glass sheets stopping ghosts from shoplifting. The chill of possibly getting caught walked along my shoulders. If any cops showed up, I'd get busted for possession of a weapon and God alone knew what else.

Stop worrying, Dru. I sighed, the tension leaving my neck for a few seconds. I felt a little naked without my bag, but I couldn't carry it everywhere. *If you could get caught, Graves wouldn't be here. He's smart enough.*

Matter of fact, he was distressingly smart. He didn't *look* like a math geek; I wondered if the goth bit was camouflage. It's not every teenage boy who wants to be a physics professor when he grows up. He probably had a nice rational mindset that would think I was batshit if I started telling him about some of the things I'd seen.

What did I care, anyway? It wasn't like he was going to be a permanent fixture in my life.

You have other problems. Start by figuring out how Dad got turned into a zombie.

I needed to go back to Dad's books and do some research. The second and last group of zombies we'd run across had been near Baton Rouge. And that had been straight-up voodoo like that guy in South Carolina, not native to the Midwest. There might be other stuff in the books about zombies, stuff we hadn't looked at last time because we hadn't needed it. I'd been too busy with unhexing to really pay attention to Dad putting the corpses down again.

The books were in the living room. Had the neighbors even heard the gunshots? The thought was like poking at a sore tooth with your tongue. All I could answer was probably not, since there hadn't been any sign of cops when I'd left. But still . . .

I didn't know nearly enough, and sneaking around a mall at night wasn't going to answer the questions.

Just what are you thinking of, anyway, Dru? I turned to my left and stuck my hands in my pockets, the cold weight of the gun against my right-hand knuckles. If I inhaled really deeply, I could smell fabric softener and the ghost of Dad's aftershave. It wasn't nearly as comforting as it should have been.

I put my head down and ambled along the gallery, past the Hillshire Farms—breathing out smoky meat and processed cheese even through the glass door—and a chain store selling cheap jewelry by the ton. My boots made almost no noise against the short, tough-as-nails industrial carpet, and it was dark.

It was nice to be in here after everything was closed up. The silence was vast and downy, like soft feathers. The half-light was restful; it hid everything. There was nobody around to see me if I chose to smile or frown, nobody looking to see what I was wearing, nobody I had to lie to or watch out for. I could stare in the windows or stop outside Victoria's Secret, examining spindly lingerie-clad mannequins spotlit for the night, and nobody would think I was strange.

It wasn't as cool as I thought it might be. After about ten minutes of wandering around I began to get a little nervous. I couldn't even hear the wind. With that much silence, the inside of my head started to get a little crowded with other sounds. Remembered sounds.

Like the tapping of fleshless fingers on glass. Or the hideous, scratching, frozen-throated bellow of a zombie.

Someone turned *him into a zombie.* It was the thought I'd been avoiding ever since I'd pulled the trigger again and again. *You don't just happen to trip and fall and turn into one of the reanimated. Someone did it* to *him. Who? Probably the same someone he was after.*

Someone, or some*thing*? The thing behind the door? I was awful certain my dream was real, and that I'd seen Dad's next-to-last moments on earth.

Which led me to the not-so-comforting thought that I might start dreaming of really gruesome things. It wasn't going to be fun if I did. Gran had never taught me much about dreams; we'd been too busy during our waking hours. All she'd ever said was, *Dreams are false friends, honey Dru. They don't show you what you need or what's sure; they most just show you nothin' you can hang onna peg. Just maybes, that's all.*

I stopped just outside the movie store and rubbed at my forehead with the heel of my left hand. If I rubbed hard enough, I wondered if I would come up with something that would fix the huge hole in the world.

Things like this weren't supposed to happen. It was like a regular bad dream, except it *kept* happening. Dad was gone. Really gone, not just coming back near dawn bloody and exhausted. He was irrevocably, absolutely, finally gone.

Just like Gran. Just like Mom.

I was alone. The fact that I'd been trained to be self-sufficient wasn't comforting at all. I wanted my dad.

I was just about to go down *that* particular mental road when I heard something I shouldn't have, something that froze me in place, staring at the blank TV screens that during mall hours showed whatever movie the employees had been told to push that week. My own reflection—curly wild dark hair, big white-ringed eyes, glaring white cheeks, and camo jacket—stared at me, replicated in each glass shield.

The crash and tinkle of broken glass was followed by a crunch and a low, sonorous growl that scraped not only at my ears but *inside* my head, dragging through the center of my brain. Pain flared behind my eyes, and I pitched forward, catching myself on the window with my left hand and forehead. The jolt clicked my teeth together *hard*. Copper bloodtaste spilled down my throat as my heartbeat slammed into overdrive, pounding so hard in my belly and chest black spots whirled and danced through my vision.

I found myself on my knees, shaking the growl out of my head. The pain vanished as soon as it had arrived, and I was only disoriented.

Get up, Dru! Dad's voice barked at me. *Get under cover! Do it now!*

I set my teeth and breathed in the way Gran taught me, pulling myself back into a compact ball inside my own skull. The growl slid into a lower, purely physical register, and I lifted my head, peering with watering eyes down the long empty hallway broken only by potted plants, benches, and carts full of useless crap covered for the night. There was a ruddy glow creeping up the walls, and I heard a rushing crackle under the growl.

Now that the thing wasn't echoing inside my head, I could think. I scrambled on hands and knees to the shelter of a huge potted palm, probably fake, and smelled smoke. I wasn't sure if it was real smoke or just my own panic. My right hand dug in my jacket pocket, the weight of the gun cold and reassuring. I slid it free of the fabric, bringing it up nice and easy and clicking the safety off as the growling swelled, plucking at the outside of the small ball I'd made of myself inside my head.

Another thing they don't tell you about this sort of thing is how much it makes you want to pee. I *really* wanted to find a bathroom, my bladder suddenly incredibly, painfully full. No time for that—I slid over to the side and peeked down the hallway.

Whatever it is just broke the glass on a second-floor window. Then I realized entrances to the top level of the parking lot were on the second floor, and a quarter of the way up this arm of the mall was one of those entrances. It was just past the shop with the funny-smelling lotions.

What the hell? I breathed in, tasted smoke and something else, something icy and fresh, with an iron undertaste.

Outside air.

Then it padded into view, long and lean against shifting shadows. It was the size of a pony, covered in weird glassy hair, shaped like a mother of a big shaggy dog. My head hurt, the way it did when an apparition was getting ready to materialize, draining the warmth out of the air and sucking up all the ambient energy most people barely recognize they're swimming in.

I sucked in another soft breath, catching myself before I made a noise. It was a close call. *Be quiet, Dru. Be really quiet. This is so not good.*

I suppose I get a prize for stating the obvious, even inside my own skull.

The dog-thing inhaled, snorting through a nose the size of the Grand Canyon. As it exhaled, its jaws parting and the huge obsidian teeth sliding against each other, it made a sound like a match applied to a gas leak. Smoke fumed off its shoulders, lifted from its spine.

It *ignited*. Orange and yellow flame raced along its back, dripping down the glassy fur, spattering the flooring. The scorch of it rolled down and hit the back of my throat—burning plastic.

The thing was on fire.

I was stupid. I gasped. I couldn't help it.

It heard me.

Its blind fiery head swung around, questing. Then it snorted, and the heat of it rolled down the hall and brushed the leaves of the fake palm tree above me. The quiet rustling was almost lost in the sound of its claws snicking as it loped unerringly forward.

A burning *dog*. The size of a Shetland pony. Running straight at me.

I scrambled to my feet, my mouth dry and tasting like thick liquid copper. I bolted. My boots slapped the linoleum as the thing let out a howling growl with the rush and crackle of flame underneath it, belching with foul, sulfur-impregnated, roasted air.

I put my head down, barely aware I was screaming like a goddamn cheerleader in a horror movie, and ran for my life.

CHAPTER 9

I pounded down the hallway and jagged to the left as the mezzanine opened up in a well of darkness, my legs thick with terror and refusing to work right, the gun clutched uselessly in my right hand as my arms pumped. The escalators were turned off for the night, but I skidded around the corner and took the frozen stairs three at a time anyway, my hips and shoulders jolting each time I landed. The thing behind me—*it's burning*, the rational part of my brain howled, and the other part, the part Dad had trained into me, replied with an iron imperative to *fucking move I know it's burning!*—gave out another roar as it thumped into something with a crash, and the whole thing began to seem like a nightmare. I'd wake up any second now, safe in my bed, with Dad downstairs watching cable.

It smelled horrible, rotten eggs and burning foulness. I ran like a rabbit, fleet with terror, my boots slapping down with little squeaking sounds. Something that sounded like Dad was screaming in my ear, but I didn't listen. I *couldn't* listen.

Instinct saved me. I threw myself aside as a bullet train of compressed air screamed past, holding the smearing crimson and orange of the burning thing, stretched out in a full leap. I fell heavily, not bothering to try and stop myself, barking my head on something. Warmth dripped down the side of my face. I scrambled to my feet and tripped again, knocking over chairs—overflow from the food court, a nice little nook where people could sit and eat their fast food while looking at the fountain—

The fountain! The click inside my head was so loud I almost didn't hear the burning thing howl again, a long, cheated rasp of ignited rage. I made it to my feet with hysterical speed and bolted, my back burning with pain and something torn loose in my side.

Behind me. It was behind me again, and it was fast. I couldn't hope to outrun it. Twenty feet between me and the fountain, and I wasn't going to make it.

MOVE! Dad's voice bellowed in my head, as if we were in Louisiana again with the cockroach things scuttling in the basement and the ammo clips jittering in my shaking hands.

I *moved*. I don't know how. One moment I knew I wasn't going to be able to get there in time, the next I was *there*.

Water gushed up in a sheet as I threw myself over the lip of the fountain in a wide receiver's dive, getting a sudden mouthful of chlorine and stale chill, my head barked something else—the concrete holding up some ridiculous Swiss-cheese sheet metal the water cascaded down while the fountain was turned on. More pain jolted down my neck. I was really racking up the score here. If this was a video game I'd be yelling at the stupid screen right now. Or throwing my controller at it.

The burning thing howled. Spattered with filthy mall-fountain water, it landed heavily as I scrabbled, a gout of foul-smelling steam belching up. Heat rolled through the water clawing at my arms and legs. I grabbed the sheet metal and *pulled* with both hands, my right clumsy because of the gun clicking against the rattling flimsy edifice. I pushed myself aside and fell again as the creature smashed spastically into the metal with a hollow *bong* that would have struck me as goddamn hilarious if the water hadn't been boiling. I landed hard again, breath driven out of me in a howling scream, and heard a yammering electronic sound. Had that been going on the whole time?

It slid down the metal and landed with a splashing jolt.

Steam drifted in great eddies from the once-placid water. The fountain bubbled and buzzed. I scrabbled for the stone ledge and just made it, hopping up and perching like a frog with trembling legs.

"Holy shit," someone was saying, someone with a high trembling voice very much like mine. I felt my lips shape the words, numbly. My hair dripped in my face and something warm and sticky was in my eyes. "Holy *shit*. Jesus Christ."

I coughed, water blowing out of my nose. Red drops pattered in the bubbling froth of the fountain. I was bleeding, but it didn't seem important. I was soaked to the skin and my fingers ached around the butt of the gun. My clothes were too heavy, full of blood and sulfur-stinking water now. I was shaking like an epileptic.

"Jesus Christ," I whispered. "Jesus *Christ*."

A slight movement caught my eye and the gun leveled itself, my finger cramping on the trigger. My gasping shallow breaths were suddenly audible even over the racket. Smoke and steam drifted in the air. Dots of coolness spattered me from overhead. The sprinklers were going. It was raining inside the mall. The burning thing lay in the water, twitching hard enough to send up little splashes and waves of froth.

Graves stared at me. He was on the other side of the fountain, wreathed in steam, his mouth ajar and his eyes wide.

Where the hell did he come from? The gun didn't care. My arm was straight, my aim was good, and I could hardly miss from this range. I gasped, my ribs heaving as I struggled to *breathe*, to get enough air into my starved lungs. I made harsh racking sounds, coughing at the reek in the steamy air. It was a sauna in here, and the sprinklers weren't helping.

Graves rose, his hands palm-out, the classic *don't shoot* stance. His mouth was ajar and his eyes were dilated. His gaze kept flicking between me and the thing thrashing in the fountain as it drowned in something inimical to it, still superheating the liquid. It was dying; I knew it was dying. I choked on the smell, shaking, but the gun didn't waver.

"Dru—" He shouted it, over the wailing of the fire alarm. My entire arm cramped with the need to do something.

I pulled the trigger.

CHAPTER 10

The second shape—the thing that was leaping for Graves—was longer, leaner, and its fur was shorter, gray instead of glassy and smoking. A white streak bolted up the side of its long, oddly-shaped head. It stretched out in full leap, its snarling muzzle starred with ivory teeth sharper than knives, strings of saliva pouring out of its mouth. My first shot went wide, and the thing bowled past Graves, knocking him aside as easily as I might shoulder a grade-schooler out of the way. Goth Boy went flying, his coat flapping once with a sound like a sheet snapped out to lay flat while making the bed, and the gun spoke again.

I tracked the thing just like Dad had taught me, training taking over. Blood bloomed on its pelt. It looked like a steroid-pumped fur rug, muscle rippling under its fur, and its eyes were alight with unholy yellow.

The werwulf screamed a high yip of pain and tumbled off to the side, landing on the fountain's lip with a sickening crack. I would like to say I hopped gracefully down off my perch, but the truth is that I fell and scrambled around the other side of the fountain, looking for Graves. Cordite pulled sharp against all the other smells filling the mall. I retched once, a heave that came all the way up from my toes and kept crawling.

Graves shook his head, dazed. He'd levered himself up on his elbows, blinking in befuddlement. He saw me, and his eyes widened. They were a thin ring of green around a dilated pupil, the whites rolling like a terrified horse's. Still, the green rim was a line of emerald fire.

"Get *up*!" I screamed, and scrambled to my feet, grabbing his arm in my left hand and hauling with every ounce of strength I had left over. He came up a little more gracefully than I might have under the circumstances, and his cheeks were flour-pale, spots standing out high along the arches of his cheekbones. The silver earring swung, smacking my face as he ran into me, blind with fear. "*Move, goddammit!*"

It wasn't my voice. It was Dad's harsh bark transplanted to my throat.

I had no idea whether I'd wounded the werwulf enough to keep it down or not, and the walloping electronic noise plus the steam was making it hard to think. I *had* to think if both of us were going to get out of this alive.

This one's all about you, Dru. No Dad around to bail me out.

Our feet slipped in spilled water. I dripped blood and fell heavily to my knees in the tide. That was why it was my fault—if I hadn't tripped, almost biting a chunk out of my tongue when I landed, the werwulf would have hit me instead of Graves. They collided with rib-snapping force, and he screamed the high girlish scream of a squirrel in a trap.

I yelled something unrepeatable and shapeless anyway, brought the gun around, and *kicked*. My boot connected solidly with the werwulf's sleek canine head, and, like a gift, the thing crouching over Graves's body turned around and snarled at me, the eyes glowing like diseased sunlight, its gray streak shocking against the wiry darkness.

My voice cracked as I screamed, and I squeezed the trigger again. The sound was deafening. Gore splattered, the nine-millimeter's barrel smoking with cooked splashback. The werwulf spilled away, its muzzle gaping.

I'd shot it in the jaw.

It fell over the lip of the fountain and began to throw up stinking gouts of reddish, steaming water, the smell of cooked fur adding to the thunderous stench.

Graves moaned soundlessly under the noise of the alarm. I realized it was a *fire alarm*, and cursed in a long gasp. The boy's shoulder was shredded. The wulf had bitten him.

Shit. Oh shit.

I struggled with myself. The best thing to do was leave him. He was *bitten*, and that was bad news. I needed to get the hell out of here quick. The cops and the fire brigade would be here any second despite the snow, and how was I going to explain all this? Even my well-honed talent for creative lying wasn't up to the task.

Graves opened his eyes. He stared at me, his mouth working under the braying alarm. Water plashed. I snapped a glance at the wulf, which was rolling around holding its jaw with two lean, furry hands, producing an amazing bubbling howl with each heaving of its ribs. I looked back at the boy and for a second, I couldn't remember who the hell he was or what I was doing here. All I could think of was the hideous, horrible smell as Dad's body rotted away right in front of me.

I was on my own. *This one's all about you, Dru. You're making the call now.*

"Get up." I didn't recognize my voice this time, either. "Get the fuck up, kid. We've got to go."

Amazingly, he set his jaw and struggled to his feet, holding his shoulder. Blood spilled between his fingers, black in the dimness.

First thing to do is get us away from that wulf. It'll heal quick and it'll be pissed. We can't go back to the room; it'll come after us there and we'll be trapped like rats in a hole. Where can I take him? Think!

There was only one place. I had to hope the cops weren't there—and that nothing *else* was there, either.

Which meant I had to get Graves moving, treat him for shock, and navigate both of us through a blizzard.

Oh, jeez. Blood dripped down the side of my face, warm and wet. My back spasmed, and I'd pulled something in my arm, too. I was a song of aches and pains, and I wanted to lie right down and let them do whatever they wanted to me as long as I didn't have to move or think anymore.

Great.

CHAPTER 11

Once I'd scrubbed the blood off both of us and gotten a pressure bandage onto Graves—the strips of his shredded shirt, actually, ripped up in the food-court restroom—the long dark coat buttoned up didn't look half bad. Neither did he, except for being so pale and shock-eyed.

I got us out of the restroom and up onto the second level of the mall into another one just in time. We weren't leaving a trail of water and blood now, though we still both stank to high heaven. I used plenty of paper towels to scrub the worst of the gunk off, shivering as adrenaline wore off and the fact that I'd just been dumped in a fountain by a big burning thing and shot a werwulf in the *face* occurred to me over and over again.

Like this. I'd look in the mirror at the long nasty gash along my hairline and think, *I'm going to have a scar when that heals.* Then my mind would shiver sideways, and I would hear the zombie again, tapping its bony fingers on the back door. Or the streak-headed werwulf's snarl. Or the burning thing's thrashing as it drowned.

And I would let out a hurt little quivering sound, clapping my hand over my mouth in case any of the cops were looking around the mall. I didn't think they would—there was a clear trail of scorching from the broken windows to the fountain, and it was so messy around there it wouldn't be immediately obvious *what* had happened.

The thing that worried me more was the wulf. Had he been rabid, newly changed, or just pissed off? Wulfen don't normally go after humans; there is too much fresh raw meat you can get easily in a supermarket. The exception is right after they shift the first time, but it would make no sense for a first-time wulf to want to get *inside* a building. From what I've heard, they usually want to run out and get some fresh air.

The thing that worried me most of all was a big burning dog the size of a Shetland pony. Had it been after me? After Graves? Or just pissed off because it had to buy some new clothes?

I didn't hear any footsteps, but after a while the alarm shut off. I waited. Graves was propped against the inside of a stall, shivering so hard his teeth clicked together rapidly. He was in shock, and I didn't know what to do for him. The bite—would he begin to change? I should have left him behind. You don't fool around with werwulf bites. You just *don't*. It was a law. When he started to get hairy and hungry, I'd have to—

Christ no. Don't think about that. I checked my watch again. Still ticking, even though it took a licking. Just like me.

My legs shook, tired all the way down to the bones. My head was full of cotton wool. I hurt *all over*, adrenaline fading in fits and starts.

I went to the entrance to the restroom, where the hallway

did a sharp bend so nobody could peek into the girls' pee-palace. I listened with every fiber of my being, focusing out, my entire body becoming an aching pair of ears. The compact ball of my *self* inside my head relaxed too, sending little fingers out, searching for any disturbance.

I heard nothing. No voices, no sounds of movement.

Okay. How do I get us out of here?

I could bet that the werwulf, if it was still alive, had fled. They're strong and unholy quick, but they avoid the authorities just like suckers. A cadre of cops with firepower and vests can cause plenty of damage, and neither wulfen or suckers want to be caught in the open like that. It attracts too much attention. They live by staying at the edges of things, under the cover of night.

Of course, the cops and other authorities didn't want news of the weird getting out; it might cause a panic. Cops, EMTs, firemen—they cover up this sort of thing as a matter of course, consigning it to the dead-file section. Dad always argued with August about whether it was a Conspiracy or just the human need to have things fit into neat little boxes.

So neither side, Real World or officialdom, wanted to meet each other face-to-face. Even if cops had vests and greater firepower, a wulf could wreak a lot of havoc. They're expensive to replace, fine officers of the law. Freelance hunters like Dad have to make do with even more firepower and sneaky cunning, understanding their prey in order to think three steps ahead of it.

Too bad I was just a kid. Dad was the brains of the operation. I just tagged along and told him where to find the biggest weirdness, or broke a hex or two. I mean, I was a great *accessory*, the best weirdness detector around, but he was the boss and the brains and the one with the guns. I was worse than useless on my own, and I had someone else to worry about now, too.

But *the situation is what the situation is*, Dad always said. There was nothing else to do but keep going. If I stopped now I'd drown without even a bubble.

"What's going on?" Graves whispered. He sounded about three years old and scared of the dark. "Jesus Christ, what's going on?"

"It has nothing to do with Jesus," I whispered back, checking the gun for the fiftieth time. If I'd had a spare clip for the gun I'd have racked it in, on the theory that it was better to have a full one than a half-empty one if something else happened.

Dad, you should be proud of me. I'm thinking like you. Trying to, anyway.

I just hoped I could think enough like him to keep us both breathing.

Graves blinked at me. "You shot it." His voice shook like a bad engine. "I thought you were going to shoot me."

I should. Dad probably would. I shut my eyes, leaned the back of my head against the tiled wall, my wet hair finally stopping its dripping. "I wasn't aiming at you."

"What was that thing?" His hand clamped over his shoulder, the pressure bandage mercilessly tight. "It had teeth. It had big teeth. It smelled."

"It was a werwulf." *I shouldn't tell him anything. I should put a bullet in his brain. Dad would put him down as a casualty before he changes. Once bitten, you have twelve hours, sometimes less. That's a fact.*

And a wulf who knew about a hunter was a liability. Dad always said "liability" like it was a filthy word. To him, it probably was.

"You *know* about these things?" The question ended on a squeak.

I shushed him. If he made noise and the cops heard it—were they still around? I checked my watch again. Eight thirty-eight p.m., or 2038 hours if you were all military. Fifty-three minutes since I'd moved us to this bathroom. Was it enough time for the cops to clear a scene this weird?

Outside it would be getting colder. I was bruised and exhausted. I walked cautiously past the stalls to the sinks, where I took another deep breath in, all the way down to the bottom of my lungs, and looked in the mirror.

There was that long but freshly scabbed-up gash along my hairline, but if I left my hair down I'd just look wet and scruffy. Anyone out tonight would probably be wet as well. If I could get us downtown I could probably hail us a cab—if the cabbie was suicidal—and take it to three streets over from my house, and hope nothing was waiting for me inside.

Yeah. And I could fly to the moon, too. If it was bad enough to shut the mall down early, there was little chance of a cab, right? But these people were serious about snow. Maybe they had everything scraped now.

There was a sound behind me. Graves floundered around the end of the stalls. "Don't leave me here." At least he didn't shout it, but he might have thought he was shouting, his voice was so hoarse and constricted.

My throat closed up on me. Dad had told me over and over again what to do if something happened to him. I usually tuned it out—who wanted to think about *that*? Not me, that's for sure. But still . . . *Don't take on any weight; you'll drown. You remember that if anything happens to me. You take care of yourself, Dru. You be strong and do what you have to do.*

But this kid wasn't a sucker or a werwulf yet. He was just a kid.

He'd brought me food and let me see his private hideaway. I got the idea he didn't do that a lot.

He'd *trusted* me. I couldn't just leave him.

Could I?

"I'm not going to leave you." I sounded funny even to myself—breathless, as if I was running up a hill. "You're going to have to do what I say."

Amazingly, he smiled at me. "You're bossy." His pupils were still huge, but a little color had begun to come back into his face, especially along his cheekbones. "I like bossy chicks."

Jesus. At least someone around here was feeling better. "Shut up. You're going to have to do *exactly* what I tell you to do. Got it?" *Or we'll get arrested. Or maybe just killed.*

"Sure. You do this to all your dates?" It was a type of courage over a screaming well of panic. He was really a brave kid, or maybe it was just the shock.

"I don't date." *I never stay anyplace long enough to date.* "Is that silver?" I pointed to his earring, forgetting I still had the gun in my hand until he flinched. He covered it well.

"I guess so. The guy I bought it from said it was."

"What about that? The chain?" This time I used my left hand to point at his necklace. *My bag's down in his room. I need my bag.*

It was too risky. All of this was too risky. If I went back down to Graves's little bolt-hole, we could be caught by the cops (bad) or caught by the possibly rabid werwulf (even worse), healed and ready for round two. They recovered *quick.* I had to get both of us out of here.

I need my bag. The urge was like the urge to pee. I wanted my bag the way little kids want a hug after they've scraped their knees, the way you want sunshine after a long rainy month, or a drink of water in the desert.

"The chain's silver." Some sense came back into his eyes. Giving him questions to answer was a good idea.

"Good. I'm going to go get my bag. You stay here."

That made his eyes wide and wild, the pupils shrinking so the green irises showed. "Don't *leave* me here!" He scraped himself away from the stall, his voice bouncing off tiles.

I shushed him again. "Look," I whispered fiercely, "you don't know how to move under cover. I'm going to go down and get my bag. I'll come back for you and I'll take you somewhere safe."

"It's not safe here?" Sarcasm tinted his tone, but at least he said it quietly. "Jesus. What was that thing?"

"Werwulf. I told you." I looked nervously at the entrance, hoping nobody heard us, hoping nobody was in this part of the mall. Were they gone? It wasn't like the cops to clear a scene in under an hour. Then again, if it just looked like a really weird vandalism thing, they might not stay too long. There had to be plenty of other stuff happening out in the world tonight. Bad weather always strains the emergency infrastructure.

I chewed my already-sore lower lip, tried to think. I *needed* my bag, and I needed to get us both out of the mall and back to the only safe place I knew. How would Dad do it?

If I thought about it that way it seemed almost doable. Almost. Except for the not-having-any-idea-what-to-do-next part.

"Stay here." I was already thinking about cover, plotting out routes and backtracks.

Graves grabbed my arm with surprising strength. "Dru. Don't leave me. *Please*."

I opened my mouth to tell him to shut up and do what I told him, but then I got a good look at him. Deathly pale, the high spots of feverish color still standing out on his cheeks, about ready to fall over by the way he swayed on his feet, his fingers biting into my upper arm. His other arm hung limp and useless.

If I left him here in the girls' bathroom, I might come back and find him unresponsive or already changing. I struggled to *think* clearly, but my clear-thinker seemed busted. I should have left him there. Dad might have shot him just to cut down on the variables; he would *definitely* be telling me to get a move on. The longer I stayed here, the more dangerous it was.

I didn't have anyone else, and I was the reason Graves had been bit. It must hurt like hell.

"Dru." He couldn't speak louder than a sandpapery whisper, and his fingers dug in with feverish strength. I was going to bruise there, too—if I hadn't already. There didn't seem to be an unbruised place on my body. We were both in pretty bad shape.

Another thought rose: Graves's arm awkwardly around me while I cried. He hadn't asked questions or tried any funny business.

I couldn't leave him here.

"All right," I told us both. "Stay right behind me. Move the way I do. We're going to try to stay under cover. How many different ways can you get me down to your room?"

The relief crossing his transparent face bit me hard in the chest. If he hadn't been so pale, he would have looked like Christmas. "Four or five. Take your pick." He swayed, caught himself, and tried to straighten. "I'll keep up. Just don't leave me."

Four or five different routes was good news, if I kept him conscious enough to navigate me. "Okay." I tried again to think clearly, failed just as miserably as before. "I need my bag, and our best option's a bus route that's still going out east. Are any going to be running?"

"The 53." He nodded, his hair flopping in his face. Even his nose looked pale, for God's sake. "Runs all night, even when it snows. I can get you there."

I took an experimental step toward the entrance. He swayed after me, and I thought I had maybe twenty minutes before I had to hold him up.

Move it, Dru. "Okay," I said again. "You and me, Graves. Let's go."

CHAPTER 12

The buses were still running. Chained up and slow as hell on their nighttime schedule, but they were still running in the right direction, and we had our first bit of luck catching the 53 almost as soon as we got to the stop across the main thoroughfare from the mall.

We looked normal enough, shivering and cold; bus drivers don't look too closely if you don't seem actively inebriated. A cab was a lost cause—it also occurred to me during the wait at the bus stop that cabbies are probably inordinately curious about their passengers. *That* was no good.

I watched my house from the corner, shivering in my boots. Graves slumped against me. He'd been almost okay on the bus, but now his head hung and strings of wet curly hair fell in his eyes, curtaining his milk-pale face. His eyes were dilated again, and his lips were close to blue.

Snow in my front yard was pristine. The truck was still missing from the driveway. The light in the living room was on, a rich golden glow in the gloomy orange snow-city light. Thick flakes of white whirled down; both of us were covered in the stuff because I'd dragged Graves off the bus two streets away. He'd almost pitched headfirst into a drift, and we had to walk in the road because of the snowplows racking up mountains of frozen, slushy chunks of ick in the gutters. The sidewalks were damn near iced over and impassable, and sand crunched under my boots. Our tracks would be obliterated in less than half an hour.

Can werwulfen track through snow? Especially if they have a blood trail—I'll bet they can smell it. I shivered at the thought. I didn't even want to think about what the burning dog and the werwulf had been looking for.

Because there was only one answer for that, wasn't there? It was an answer I'd run up against on the bus, the gun a cold weight in my pocket and Graves slumped against me, his head bobbling a little bit as we were bounced around.

It looked like nobody had messed with the house. It looked like the shooting had gone unnoticed. Snow made sound carry itself around weird, and the house had been pretty closed up. I wondered if anyone would have found me yet if the zombie had done what it set out to do.

Now *there* was a nice, happy thought.

There was no cover, but I didn't want to struggle around through the drifts to the back. For one thing, I didn't want to see the shattered debris of the door the zombie had come through any sooner than I had to. For another, Graves was slumping more and more heavily each passing second. I was doing okay keeping him moving, but I didn't feel up to carrying him if his legs gave out.

"Come on." I didn't say it nicely. I all but dragged him up over the mountain range of road-snow piled at the bottom of our driveway. Then it was slogging through snow midway up my shins, each step dragged down with powdery, icy weight. My nose dripped and my cheeks were raw. My fingers felt like frozen sausages. Graves started making a thin noise in the back of his throat, like he was going to pass out.

I didn't blame him. I bet his shoulder hurt like hell. Wulf bites are messy; they grind a lot when they clamp down. He was lucky to still have some use of his arm, his hand tucked limply in his pocket to keep him from looking like Frankenstein's monster. The wound had been still raw and messy when I peeled up the bandage to check it, just after we got off the bus; a good sign for him not changing just yet but a bad sign for him possibly staying out of unconsciousness.

I dug in my coat pocket for my keys. "Don't you dare pass out on me now, soldier," I hissed. The strap of my bag cut into the space between my shoulder and neck, and with Graves's unwounded arm over my shoulders I felt like Atlas holding up the world. I was so tired even my eyelashes hurt. My back was a solid chunk of pain, my side flaring with a red sensation, just under a really bad stitch, with each breath.

The key went into the doorknob; it took me two tries and a round of cursing before I could get the deadbolt open, too. I pushed open the door and was faced with the remnants of zombie stink, not too bad considering how we both smelled now. The house'd had time to air out through the back, I guess.

Graves stumbled. I propped him against the hallway wall and closed the door. Then I got out my gun and I swept the house just like Dad had taught me. Every place we lived we went through the drill, covering fire angles and searching as a two-man team. He also made me do it alone while he timed me. I'd only done it four or five times with the stopwatch in this place, but that's enough when you've been doing something like that for years.

The living room was a shambles, but the only sign remaining of the zombie was thick, fine powder-ash ground into the carpet, a meaningless smudge inside tattered clothes. There was a bullet hole in the wall, and another one lower down I hadn't noticed before.

A little paint and spackle will fix that right up. I shivered, let out a shapeless sighing sound like a sob. My nose ran, clear snot dripping down my lip. I wiped at it with my sodden coat sleeve and continued.

The kitchen was icy and unfamiliar in the dark. The back door hung on its hinges, sound except for a huge hole in the middle of it. There was plywood in the garage—I could nail something up there and hang a blanket over it for insulation. The enclosed porch was cold and dank, smelling like a root cellar, and the glassed-in screen door was miraculously undamaged. I wrestled it closed through a wad of wet snow and looked for something to brace it with, found exactly nothing, and gave up. The snow would drift up against it and keep it closed if I was lucky. Besides, if we had to get out in a hurry, I couldn't lock or block it. I still hadn't swept the upstairs.

Upstairs everything was as I'd left it. The whole house was still.

Quiet as a tomb.

Downstairs, Graves's eyes were half-closed. "Nice place," he mumbled, but the words had a slurred quality I didn't like. His lips were bluer than I liked, too. Pale drops of sweat and water stood out on the ashen gray his skin had turned into, and his pupils were so dilated I could barely see the irises, just dark holes.

I locked the front door and got him upstairs, bullying him up each step. I was sweating and clammy by the time we finished. Then the hard part started. I got him out of his wet clothes, ignoring the snickers as I stripped him down to his tighty-whiteys. He went into my bed under the blankets, and his eyes closed the rest of the way. He sighed just like an exhausted little kid and was out.

I dropped my bag, shucked my coat, and started struggling down to sports bra and panties. I didn't think he'd die of hypothermia—he'd been bitten, and the fever from the bite might help.

What, so he can tear open your throat when he changes?

I wasn't thinking clearly. I was so cold I didn't feel cold anymore, which was a bad sign. I just felt tired. So goddamn tired.

I climbed into bed, stacking the blankets on top of us. Then I took him in my arms, shivering. He was icy, I wasn't much better, and he was making that thin, hurt sound again. I realized I was lying on his shoulder and tried to rearrange myself, managing to move so I wasn't grinding down on his injury. His shirt, torn up and used as a bandage, was chilly and tacky-wet.

"What're y'doin'?" His tongue was too thick for his mouth. I hoped he wasn't changing. His skin was smooth enough against mine.

All the wulfen I'd ever seen were bad shadows in the rearview mirror, or looking just like everyone else who hung out in a bar catering to the Real World. In other words, weird as all get-out. If he changed . . .

I couldn't even finish the thought. My bones had turned to lead bars, along with my eyelids and even my wet hair. If we both died of hypothermia, all of this would be academic anyway.

Graves shifted uneasily, stilled. The prickle of hairiness would give away the change, and the sound of bones crackling. Dad had talked about it—the sound of their bones reshaping, the snarling, the fur rippling out.

God, I hope that's not happening. I let out a long, shaking breath. "Warming you up."

"Jesus." His eyes dropped closed, struggled open. "Y'cold."

"So are you." The gun was on the nightstand. If he changed, he'd probably start to scream when his bones began to remodel themselves. I'd have enough time to take care of the problem.

Dru, you're not thinking straight.

I knew I wasn't. But I was so completely exhausted.

The wind started to moan outside, but inside my room everything was hushed. My fingers and toes hurt, needles rammed all the way through flesh and bone. I hoped we weren't going to lose toes to frostbite. But it wasn't as cold as it could have been if it was still snowing, was it?

I couldn't think. My head was full of mud. I should have warmed him up and gotten something over the hole in the back door. Snow would trickle into the porch if the screen door didn't stay closed, and I'd have a hell of a time cleaning it up.

A little warmth began to steal back into me, then a little more. Graves's cheeks flushed, and he started to sweat. He stopped making that noise, and would jerk himself awake every time his eyelids fell. The time between those little twitches got longer and longer, his breathing evening out.

"Dru?" he finally whispered.

"What?" I roused myself with an effort. *Tired. Got to get up and fix the back door. Then have to think of something. Something I have to do.*

I couldn't remember.

"Are you naked?" His eyes fell shut again, and he made a little hitching sound like a snore.

Oh, for Christ's sake. But I fell asleep before I could work up the energy to be pissed off.

CHAPTER 13

I **woke up with** a pounding headache, stiff and sore all over, with a back made of torn-up iron bars and something wrong with my left arm because Graves's heavy goddamn head was lying on it. I sat bolt-upright and flinched as still, cold air met bare skin. I was sweating—he was *warm*. Sweat cooled rapidly on my back and shoulders. My mouth tasted like day-old coffee mixed with ash.

Graves was on his back. He didn't protest when I scrambled painfully out of the bed, because he was utterly, deeply asleep, his hair lank over his face, his nose lifting proudly. The very, very slight suggestion of epicanthic folds made his closed eyes exotic, the fan of his charcoal lashes even and regular against his cheekbones. The bandage was crusted with blood and something yellow, traceries of blue-black spreading along the vein map up his neck and down his arm, onto his chest.

Doesn't look good, does it?

I looked around for clothes. I still smelled traces of the burning thing from yesterday all over me, but I needed to get something on my shivering skin. I was also hungry as hell.

First things first, though. I pulled on a pair of jeans and a sweatshirt, scooped the gun off the table, and went into Dad's room. I came back with nylon rope—good for rappelling, tying down a load in a pickup, and, not so incidentally, for tying up a kid who might turn into a werwulf.

Werwulfen, especially new ones, have a real problem with silver. That part of pop culture is real enough. The chain around his neck wasn't rubbing red blisters into his skin, which was a good sign. Neither was the skull earring, pressed against his cheekbone by the way his head was turned slightly to the side. A pulse beat strong and steady in his throat. He was skinny but had a lot of good muscle—and if he started to change on me, he would have the kind of hysterical strength that could throw me across the room without thinking twice about it. Or even noticing.

He'd be too busy looking for his first chunk of raw meat.

What am I going to tie him to? The mattress? Jesus, a fine time to wish I had a four-poster.

Fortunately, Dad taught me a lot about knots. A trucker's hitch will cinch someone down—it just gets tighter the more you struggle—and if he couldn't get enough leverage, he couldn't come after me. First I trussed his wrists and elbows, then his knees and ankles; then I ran four more lines between the mattress and the box spring. *That* was a trick. Each one I secured with a trucker's hitch.

If he had to go to the bathroom, he was out of luck. I could always get a new mattress. I couldn't buy a new trachea.

With that done, I washed up. No hot shower for me—I couldn't afford the time. But clean clothes and a scrubbed-clean face does wonders for any girl's mood—even if that face is dead white, hectic flares of color on the cheeks, and with pupils wide enough to look half-wild. The zit on my temple had vanished, and no more seemed to be rising.

Go figure. My hair was a total loss, though. Humidity and cold made me look like the Bride of Frankenstein, except without the cool white zigzags.

That made me think of the streak-headed werwulf, and I shivered. I found a dry pair of sneakers because my boots were still sopping wet, and was ready to start solving problems.

Downstairs, snow had spilled in through the screen door on the little porch, and it was bastard cold. I looked longingly at the box of Cheerios on the counter—my stomach growled just thinking about it—but went to hunt in the garage for plywood instead. My scrounger's luck was good, and in less than ten minutes I had the snow cleared away and plywood bracing the screen door; I nailed more plywood up outside over the hole in the actual back door. I swept up broken glass, listening to the wind moan outside. My fingers were numb and my breath made little clouds in front of my face. I began to regret ever waking up.

I rigged some blankets on a line over the back door to insulate it, taping it down with duct tape, every girl's best friend. Then, finally, I turned up the heat and shivered through my first bowl of cereal. The milk burned, it was so cold. The entire house smelled like fresh air plus a faint, rapidly fading taint of zombie. I was so hungry I didn't even mind.

As soon as I finished the cereal, I put a fresh clip in the gun and checked on Graves. He was still out cold, breathing through his nose and mouth the way little kids do. The house began to warm up, and I sat on the stairs for a long time, hugging myself and staring down the hall at the boxes and the bullet holes blown in the wall.

What are you going to do, Dru?

The hollow place inside me didn't answer. I knew I should get up and eat something else, but I just kept staring at bullet holes. Nothing sounded good now that I had a lump of cold cereal in me.

I held the gun loosely in my right hand. If Graves started to change . . .

Well, technically you've already killed one person, sweetheart. Dad's voice, cool and calm, like every time I was being an idiot. *One more shouldn't be that hard. Just wait until he changes and put him down. You should have done it at the mall.*

Still, it was oddly comforting knowing there was someone in the house who wasn't going anywhere. Kind of pathetic, but I've spent so many nights alone waiting for Dad to come back it was nice to hear the silent sound that means someone else is breathing in the same space. So what if he'd turn into a big hairy beast and try to kill me? The first time a werwulf changed it was unstoppable until it got blood.

That's what the books said. I didn't have any reason to doubt them. Or Dad, who said the same thing.

This is rapidly getting out of hand. Dad's phrase, delivered with a straight face and usually a gun in either hand. *What are you going to do next, Dru?*

I needed a plan. The trouble was, I didn't have one.

"I suppose I should get the living room cleaned up," I said to the quiet. "Wait for him to wake up. Then we'll see."

The hollow place inside me wasn't satisfied by that. Dad was dead. He wasn't coming back. I was alone in the world, and I'd gotten some kid who had tried to help me bitten by a werwulf. There were other things I had to think about, but I was damned if I could remember them. I felt very small and very alone, sitting there on the stairs.

Racking up the score here, kiddo. I shivered, hugging my

knees. The snow was really coming down, wind moaning against the corners of the house. It was 8 a.m. and dark out there, except for the directionless glow between the whirling quarter-size flakes from reflected city light. *Gonna need a new back door. Unless you're blowing town.*

I *couldn't* blow town. Graves would need someone to explain to him what was going on. And someone had killed Dad.

That was what I'd been trying not to think. I mean, I'd killed Dad. But it hadn't *really* been Dad. You can't make a zombie when someone's still alive.

You just can't.

Someone turned him into a zombie. You don't wake up one morning as one of the reanimated. Someone killed him and turned him into a zombie. He wasn't in good shape, either. There was a lot of trauma to those tissues—they rot quicker when they're injured before they die.

I felt like I was in one of those snow globes—you know, where you shake them and the entire inside fills with whirling white. Everything inside still and motionless, surrounded by floating bits of ice. I was trying not to think what I had to think next, and succeeding only in filling my head with static.

I don't know how long I would have sat there if I hadn't heard a sharp, surprised half-yell from overhead.

Graves was awake. I hauled myself up and trudged up the stairs, the gun cold and heavy in my hand.

I didn't want to do what I thought I was going to do.

Tough luck, chickie babe. You have to.

***

He stopped struggling against the ropes as soon as he saw me. The blankets had rucked up away from his toes. The room was warmer, and sweat plastered his long, dead-black hair to his face.

We stared at each other for a few moments. Then he lifted his chapped fingers—lying on his side, it was about all he could do. His voice was husky, and he said the absolute last thing I'd expect a kid who'd gotten bit by a werwulf and tied to a bed to say.

"Kinky." He arched one half of his unibrow, his eyes burning green around the holes of his pupils. He didn't look ready to sprout hair or fangs.

We were coming up on twelve hours since he'd been bit.

"I never figured you for the bondage type," he continued. "How the hell am I going to piss?"

Smart kid.

The gun was loaded with one in the chamber. I clicked the safety off, praying that the next five minutes would go well. I advanced nervously into the room, giving myself plenty of time. The knots looked like they were holding just fine.

"I'm going to ask you a few questions." I managed to keep my tone even. "If you give the right answers, I'll cut the ropes off and we'll go from there."

He licked his lips. His eyes flicked between the gun and my face, and he went very still.

Something told me he knew I wasn't bluffing.

That was great. Because I wasn't so sure. I couldn't kill him on my bed. I couldn't shoot someone like that. Sure, I'd shot the werwulf. It had been just like a video game, just like Dad trained me.

But . . . I *knew* this guy. I couldn't shoot him. He was *human*.

He was the closest thing to a friend I had now.

I stood beside my own bed, near our scattered sodden clothes from yesterday. I leveled the gun. "First question. Where did you get your necklace?"

He swallowed. He'd gone ghost-pale. His pulse throbbed frantically in his throat. "Hot Topic, in the mall. You're not going to shoot me, Dru."

I wish I was half as sure as you sound. I was nerving myself up for something, that was for goddamn sure. "Do you know what it means?"

"Hell, I just got it because it was on sale. People leave me alone if they think I'm crazy and into that cult shit." His Adam's apple bobbed as he swallowed convulsively. "Christ, you're not going to shoot me, are you?"

It's either that or have you tear out my throat. Twelve hours is the limit for werwulf changes. If you haven't changed by now, there's only a couple of reasons why. I leaned down a little, bracing the gun in both hands, and put the barrel to his temple. Kept my fingers carefully locked outside the trigger guard, because accidents can happen. "Do you believe in ghosts, Graves?"

He swallowed again. His throat worked. "Shit, I don't know. Don't shoot me. Please." His voice cracked.

If he knew about the Real World, he would have answered differently. Was he lying?

I didn't want to think so. He hadn't acted like he knew jackshit about it. So that narrowed down the reasons why he wasn't getting all hairy.

I swallowed. My throat was as dry as the stuff you drop into water to get fog for parties. Frozen carbon dioxide. It burns like hell and you can use it in swamps to make gator spirits angry. "Answer this question very carefully, kid. Are you a virgin?"

The silence was so long I thought I was going to have to ask him again.

"What the hell?" He sounded honestly perplexed.

"Yes or no? *Are you a virgin?*" I lost control halfway through. My voice spiraled up into a scream.

He flinched, and I ached to hit him. I wanted to hit *something*, that's for sure. I wanted to *do* something instead of just stand there and threaten him.

"Sonofa*bitch answer me!*" My voice bounced off the walls, made the whole room whirl around me. My blood pounded in my ears. Adrenaline poured through my blood, copper winding me tighter and tighter.

"*Yes!*" he screamed back. "Yes, I'm a fucking virgin, *don't shoot me goddammit fucking please!*"

I froze. My fingers were cramping outside the trigger guard.

His chest heaved. Tears slicked his cheeks and his eyes were squeezed shut. He strained against the ropes without moving, and my entire body had gone cold.

Almost twelve hours, and he was a virgin.

It might be okay after all.

I didn't recognize the hoarse rasp coming from my throat as mine. "All right." I eased the safety back on with a click, *after* I pointed the gun away. Far, far away from both him *and* me. "All right. Fine. All right."

Graves made hoarse little sobbing sounds. I backed off, retreating from the bed.

Jesus. What had I done? I should have asked him that first off instead of putting a gun to his head. I felt sick.

I stumbled for the bathroom and threw up every inch of cereal I'd eaten. Then I cried too, shaking over the cold porcelain. I had to blow my nose three times. When that was done, raw-eyed and sore, I went slowly back down the dark hall into Dad's room. I found a spare holster and put the gun in it, and I got out a bowie knife. The knots would be cinched down too tight to loosen now.

Graves was lying on the bed with his eyes closed, his lips moving soundlessly. I'd just scared the shit out of him.

So what? Better to scare him than get your throat ripped out. The first time a wulf changes, it's unstoppable.

I told Dad's voice to take a hike for once, and began sawing through the ropes. "You were bitten by a werwulf. I had to be sure," I said as I avoided cutting his forearm. My hands were shaking just a little. "Just stay still. We'll have you out of these in a jiffy."

He didn't say anything.

I managed to get the ropes around his ankles and knees cut through, then the ones at his elbows and wrists. He just lay there, limp, breathing heavily.

"I'm sorry." I sounded five years old. The words were empty. It was the kind of thing you say to someone when you've broken a toy or something, not when you've just held a gun to their head and shouted at them. "I had to be sure. If you're a virgin, it's okay; you won't change like a regular wulf. The imprint won't take, because you're a closed door. At least, that's what Dad told me. He was almost always right. I—"

"Shut up," he whispered. His eyes squeezed shut. Tears made his lashes into a damp mat. "Leave me alone."

I backed away on my knees, holding the knife. "I'm sorry. Really. I just—"

"I said, leave me *alone*. Shut *up*." His voice broke.

I wiped at my cheek with my fingers. There wasn't anything else to say. So I just made it to my feet with each piece of my body creaking and left him alone.

CHAPTER 14

I sat on the stairs again, listening to the heater run and the silent un-noise of snow outside. I heard Graves moving around—the toilet flushing, water running, shuffling feet and creaks I hadn't had a chance to learn in this new place yet. Each house has its own set of sounds, and each person sounds different.

He didn't sound like Dad. But still, just hearing someone breathing and walking around was better than nothing. *Way* better than nothing.

My eyes were hot and grainy. I stared at the gun in my hands. Nine-millimeter, dead black, and heavy, its nose sleek and sharp. It was a good gun.

What are you going to do, Dru? Go back to high school and be prom queen? What the hell. Why not?

The answer was right around the corner—I just couldn't think of it. There was something I was missing, something I was trying not to think. It had to do with that door, and the concrete corridor, and the dream hanging heavy in my head, like a lead bowling ball.

Someone turned Dad into a zombie. While he was out hunting. So someone knew about what he was doing, right?

But who could know? What had he been after? He hadn't said anything to me.

The questions revolved inside my head. Then the thing I'd been forgetting since waking up slid into place with a click like racking a bullet into the chamber.

Contacts. Dad had contacts. I should call someone.

Relief so intense it was ridiculous poured through my entire body at the thought. Someone adult, older than me, better-armed and more experienced, who could come out and . . .

. . . do what? Set up housekeeping? Adopt me? Take me on as an apprentice? Make everything okay?

Yeah. Sure. None of the other hunters Dad had let me hang around with were in the *least* parental. But they were older, right? And they'd be interested in something that killed him. They were his friends. Combat buddies. Comrades in arms.

Right?

I closed my eyes. Leaned against the wall, dangling the gun in my right hand.

The stairs squeaked. Graves shuffled down each one like it hurt. There was a dragging sound.

I didn't open my eyes.

When he sat down beside me I was only mildly surprised. We sat like that for a few minutes, until my eyelids flew up and the world came rushing back into my head again.

He had Mom's sunrise quilt from my bed wrapped around his shoulders, and his face was set. He'd pushed his hair behind his ears. He was barefoot. The house was warm enough now.

The messy lacerations of wulfbite were closing, angry pink instead of bleeding crimson or the crusted yellow. The blue-black mapping of his veins had vanished. Their bites heal really, eerily fast. Nobody knows why.

The ticking silence of the heater filled up the space between us. We both fit on the step, he was so birdlike thin.

I'd told him I was sorry. Did he have any idea how sorry I was?

He sat there for a while, fidgeting in that way of his. Then he spoke, quietly. Almost gently, as if I was crying. "Why'd you do that?"

I had to. "You might have changed."

"Changed." He said it so flatly I almost might not have known it was a question.

"Into a werwulf. Like that thing back at the mall that bit you."

"A vherr-what?"

"A werwulf." I considered spelling it for him, decided not to. "As in howl at the moon, silver bullet, Lon Chaney type of thing. Only it's not really like that. They're responsible for some disappearances, but mostly they eat a lot of raw meat and play head games with each other. Humans aren't enough fun. Plus they've got a running feud with the suckers."

"Suckers?"

You don't even want to know. Dad *never even wanted to know.* "I had to know if you'd change."

"So you tied me up and asked if I was a virgin? Help me out here." He shifted, wrapping the quilt more tightly around his bare shoulders. He was shirtless. Of course—his shirt was ruined and his coat was probably still wet.

I glanced down. He wore a pair of my workout pants. They hit him at mid-calf and sagged around his narrow waist. Boy had no hips at all. "It's near twelve hours. Generally, if you don't change by then there's a reason, and you're probably safe. If you're bitten while you're a virgin, some of the transfer of werwulf stuff doesn't get done. It's all theory, but virgins have a higher incidence of not changing." I watched him out of the corner of my eye, waiting for the leaning backward that would tell me he'd stopped listening. People don't want to hear about the Real World, and if you ever try to explain, they just quit listening real early.

He didn't move. Just stared at me. I took a deep breath and forged ahead. "It has to do with magic, I guess. Stuff like that. See, when a werwulf bites and doesn't finish his kill, there's an . . . an imprint, I guess you could call it. If you're a virgin, the imprint doesn't get made right. It's like you're a closed door, and once you have sex that door is opened and some things can take hold. Infect you, almost." I looked down at my knees, just talking to hear myself talk now. Or maybe I was afraid of what he would say once I shut up. "Congratulations. You're mostly safe from wulfbite for the rest of your life. Like . . . like an inoculation." It was a pretty good explanation, and about the sum total of my knowledge of werwulfen. The silent house ate the words. I couldn't think of anything else to tell him.

"Well. That's comforting." He swallowed so heavily I heard it. "Look, Dru, I— "

"I'm glad you didn't change," I said all in a rush. "Because I don't know what I'd have done."

"Shot me." The raw edge of anger smoked under the words. I closed my eyes against it, leaned against the wall. "I guess. Right?"

Yes. No. I don't know. I shot someone else. Hopelessness turned into a rock inside my chest.

"Dru?" As if I wasn't listening.

"Fuck off." *Don't lecture me.*

He persisted. "That was real, wasn't it." It wasn't a question, but he was still trying to convince himself. "I saw a huge-ass dog burning and running after you. I saw the thing that bit me, and the bite's closing up like I'm Wolverine or something. It was *real*."

"Bingo. You get a prize." The gun was so heavy. If I let it slip through my fingers and tumble down the stairs, what would it do? Probably go off and kill someone else. Just my luck.

He asked the question that got everyone in trouble. "What else is real?"

You don't want to know. "You wouldn't believe me if I told you." *Some things you just have to see for yourself. But you're not going to see it, are you? You're going to head for the door and leave me to get through this myself. It'd be better for you if you did, I guess.* Sour heat boiled in my throat. I pushed it down before it could make my eyes prickle.

"You could tell me and see. I mean, I was okay with everything else, wasn't I?"

Wind mouthed the corners of the house. It wasn't as lonely a sound as it usually was, because someone was sitting right next to me. "You got bit for it. I'm sorry." There they were again, those two pale little useless words.

"Well, you're an interesting chick, Miss Anderson." When I didn't reply, he moved, bumping his shoulder against mine. "Did you feel me up when you were tying me down?"

What? My jaw threatened to drop. "Um, no. Did you want me to?"

"Well, it would have been nice." His shoulder bumped mine again. "Can I ask you something?"

I didn't answer. He was going to ask me anyway. People don't say that if they don't want to pry something out of you.

But he surprised me. "What happened to your dad? I mean, really happened?"

"He got t-turned into a z-zombie." I thought I was going to choke on the words, but they came out. Hoarse and broken, but they came out. "Someone did it to him." There it was. Someone had beat Dad up *bad*, and then turned him into one of the reanimated.

I'd said it out loud now. Any chance of waking up and finding it all just a Really Bad, Really Lifelike Dream was now straight in the scupper, as Gran always said.

"A zombie. Okay. Whew. All right." Graves let out a huge sigh, like he'd just finished carrying a heavy container up a steep hill. "So what are you gong to do?"

How the hell should I know? "Make some lunch, I guess." I used the wall to push myself up to my feet. The heater clicked off. "You want something to eat?"

"I wanted to ask you something else." His chin tilted up a bit, and he met my eyes. The skull and crossbones earring fell back, touching his hair. He'd taken off the necklace, and his muscle moved in his bare chest under the quilt. "You got anyone you can call? Like your mom or something, since your dad's . . ." Graves had to swallow before he said the word. "Dead? He's dead, right? That's what zombie means."

I shrugged. "It means dead and reanimated. My mom's dead, too. So is my grandmother." *Everyone's gone. They all keep disappearing on me.* The words were full of old bitterness. "I'm going to make lunch. You must be hungry."

"So you just live here by yourself? In this house?" He was a persistent one. He scrambled up off the steps, wrapped himself up in the red-and-white quilt like a mummy, and shuffled after me.

"For a while. Until I can't anymore." I led him into the kitchen and flicked the light on, setting the gun on the counter within easy reach. "Pretty much all I feel like making is grilled cheese. You want some?"

His eyes roved the surface of the counters like he was looking for contraband. "Why was that dog thing after you?"

That was another question that bothered me. I shrugged. "I don't know. Do you want some goddamn lunch or not?"

"Sure, I'll take some. If you promise not to hold a gun to my head." By the time I rounded on him he was smiling, and had both his hands up in *hey, man, I'm harmless* mode. "Just kidding, Dru. Lighten up, okay?"

Lighten up? I stared at him like he was crazy before getting the cheese and butter out of the fridge. *I tied him down and nearly shot him, and he's telling me to "lighten up"?*

The grin widened, his eyes very bright green now, no hazel tint left. He shook his hair down over his face and puckered his lips, making kissing noises. That strange heat crawled up my cheeks again. It got to me and I laughed, with the butter in one hand and the cheese in the other. We had bread in the freezer—it probably would have frozen on the counter too. That's a good way to keep it fresh down South, especially if you eat a lot of toast. Or grilled cheese.

"That's better." He leaned against the counter, wrapping himself more securely in the quilt. "We're in the same boat, you know. I don't have anyone either. Not anyone I can call or anything. I've been on my own since I was twelve."

Great. What am I supposed to say to that? I got the frying pan out. He didn't mention the plywood and taped-down blankets over the back door. I didn't mention the closing and healing flesh on his shoulder. We were mostly silent, and the wind moaned against the corners of the house.

But I opened up a couple cans of tomato soup and dumped them in a pot, and I didn't feel quite so lonely. Having someone in the house—someone who wasn't going to leave just yet—helped. I even poured him a glass of milk.

Call me domestic.

CHAPTER 15

Holy *shit*." Graves peered into the ammo crate. "Jesus. Was your dad a survivalist?"

He was helping me clean up the living room. He didn't ask about the bullet holes in the wall, or about the faint, horrible smell of rotting zombie. He also didn't ask about the clothes he'd seen me scoop carefully up off the floor and set to soaking in the washing machine. Dad's clothes were torn up and stinky, all his weapons and his billfold missing, along with Mom's locket on its supple silver chain.

I didn't want to think about that.

Snow whirled down thick and steady outside, each flake a muffled erasure of the world. The radio said some people had lost power, but not us. Not yet. I was glad about that—even with the duct-taped blankets the kitchen was chilly, the heater working overtime until I scrounged up more blankets and another two pieces of plywood to create a baffle. It worked pretty well, actually.

Especially since I'd braced the door to the porch.

I opened up the fire-safe box, sure I'd find what I was after. After a bit of digging through papers—birth certificates for both of us, my immunization records, a fat file of records from each school I'd attended—I found the ragged red address book, duct tape clinging to its vinyl cover. Dad's kill book would be in the truck, but contacts were always kept separate.

Okay, Dad. Let's see who can get me out of this, since you've ended up a stain on the living-room rug. A stain I should vacuum up, by the way. In a fresh bag so I can keep it.

A hot bolt of nausea scored through me. That was no way to think about my dead father, was it? But it was either find something snarky to say or start crying, and if I started sniveling now, I might never stop.

Dad hated sniveling. "Bingo," I muttered.

"I mean, what do you use all this stuff for?" Graves continued. I'd given him a pair of Dad's sweats, but he'd turned down my offer of a Peter Frampton T-shirt. So his narrow back was pale and goose-pimpled despite the heater. I could have found him something else to wear, but he made such a big deal over the Frampton I decided he could go shirtless if he was going to be picky. I mean, it's not like it was David Cassidy or something.

I kept trying not to look at his bare skin, though. It made me feel weird. "Hunting." I closed the top of the safe box, made sure it was shut and locked down. "Get out of there, that's live ammo."

He was still poking around. "This isn't really a grenade, is it?"

"Of course it's real. You won't clean out a roach-spirit nest with a fake grenade. Get *out* of there, you're not trained."

"Did your dad teach you how to use this stuff?"

"Most of it. He told me to leave the AK-47 alone, though." I paged through the address book, deciphering Dad's scrawl. Most of the numbers were down South, with a smattering in California and up around Maine. Nothing *near* the freaking Dakotas. I even recognized some of them—the hunter in Carmel who surfed almost every day unless he was too injured from clearing out sucker holes with a team of hard-faced mercenaries; the women who lived out on the back bayou miles away from anywhere and kept the gator spirits pacified and cleared out; August in New York who swore in gutter Polish when he drank with Dad and could make a thin shining yellow flame spring from the tip of his index finger if he was in the right mood.

Graves almost choked. "You have an AK-47?"

And a flamethrower, but that's in the truck. "Only for emergencies." I found a scrap of paper tucked three-quarters of the way back with a number in our new area code. Nothing else. No name, no inked cross that meant it was a safe number for me to dial, no ident info.

Great. Who would take a plane ride out here just to make me feel better? I'd have to explain what happened to Dad, too. Or as much as I knew about what happened to him. Which wasn't much. But still.

The way my stomach turned over at the thought threatened to push out every bit of grilled cheese I'd eaten. It was my fault; I hadn't told him about the owl. "Jesus," I whispered, staring down at the number. It was on the back of a receipt from an occult shop in Miami, the one where Dad had found a glassy shard of obsidian good for taking down chupacabras. He'd FedExed it out to Tijuana for Juan-Raoul de la Hoya-Smith.

The goatsuckers were really bad around Tijuana. Juan-Raoul said it was the heat and the *tamales*.

Dad had stayed closeted with the dreadlocked, scary-looking owner of that shop for a good two hours after it closed, while I wandered around looking at things and getting hungrier and hungrier. When he'd reappeared, his face had been stony-set and white, and he'd stayed up drinking in our hotel room all that night. I'd ordered room service and watched old cartoons until I fell asleep.

Now I wondered if Dad had gotten this phone number there. I wondered if it was safe—the inked cross meant "safe"; the slashed circle meant "unsafe except in an emergency"; and no sign could mean anything.

It was Dad's handwriting, no doubt about it. Nobody else had access to the book, and there was his way of making a 9 from the bottom with a single line. I wondered whose number it was.

I was going to have to go to a pay phone and find out. It was the only number in this area, but it didn't have a mark next to it. It wasn't like Dad to forget a thing like marking a safe contact.

It wasn't like him at all. But he hadn't been himself since that shop with the cottonmouths hitting the glass with hard, padded sounds, making that horrible ratcheting noise. I looked up at the living-room window. The blizzard wind made a low chuckling sound, mocking me.

"Dru? You okay?" Graves was suddenly there. I hadn't seen him moving as I stared at the window, lost in thought.

Woolgathering, Gran would have called it. As in, *Don't woolgather when they's work to be done, Dru. Go milk the goats and look'n fer eggs, and when you come back I'll teach'n you how to use a pendulum. Won't that be fun?*

Only with her thick Appalachian accent, it sounded slow as molasses inside my head. I could get out the pendulum now, but it wouldn't be any good when I was wishing and hoping too hard.

Sometimes things like pendulums or tarot cards will just tell you what you want to hear, not the truth. Gran always said you should see it for yourself instead of using "crutches," but the crutches were good when you didn't have time to put yourself in a trance or wait for a dream or omen.

"I'm fine." I shook the idea away and copied the number on a plain piece of anonymous scrap paper, then shoved it in my pocket. The receipt was Evidence, and we Minimized Evidence, so it went back in the book. The contacts went back into the fireproof box, and I looked around the living room. There was nothing to do for the time being while we were snowed in, so I searched for something to say to get the conversation off me. "You can't go anywhere in this kind of weather, you know."

"I thought I'd just stay with you anyway. Seeing as how you're so interesting." He waggled his eyebrows, but the effect was lost under his mop of hair. He rubbed at his shoulder gently, the pink traces of werwulf bite already fading. The scars would be white and star-shaped before long, little puckers where the teeth had punctured the skin. "Besides, I can't get back into the mall just yet. Or anywhere else."

The quick healing was eerie, and the wounds just *looked* wrong, the way all wounds from the Real World do.

I'm sorry. I didn't say it. Instead I pushed myself to my sock feet and shivered, staring out the front window. The snowflakes were amazing, thick and cottony. "How often does it snow like this?"

"About four or five times every winter. School will be back open tomorrow; they'll have the snowplows going all night. You should think about going."

Yeah. I'll get right on that. I rubbed at my temple, where the zit was gone. It still hurt a little, though, deep under the skin. I hate those zits that burrow underground. You think they've vanished, but no, they just barricade themselves right next to the bone and hurt.

And my back twinged as I stretched carefully. "I don't have any big dreams to keep me in school. What are you, a guidance counselor?"

"You have to think about the rest of your life." He sounded serious, just like an ABC After School Special, pushing his dead-black hair away from his forehead. "Seriously. High school isn't forever. If it was, I'd kill myself."

That makes two of us. "High school doesn't even *matter.* When I turn eighteen I'll be able to smoke and vote, not to mention get a decent job."

"Not if you keep skipping. The way to get a decent job is to play the game well enough in high school, so you can get into college on a good GPA. That way you don't end up poor and sucking on forties out in the Circle K parking lot, like my stupid stepdad." Graves stretched. His eyes had turned a sleepy moss green. "Can I have another sandwich?"

"You know where the kitchen is." *I need to find the truck. Then I need to find out who did that to Dad. And who this number belongs to.* My left hand curled into a fist, shoved inside my pocket to touch the paper. It was the only lead I had for now.

I thought Graves would keep bugging me, but apparently he was *really* smart. He left me alone in the silent living room with its faint horrible smell that lasted even after I got the ancient vacuum cleaner out and sucked every last trace of ash into a fresh bag.

It was the only way I had to keep some piece of Dad. He deserved a funeral. He deserved to be buried with Mom.

That was the wrong thought, and it made everything even worse. Something inside my chest was tearing open, and it was hard work to try to keep it closed over. That's the funny thing about old hurts—they just wait for a new heartache to come along and then show up, just as sharp and horrible as the first day you woke up with the world changed all around you.

I taped the bag shut and tucked it in the fireproof box; then I had to lean over the top of the box for a while, shaking and keeping the sobs muffled in my throat while Graves clinked around in the kitchen, listening to the weather report on the radio and occasionally bursting into snatches of song.

I was glad he was in a good mood.

CHAPTER 16

The bad part of the storm lasted not a week but three days, and Graves turned out to be a halfway decent cook. I'm no slouch in the kitchen—Gran took care of that—but Goth Boy was better. He made me omelets and was a fair hand with coffee, even though he did it too weak like most civilians. He slept in Dad's cot, dragged into my room and neatly made each morning.

I got the idea he was on his best behavior. It was kind of nice to half-wake in the middle of the night and hear someone breathing, though. Like I was in a hotel room with Dad. I would half-smile and roll over, and I slept pretty okay.

By the third day I was sick of the house and in a state of nervous tension that had me working the heavy bag in the garage, shivering as sweat steamed on my skin and I popped punches like a boxer, shuffling, and did my katas. It hurt, but I was used to that, working through the flinches as my muscles reminded me I'd mistreated them.

The tai chi helped a little bit. The breathing and the quiet movements—full moon rising over the water, single whip, play the guitar—cleared out the inside of my head. It was the only time I wasn't chewing myself into little mental bits. The problem was, as soon as I stopped, listening to the broken garage door bend and flex as the wind plucked at it, all the problems started crowding back inside my skull again.

At least while I worked out I could sometimes hear Dad's voice in my head. Better than nothing. But I didn't touch the weight bench in the corner. Dad was always picking up cheap barbells at garage sales, since it didn't make sense to tote them around the entire continent with us. The bench itself was a remnant from two cities ago, and one of the first things I'd pitch if I was packing to leave.

Except I kept thinking Dad would stamp out into the garage, growl a greeting, and expect me to spot him for a set or two.

I worried about the truck outside in this kind of weather, I worried about *finding* the damn truck so I could get out of town, and I most especially worried about whatever had turned Dad into a zombie.

The snow had blown itself out, and the weather report said it would be clear and chilly the next few days. School was set to open up, and Graves had a bad case of cabin fever as well. He was getting tired of wearing Dad's clothes, since they were all pretty much too baggy for him. I washed his jeans and he even condescended to compliment my long-sleeve Disco Duck T-shirt. We watched cable until I could hum along with all the advertising jingles again. We could agree on old sci-fi B movies, but he didn't want to watch the horror flicks.

I didn't blame him. So we stuck mostly to cartoons.

The fourth day turned over into the quiet cold before dawn,

and I woke up in my bed with Graves leaning over me in only his tighty-whities, shaking me with a clammy-cold hand. "Someone's at the door," he whispered, and I bolted out of bed so fast we almost cracked skulls.

"Who is it?" I grabbed a sweater and struggled into it, hearing the knocking—dull thuds muffled by the acoustics of snow—that hadn't managed to dent my dreamless sleep.

Or had I dreamed? I couldn't be sure.

I made it halfway downstairs just as the thudding stopped. Graves bumbled along behind me until I turned around and gave him a glare, putting a finger to my lips. He froze in the act of opening his mouth, scratching at the lower curve of his ribs on the right.

Three more thuds, each very distinct. I froze, my skin going cold and prickling, every hair on my body standing straight up and doing its best to escape my skin.

I knew that feeling. Gran had called it the singing willies. Dad called it the tingles.

I called it *something nasty on the other side of that door.*

And me without a gun or anything.

It tasted like old sludge and rust, the tang of iron against the back of my palate in that special place ordinary people don't have. Dad said he always knew when I was getting the tingles by the look on my face, and it must have been true, because Graves went white as milk under his coloring, his nostrils flaring and his messy hair quivering as he shook like a dog caught between cowardice and outright peeing itself with fear.

I caught something shifting over the surface of the door, a ripple like blue lines, just caught out of peripheral vision. The bolt of pain searing through my head caught me unaware, and I let out a hard, whistling breath.

I snapped a quick glance at the entrance to the living room. Stopped myself—the blinds were up, I hadn't pulled them before bed. No cover. There were weapons up in my room. I'd have grabbed one on the way out, but if a cop was at the door—or another adult authority figure—I would have gotten myself in trouble.

This is getting ridiculous.

One last knock on the door, a playful tap. *Little pig, little pig, let me in.*

I let out a soft, shallow breath, just a sip of air. Pointed at Graves, pointed upstairs, and made a gun with my forefinger and thumb. Raised my eyebrows meaningfully.

He nodded, the pink scars on his shoulder standing out vividly against pale skin. His undies had ridden up into the crack of his narrow ass, of which I was treated to a full view as he turned and tried to go as quietly as possible up the stairs.

I settled down into a crouch, watching the door, my entire skin alive and alert to every sound I could possibly pick up. Whoever it was, they were on the front porch, waiting. I knew it as surely as I knew my own name. It's like being able to see the heat shimmer off pavement on a summer day, the disturbance created by something weird standing in the normal world. The blue lines trembled on the edge of being visible, the house's space rejecting something inimical.

Every place we lived, I usually snuck out of my room the first night and traced the windows and outer doors with the wand Gran left, feeling my will bleed through the rowan wood and into the fabric of the walls themselves. She called it "wardin'" or "closin' up the house." Dad called it "that old Appalachia foolishness," but never very loudly, and he never stopped me.

Too much of what Gran taught me was useful. He just made a

token protest, that was all. I never pointed out that the protest was ridiculous, considering *his* line of work. It was just one of those things.

Sometimes I almost saw those thin blue lines running like lightning over the physical texture of the walls and windows. This time, it seemed like they were getting stronger, the lightning crackling together and concentrating, repelling something.

Holy shit.

The stairs creaked. The house responded, singing its almost-morning song under a blanket of snow. Yesterday the front yard had been a carpet of white, only barely broken by nubs where the picket fence stood guard, buried under a drift.

The front door did not creak. It just stood there, radiating the secret of something behind it, running with blue light I could almost, *almost* see. My palms had gone slick with sweat, my mouth cotton-dry and tasting funny, like morning and rust all swilled together.

That's not rust, Dru. That's blood. The voice of instinct announced it quite calmly. *It's something weird and it smells like blood. It's on your front porch, maybe looking at the dead plants in plastic pots you never bothered to move. If you look out the window in the living room, what do you want to bet you'll see it grinning back at you?*

A faint rattling, scratching noise touched the door. I began to feel woozy, thinking of Dad's bone-scraped fingers screaking against glass.

Little pig, little pig, let me in.

There's a lot of things in the Real World that can't cross a threshold without an invitation. Zombies aren't one of them—but maybe this thing was, and maybe the old ritual of closing up the house Gran had taught me was doing some good.

Maybe? No, *definitely*. "Not by the hair on my chinny-chin-chin," I mouthed, as Graves tried to move quietly down the stairs behind me. A board groaned sharply under his weight, and he let out a breath and froze.

The sense of presence leached away, like oily water sliding down a drain. I heard a thin sound that might have been a chuckle or a scream, depending on how far away it was.

I sat down hard on the stairs because my legs wouldn't hold me up. They were shaking too bad, and weak as wet noodles.

Graves handed me the gun over my shoulder. I took it, not having the heart to tell him the thing at the door was gone. My legs jittered like I'd had a jolt of pure caffeine laced with terror.

Well, I certainly had the terror. It spilled through me, dark as wine and tasting of ash and metal.

"It smells bad," Graves whispered. "What is it?"

I don't know enough to even guess. Except just one thing—it's bad. Really, really bad. I swallowed four or five times, my throat dry as silicon chips. "You can smell that?"

"Yeah. It smells nasty. Something rusting." His nostrils spread slightly as he inhaled, taking in a gulp of air that flared his rib cage. Muscle stood out in his neck and shoulders. He was shaking, too.

"That's not rust. It's blood." We both let out the breath at the same time, me at the end of my sentence, him as if he'd been waiting for me to exhale. "Are you psychic?"

"Me? No. I can't even get a date." He gave me a glance, and his eyes burned sickly phosphorescent green. Against his deadly paleness, the ethnic coloring of his skin drained away to stark white, the glow of his eyes was an insult. "It's gone, isn't it."

"It is." I wished my legs would stop shaking. "I don't know what it was." *But I can guess, can't I? It pretty much means one thing—something so bad even Dad would turn tail and run hard from it.*

I just hope I'm wrong.

***

Dawn came up clear and cold, snow throwing back thin sunlight under an aching-blue sky brushed with high white horsetail clouds. I put on Dad's Army sweater and his surplus coat, threw on a pair of jeans, stepped into my boots and stamped downstairs. I squinted at the ammo box, which was better than staring at the grease-dusty stain on the carpet.

Did I want to go around armed in broad daylight? It was looking more and more like a good idea. But still, the thought of getting caught with a firearm, no good ID, and no good explanation why I was packing heat was daunting.

To say the least.

"I still think I should go with you," Graves said. He leaned against the door to the living room, hands stuffed in his jeans pockets.

I shook my head, my braid bumping my shoulder. I'd drenched my hair in conditioner and braided it back, wanting it out of the way. "Dad would kill me if I dragged a civilian into this." I winced inwardly as soon as I said it, soldiered on. "Best thing for you to do is forget you ever saw any of this and go back to getting through high school." *Since something hinky is knocking at my front door and I can't blow town unless I have the truck. You're already too involved.*

"Yeah, well." He shrugged, thin shoulders rising and dropping. "Fat chance. What are you going to do, anyway?"

I cast another longing look at the ammo crate and picked up my backpack. The glare of snow outside made the bare walls even whiter, the bullet holes next to Graves standing out in sharp relief. "I'm going to make a phone call."

"Who you calling? Ghostbusters?"

I suppose you had to make that joke sooner or later. I mentally reviewed everything in my backpack, ran over how much money I had again. "I don't know yet."

"You don't know who you're calling?" His unibrow peaked on either side, forehead wrinkling as he mulled this over. "Jesus."

"Look, I've been doing this most of my life. I can do without the editorial." I thought about it for a few more moments, then strode over to the smaller weapons crate and dug for a few seconds, coming up with a switchblade. I pressed the button and was rewarded with a *snick!* as the suicide spring unleashed the stiletto. I studied the silver coating along the flat.

Silver doesn't belong on the edge where it can be sharpened off. If you load a blade along the flat, it might disturb the balance, but it stops a lot of things cold. And I could explain a military-surplus stiletto-style switchblade a lot easier than a firearm. I was pretty sure I could even talk myself out of getting detained if all I had on me was a blade.

I pressed the button and used the top of the weapons crate to close the knife, stuffed it in my jacket pocket.

Graves shrugged and peeled himself away from the wall. "I'm going with you."

"Look—" But he was already gone. I heard him take the stairs two at a time and guessed he was heading for his coat.

What could I say? He'd already been bitten. Once the Real World gets its teeth in you, it's hard to go back to nine-to-five and Happy Meals.

And . . . well, I listened to him moving around upstairs and could almost pretend he was Dad.

My conscience pinched me, *hard*, right in the middle of my chest. *Dru, you can't let him in on this. He's already been banged around and bitten. He might get worse if he gets mixed up further.*

But I was a kid too, and on my own. I wanted some help and he was looking like the best help I was going to get.

It wasn't fair.

But I'd gotten him bit—I wasn't naïve enough to think the burning dog and the werwulf had just been in the neighborhood and wanted an Orange Julius after closing hours. Not with something tapping at my door before dawn, too. Something the blue lines of Gran's warding—which seemed much stronger now than ever before—had sat up and taken notice of.

It wouldn't be decent of me to drag him along any further. He'd just end up getting hurt—he didn't have any experience at all.

I swallowed, hard. Slid my bag's strap over my head, pulled on a stocking cap, and yanked my gloves on. It looked bastard cold out there. When I stepped out the front door the air was like a dry suckerpunch to the lungs; I gasped and started shivering immediately, hunching my shoulders and wrapping a scratchy wool Army-surplus scarf around my neck. *Jesus. This isn't people weather. It's Popsicle weather.*

I was fairly sure Graves would lock up on his way out, so I crunched carefully down the porch steps. I was miserably unsurprised to see the snow in the front yard was still pristine. Whatever had knocked at the front door hadn't left any footprints.

Great.

I was already caked with snow up to my knees by the time I made it onto the street. The plows had come by again that morning, so the going was treacherous but not impossible. Dru Anderson, Fearless Teen Hunter of the Weird, slipping and sliding on crusted ice. But Jesus, if I had to stay home I'd start chewing on the walls.

And who was to say that something wouldn't come back once the sun went down, and bring someone with it that the warding wouldn't stop? My best chance was to try to make contact with someone now.

"*Dru!*" Graves yelled.

I didn't hunch my shoulders, just kept going. My boots had some good traction, but I couldn't go faster than a sort of skating crawl.

"*Dru! Wait up!*"

Kept going. Once I hit the cross-street I could hook down and get to the bus shelter, and hopefully the buses were still running on time. Maybe he'd get tired of yelling once I made it clear I wasn't listening.

Crunching sounded behind me, a fast light patter that sounded wrong. Then Graves all but plowed into me from behind, grabbed my shoulder, and we almost went down in a heap on the frozen roadway. I grabbed at his wrist, locked it, and found some solid footing, almost spinning him in a half-circle before he jerked his arm away much harder than he should have been able to.

I stared at him; he stared at me. His mouth was half-open, short light breaths puffing vapor into the chill. His cheeks were already raw and reddened, and his hair was even wilder than usual, almost standing straight up and spitting sparks. The effect was startling. He looked like a cat rubbed the wrong way with a balloon.

"Jesus," I gasped. "What the hell?"

"I'm going *with* you," he announced. Like I was stupid. "For Christ's sake, Dru."

"You're going to get yourself killed. And maybe get me killed too. Let *go!*" *And Jesus, how did you run like that?* A nasty supposition halfway rose in the back of my head, but I killed it. I had enough problems. I yanked my arm free.

He set his jaw stubbornly, and the breeze turned knife-sharp. My hair felt like it was freezing to my head, and the layers I was wearing weren't helping as much as I'd thought they would inside the house.

"You got me into this." His hand dropped to his side, and he squared his shoulders. "I got bit by something that shouldn't be *real*. None of this should be fucking *real*. And you're telling me to be a good little boy and run along home. No dice. I told you the first one's free, Dru, but this ain't the first one. This one you're paying for, and you're taking me with you. You *owe* me."

"I don't owe you anything." I knew it wasn't true even as I said it. If I hadn't been hiding in the goddamn mall, would the burning dog-thing have come to the house? Good luck getting the thing off my back then. He'd saved my life—and even if he didn't know it because he was a babe in the woods, *I* did.

Andersons pay their debts, Dad always said. *And quick, before they mount up.*

But what about the thing knocking on the front door? Someone knew where I lived now.

Someone—or some*thing*.

My stomach turned hard and sour. Graves stared at me like he was trying to will a hole in my forehead. Little ice crystals touched his hair, and his cheeks weren't just red now, but flaming. We were both shivering.

He didn't even have a scarf. For a native of this place, he seemed woefully unprepared.

I didn't even know what to do; I was just making it up halfass as I went along. "My dad is dead." The tone I used—flat, normal, as if I was talking about dinner—surprised me. Snow muffled the words; they plopped down exhausted as soon as they left my lips. "I'm sorry I got you into this. Do me a favor and go home so you don't get any further in."

"Hey, I don't know if you noticed, but I don't have a picket fence and fireplace to go back to. I'm on my own like you are, and for longer, too." He hunched his shoulders, already looking miserably cold. "I could've just left you sitting there in the mall. I got involved because I wanted to, and now I'm *in* it. So can we get moving before I freeze to death, or is that too much to ask?"

I took a step back, found my footing, and turned. Headed off down the street. Some of the neighbors had cleared their sidewalks, but most of them hadn't bothered. The gutters were mounded with snowplow ick.

Graves crunched along behind me. I tried to ignore him. *Good one, Dru. What the hell do you need him along for? He's only going to drag you down. Or you're going to drag him down.*

But he caught up with me as we reached the end of the block, and I didn't step away or try to keep ahead of him. He didn't say another word for a long time, and while that was okay, I kind of wished he'd talk to me.

It might have stopped me from thinking scary, scary thoughts.

CHAPTER 17

The coffee shop was one I'd never been in before, and it was jammed with people in heavy winter coats, the windows fogging with collective breath. I watched the street for a bit, Graves sitting across from me and fiddling with a paper cup, his legs stretched out and his knee bumping mine every once in a while until I shifted.

"All right," I said, finally, when I'd watched the traffic moving on the street for long enough. I took a gulp of my hot chocolate, found it was cold. "We go over it again. I'm going up to that pay phone. I'm popping in the change and dialing. I'll see who answers and play it by ear. As soon as I hang up, you get up and meet me up at the corner. If I walk up on the building side, you peel away, take the 34 bus, and meet me at my house in a few hours. If I walk up on the street side, it's safe to act like you know me. Got it?"

I got an eye roll and a shrug in response. "I got it, I got it. Very James Bond. You really *have* been doing this a while." He didn't look at me, staring at the line going up to the counter. His face squinched up as if he tasted something bitter. "This place really reeks."

I shrugged. It was just a regular chain coffee outlet, with hordes of overpriced crap crowding the shelves and rickety tables, the kids behind the counter scrambling to keep up with the nonfat, soy chai, double shot, sugar-free, dry foam, drip please, do you have a sugar substitute? People shuffled up to the counter, got their froofy java, and shuffled out the door, usually jabbering away on cell phones about something useless or meaningless.

None of them knew about the Real World. None of them were so scared their bones felt like water.

"They don't have a clue." I scooped up my not-so-hot-anymore chocolate and scraped my chair away from the table. My back still hurt, twinges running down either side of my spine like a river.

A lady the size of a pickup truck in a massive blue parka—so large she looked practically square from the back—manhandled her kid up to the counter. The poor kid looked about five, bundled up against the cold, a wide slick of snot running down his upper lip, which he kept wiping at with a crusted sleeve. He stared raptly at the wall below the counter as his mom jabbered at the tired-looking blonde girl behind the counter. The curve of the wall seemed to fascinate him, since it bulged out to hold the coffee machines off to their left, and he ran his mittened hand along it until his mother jerked him back like she wished she had a choke collar on him. He let out an indignant sound and she shook him the way a dog will shake a puppy, but without a mama dog's gentleness.

My stomach turned into a cold lump. "Not a single goddamn clue," I repeated, and tossed my still-full cup into the trash on my way out the door.

The cold was full of exhaust and a bitter metal tang that probably meant more snow. I crunched down the sidewalk—a sheet of deicer pellets that looked like blue rock salt lay unreeled in front of every downtown business—toward the pay phone. I was pretty sure it worked; it'd given me a dial tone earlier when we walked past toward the coffee shop.

I dug in my pocket for quarters and the number, copied onto a blank anonymous scrap of notepaper. I ran over the plan again, trying to look for weak spots or angles, anything I'd missed, and I suddenly wondered if Dad had ever felt this way. This *responsible*. Throat dry, stomach churning, worry like a diamond-eyed rat chewing inside my head with bright, sharp teeth.

When I was little, I used to think he could do anything. He'd show up at Gran's every few months, sometimes with bruises or walking a little slow, and Gran would bake a cake, lay out a supper with everything he liked. It got to where I could tell when he was coming in by how early Gran got up and started cooking in the morning. She always knew before he would come bouncing up the washboard driveway, even though the house had no phone.

I remembered him picking me up and whirling around until I was dizzy while I shrieked with laughter in the front yard, a field of daisies and grass Gran hacked at with a machete every once in a while. Or him taking me out into the woods a little later and teaching me to shoot—first plinking with a BB gun, then with a .22 rifle, and last of all with a pistol and a shotgun. That was my twelfth summer, the one before Gran died.

I shook the memory away and stepped up to the half-booth. The mouthpiece slipped against my gloves, and I consoled myself that not a lot of germs would be able to live on it when it was this goddamn cold. I plugged the quarters in and dialed, then stuffed the paper back into my pocket. *Leave no trace, Dru girl. Think about what you're doing.*

I waited, heart pounding, a nasty sour taste filling my throat up to my back teeth.

Ringing. The phone worked, at least. Two rings. Three. Four.

Someone picked up.

They didn't say anything, though. Instead, there was the peculiar not-quite-dead sound of a line with someone breathing on the other end. I listened, counting off the seconds. There was faint, indecipherable noise in the background, like traffic.

One one thousand. Two one thousand. Three one thousand.

There was a hissing sound, breath escaping between tongue and teeth, not quite whistling.

Six one thousand. Seven one thousand. Eight one thousand.

"Don't hang up, little girl." Male. Sounded pretty young, too, but something in the spacing of the words was off. Like an accent, and unlike.

My entire body flushed hot, then chilled. I tasted wax oranges and salt, but faintly. *Nine one thousand. Ten one thousand.*

"Quiet as a mouse." There was a short, bitter little laugh, as if the guy at the other end had a mouthful of something foul. "Fine. When you're ready for more answers, come find me. Corner of Burke and 72nd. You can just walk right in."

Fourteen one thousand. Fifteen one thousand. I jammed the receiver back down in its cradle and stepped back, breathing heavily, all my muscles threatening to turn into noodles. *Jesus. Jesus Christ.*

I glanced around. The dangerous taste of oranges intensified, coating my tongue. *Shit. What now?* My legs took care of moving me away from the phone, hugging the building side of the walk. There were even dry patches where the building overhangs kept the snow off.

I didn't wait to see if Graves peeled off and headed for the bus. I hoped he'd be smart.

Burke and 72nd. I had to find a map. The transit center would have one, and it was a good place to lose a tail. I wasn't sure if someone was following, but the thick, clotted citrus filling my mouth warned me. Sometimes Real World baddies can get a lock on you even over the phone line, Dad said—hey, they were psychic, too. It was why we bothered being cautious about phone numbers—and my best bet was getting enough distance to confuse whoever it was.

There hadn't been an inked cross, so it wasn't a safe number. But he, whoever he was, might not know for sure it was me. Hopefully he wouldn't know if Dad had given the number to another hunter, if there had been a backup, or just *who* I was.

Too much you don't know, Dru. This might have been a mistake.

Still, now I knew something. I knew where a trap was. Where there was a trap, there was a way to spring it and find out who was behind it. If I was careful, and lucky.

You might be careful, but you're just a kid. Dad should be doing this. He was smart and strong, and if someone turned him *into a walking corpse, you don't have a chance.*

But I was all there was. What else was I going to do?

Skip town. Get the hell out.

Yeah, right. In the snow. With no car. *That* sounded like a way to get caught by something or someone. And not a nice way, either.

I put my head down and lengthened my stride, still sticking to the building side. The sky was a freezing, aching blue, clouds blinking over the lens of the heavens. Some of them were heavy gray, a thick billowing edge trailing infinity in its wake.

I didn't look back to see if Graves was doing what I'd told him.

He was on his own for the next few hours, until I was sure it was safe for me to go home.

Until I was sure I wouldn't bring anything home *with* me.

The transit center was two streets over. I stood looking at a map of downtown and finally found Burke and 72nd on the edge, where the streets started to bleed away into the suburbs. Only one bus went out that way. I checked the sky, traced the route with my fingertips, looked for escapes. There weren't any.

This would be a lot easier if I had the truck. Come on, Dru. Plan. Use that brain.

I stood staring at the transit map, willing it to show me something different. I needed to make sure my trail was clear, go home, and plan.

A bolt of glassy pain lanced through the center of my brain. I sucked in a breath, flinching, but it passed as soon as it had come, leaving only a ringing sound in its wake, like a wet wineglass stroked just right. Everything else was drowned in silence like deep water.

I looked up.

The world stood frozen in sharp detail. The buses were caught mid-idle, clouds of breath hanging out of everyone's mouth, each puff of exhaust or breath solid like wax castings. A guy in a long dark coat was flicking away a cigarette butt, its smoke trailing thinly from his fingers like a leash. People stood, balanced on one foot or another, like the movie of life had just hit pause and someone had forgotten to tell me.

A snow-pale fluttering moved atop one of the buses. I stared.

There, on top of the long, blunt-nosed shape, Granmama's white owl fluffed its wings, pinned me with a yellow stare. Its head cocked to the side, as if to say, *What's up, boss?*

It was hard to move. Clear air had hardened to syrup around me.

The best I could manage was a swimming amble, fighting against drag. Three steps, four, toward the bus, which stood with its door open, the driver inside motionless, a CB handset to his mouth and his eyes shut, in the middle of a blink.

The world snapped around me like a rubber band. Sound flooded back, engines and coughs and people talking, the low moan of the wind. I stood for a moment, staring up at the driver as he finished jabbering into the radio and glanced down at me.

"Getting on the bus, kid?" He had Santa Claus apple cheeks and a full white beard, and a kerchief of the American flag knotted around his neck. His knuckles were swollen and reddened, and he looked as cheerful and nonthreatening as you'd want someone to be behind the wheel of several tons.

I climbed aboard, heart thumping, showed my bus pass, and took a seat a quarter of the way back—close enough to the driver that delinquents or crazies in the rear wouldn't bother me, but far enough back the driver wouldn't notice much of anything I did unless I had some sort of vomiting seizure or something.

The way I felt, a seizure might've been an option. I had to struggle to breathe deeply.

I was sweating under my coat, scarf, and hat. But my teeth kept wanting to chatter, and goose bumps prickled hot and hard on my arms and legs. I folded my arms, trying not to feel as if I was hugging myself for comfort, and when the bus started up and began lurching, I wondered if the owl was still on top. Or if anyone would see it.

Way to go with the woo-woo, Dru. But there was a curious comfort—Gran had taught me about running on intuition. If her owl was here, I didn't have to worry much about being led astray. I just had to go with it, and I didn't have to convince Dad that it was serious and for real instead of just kid fears or an overactive imagination. Sure,

I was supposed to watch out for stuff he couldn't eyeball, and he always said my instincts were good. . . . But still, I guess adults have problems with this sort of thing, even when they know the monsters are out there.

I'd never had the world stop around me before. And the owl had never shown up during broad daylight. It was a nighttime thing, a dream thing.

I shivered again.

Watch your ass, Dru. Just because you're getting a message doesn't mean it's a good one.

It was just what Dad would have said. Gran might have just nodded, her peaky gray eyebrows going up in that particular way, the one that meant I'd just stated something so obvious it didn't bear repeating or remarking on.

I swallowed a sudden wave of homesick loneliness. The taste of oranges faded as the bus wallowed through a turn, tires rasping and gritting on sand-covered roadtop, and crept out of the transit center. I looked steadily out the window, my eyes pricking with hot tears, and waited for the next thing.

* * *

Two hours later the sky had turned into a pale gray bruise, small stones of snow were pattering down, and my mouth tasted like I'd been walking in a citrus grove again. I heard that same ringing, like a gong after its tone has faded but before it stops vibrating, and pulled the stop cord. My hand just flashed out and caught it, really without any direction on my part.

Running on intuition is like that. You never know what crazy shit's going to happen next.

"Keep warm out there," the driver said as I passed. He'd said the same thing to every ever-loving person who got off. I just pulled my cap further down, almost to my eyebrows, and hoped I wouldn't slip and fall on my ass when I hit the ground outside.

I exhaled sharply, looked around. The bus shelter here was a shell of plastic, scarred with graffiti, and warehouses slumped all around under the iron-dark sky. The light had deepened but was failing fast, sunshine struggling to make it through whirling snow. It was late in the afternoon, and it gets dark quickly in winter this far north.

Real dark, and real quickly.

I cast around. Considered spitting to get the taste of wax oranges off my tongue. The snow hissed, driving in small particles against the bus shelter, and Granmama's owl glided in on soft muffled wings, a cleaner white than the dirty sky.

You know, I'd be diagnosed crazy if I told a shrink about this. What the hell is an owl doing out here? But I followed carefully, my soles crunching against snow that started to creak when I stepped in it. What sidewalk there was wasn't cleared out here—I had to fight through a shin-deep freeze, scramble over a heap of dirty crap thrown up by snowplows, and cross the street. Then there was another waist-high mountain of exhaust-blackened, sand-laden snow to scale, and the mouth of a dark alley to navigate. The owl glided in noiselessly as if on a string, a tongue sliding through a gap in broken teeth. The warehouses on either side were abandoned, *Sunshine Meatpacking* on one faded sign spackled with chunks of frozen stuff plastered there by the wind.

The alley had been sheltered from the worst of the snow. It was stacked with wooden pallets and other assorted junk. Good for an ambush, especially with the shadows growing by the second. The owl floated above me in a tight circle, then sailed down and around a bend.

Great. A blind turn in an alley. Dad would be motioning me back to the open end of it to keep watch. He'd go from cover to cover, but I was just strolling down the middle as if I was on rails.

Tiny little dots of snow drifted down one at a time, the alley only getting a desultory sprinkling. The wind rose with a moan, tiny ice pellets whispering wherever they touched a flat surface. I slipped my right hand in my pocket, touched the switchblade's cold handle. My fingertips were frozen solid, not stinging anymore.

The alley made an L shape, and the bend was choked with junk on either side. I halted, peered around the corner, saw more daylight.

Looks okay. I looked up—no owl. The oranges vanished, leaving only the cold and the sudden miserable feeling that I was being watched.

I slid through the gap between pallets and headed down the other half of the alley. There was less trash here, but it looked older and more rotten—a drift of decaying newspaper over a shape that might have been human.

I flinched nervously. Looked again and it was just a busted-down old couch. Overflowing trash cans, one with condensation frozen on its sides, frost flowers blooming across the galvanized surface. I shuddered at the thought of what they might have in them and hurried past, because the end of the alley suddenly seemed brighter.

I came out, blinking, in a weedy, trash-strewn vacant space. At the far end, a chain-link fence sloped drunkenly back and forth. It looked weirdly familiar. And there on the other side . . .

I turned in a full circle. Yep, there were the two buildings squinched together, broken glass staring out into the cold night. I'd seen them from a different angle. I finished the turn, squinted at the chain-link fence. Let out a disbelieving sigh, my breath louder than the snow.

Our truck hunched on the other side of the fence. It was buried under a hood of deep snow, but I'd know the camper shape anywhere. And under the snow it was faded blue, the blue of a summer sky, the best color in the world.

"Holy shit," I whispered. The buildings behind me crouched, groaning like they intended to get up and hobble for a hot bath.

I took another two steps forward, through a knee-deep drift. The wind smacked me, rising and moaning eerily, loaded with stinging snow-buckshot. My jeans were sodden, clinging below the knee, and I couldn't feel my feet. I lurched forward again, tripped over something buried under the snow, and fell headlong. My palms hit snow, and I hoped there was nothing sharp under its soft white blanket.

Good one, Dru. I floundered up to my feet, shaking like a dog to get the powdery stuff off me. Considered cursing, but another bolt of pain slung through my head, this one jolting down my neck and spreading across my sore, aching back. I let out a half-garbled sound and hunched, crossing my arms over my belly, cold burning against my cheeks.

I pulled back into my own head with an effort, clenching myself like a fist. My eyes ran with hot water, and I lurched to my feet, aware of how the light was draining from the sky.

Get to the truck. It was Dad's voice again, urgent but calm. *Get to the truck* NOW. *Run, Dru. Run.*

I made it up and staggered. My feet were so cold I didn't think I could run, but I gave it a go just as a low, hissing growl sounded behind me and something snapped like a flag in a high breeze. Snow flung itself up and the wind screeched. I leaped like a fish with a hook through its mouth.

"*Down!*" someone yelled, and habit grabbed me by the scruff. You don't hesitate when someone yells like that.

I hit the snow again, full-length, and heard something roar.

Goddamn, that sounds like a shotgun. I floundered, rolled over on my back, and the world turned to clear syrup again, snowflakes hanging suspended, the sky flushed with one last long red smear of dying sunlight, and the werwulf hanging in the air over me caught in mid-snarl, a long string of saliva flying back to splat on the lobe of one high-peaked, hairy ear. Its eyes were like coals, and the white streak up the side of its head was familiar—I had time to see almost every hair etched on its pelt, as well as the ruins of a shredded pair of canvas pants clasping its narrow hips. Its legs bent back the wrong way, fully extended for the leap. Its long, lean face was screwed up in a snarl of pure hatred.

It hung there for what seemed like forever as I struggled against deadweight, a scream locked in my throat—and the world snapped again, with a sound like ice breaking over deep cold water. Something hit the thing from the side, and it tumbled, turning in midair, landing impossibly gracefully, kicking up a sheet of snow as it slid.

"*Get up!*" that voice yelled again. It wasn't Dad's, but I know the sound of a command under fire. I scrambled, made it to my feet, found out I'd lost my stocking cap, and bolted for the truck again.

I made an amazing running leap as my back tore with pain again, the chain-link fence sagging under my weight. Fingers and toes madly scrabbling, I muscled up and made it just as that huge booming sound repeated. Definitely a shotgun, but I wasn't waiting around to find out. Adrenaline and terror boosted me up over the fence—I dropped a good five feet and jarred myself a good one when I landed, almost biting a chunk out of my tongue. It was ten feet to the truck, the longest ten feet of my life. I skidded on something icy under the snow and fetched up against the driver's side, grabbed onto the mirror, and snapped a glance over my shoulder.

Someone crouched in the snow, shotgun socked to his broad shoulder and trained on the streak-headed werwulf. I saw a flash of black hair, lying down sleek and wet, before the gun spoke again. The wulf howled and tumbled away, a high arc of blood spattering free.

My brain kicked into overdrive. *Gun. Get a gun. Keys.* I dug in my left coat pocket, dragged my keys out—spilling out a few spare pieces of paper and a gum wrapper—and found the truck key. My fingers tingled madly. *Lock might be frozen, oh God, help.*

The key went in easy. I twisted it—and was rewarded with the little silver bar of the lock inside clicking up. I tore my key free, dropped it on the driver's seat, and dug underneath the seat for the flat, heavy steel box.

The field box. It held a gun, ammo, and a couple other things you might need in a hurry if the situation went south. I was never supposed to touch it, but this was an *emergency*, dammit.

Another snarl. The sound almost made words. A werwulf's mouth probably wasn't built for human speech, but it sounded terribly, horribly almost human. As if an intelligent, murderous dog was trying to cry out.

"Come on, pretty boy. Let's see what you've got." He sounded like he was having a grand old time, whoever he was—I couldn't see out through the windshield. I got the box open, and let out a relieved half-sob. The modified Glock lay there, three clips next to it, I racked one, chambered a round—it seemed to take forever—then ducked back around the driver's door, gun pointed down.

Now that I wasn't half-blind with fear, I saw a jagged hole in the fence, just big enough to duck through. The field was now trampled, snow flung all over the place and dead grass sticking up in spikes. How had that happened?

They circled each other, the boy—because he didn't look any older than me—moving with fluid grace, his boots light atop the snow and landing like it was solid ground. The wulf limped and slipped, favoring its left side, and snarled again at him, the sound rasping at my brain like sandpaper. The streak up the side of its head glimmered just like the snow.

"I'm behind you," I warned him, wishing my voice didn't squeak halfway through. My throat was dry. The wulf's coal-like eyes flicked toward me, back at the boy as he took another step, getting its attention again.

"You should get out of here," the boy said conversationally, and I couldn't believe what I was hearing. Or seeing.

He had no footsteps. No footsteps at all. The powdery snow didn't give under his feet.

"I'm armed." I edged forward, raised the gun as he slid out of my field of fire. The circle they were drawing around each other was getting smaller with each step. "Besides, I've got some questions to ask you." I raised the gun, sighted just like Dad taught me, and put some pressure on the trigger. Snow whirled down, the flakes getting bigger, the clouds overhead losing their bloody light as the sun slid under the horizon.

The werwulf snarled again, its lean muzzle wrinkling. Blood spattered loose, the snow steaming where it landed. My palms were sweating, wool gloves sodden with melted snow and my own fear. *Hold it steady, Dru. Don't point that thing at anything you don't intend to kill.*

It eyed the boy, and me, and a shadow of madness crossed its glowing gaze before it backed up two steps, shook its slim head, snarled again—then whirled and bolted.

He fired, and so did I. The wulf howled as bullets struck home. I aimed for its back and knew I'd hit it as soon as I fired; the shotgun blast probably wasn't as effective. The wulf nipped smartly through a boarded-up window, leaving behind only a chilling howl echoed by the wind. Snow blew—and I half-turned, training the gun on the boy and breathing so hard my ribs heaved hysterically.

He lowered the shotgun and gave me a sidelong glance. His eyes were blue, like mine—but a very light cold blue, like the sky that morning before it clouded over. Winter blue. I saw this before the last bit of pink dusk faded out and the eerie orange half-darkness of snow reflecting city light replaced it, softening the sharpness of his profile.

"Who the hell are *you*?" I coughed once, rackingly, but the gun didn't waver. A thin thread of melting snow slid down the back of my neck, and a few wayward curls that had worked free of the braid bounced in my face. "And why did you tell me to go halfway across town?" *And why the hell did Dad have your number?*

He was silent for fifteen seconds, his head tilted as if listening. "We'd better move," he said finally. The odd spacing between his words didn't go away. "This is an old haunt of *his*, but still useful. *His* other pets will come back in force, sooner rather than later."

What's this we, *white man? And whose other pets? I've never heard of werwulfen being* pets *before.* "Who the hell are you?" I was only faintly relieved to see that he had a shadow, but his boots rested lightly on the snow, not disturbing it a bit. *Jesus.*

That earned me another sidelong glance. "It's Reynard, Christophe Reynard, nice to meet you. Can you drive, little girl?"

I backed up carefully, testing my footing with each step. My boots crunched right through the top crust of the snow and kept sinking until they hit dirt. "Of course I can drive. I've got my permit and everything." *And two sets of fake IDs for if I need to look a little older than I am.*

"Then you'd better see if that thing starts. Go on." He didn't move, staring at the hole in the wall the streak-headed wulf had squeezed through. He wasn't even breathing hard. His mouth drew down at the corners, that was all. "The cold around here can play havoc with batteries."

It was just the sort of thing Dad might have said. "Who the hell *are* you?" I repeated.

"I told you." Apparently deciding it was safe, he turned away from the warehouse, holding the shotgun easily. "Maybe the silver load in those pellets will poison Ash before he gets home to tell tales, but don't count on it. You need to get that truck started, Dru."

I gave a nervous little jump. *What the hell?* "How do you know my name?"

He gave a slight nod, like I'd confirmed a guess, and I swore at myself again. *Way to go, Dru, falling for the oldest trick in the book.*

"I know a lot about you." He looked like he meant it, too. Snow whirled down, flakes now the size of dimes, and following every eddy and swirl of wind. "I know you should be in school, I know you're alone, and I know you're scared. You shoot me, and you'll have more questions *and* a dead body on your hands. Go home."

I wasn't about to give up so easily. Either he was a safe contact and Dad had forgotten to mark it—which wasn't like Dad at all—or he was someone I might have to threaten to get some information out of. And if he vanished now I might never find him again, phone number or not. "What did you do to my father?" I felt like my hands were shaking, but the gun was steady as ever.

"Your father?" He measured me with those burning blue eyes. I realized he wasn't dressed for the weather—just a black long-sleeve T-shirt and jeans, snow beginning to cling to his sleek dark hair and eyelashes. Heavy engineer's boots were clumped with snow despite the way he stood balanced weightlessly on the crust, and there was a spray of it up his left side, like he'd rolled or landed in it. "I told him to leave well enough alone, that's all. I told him he was lucky to have made it this far. And I told him what I'm going to tell *you.* Go home and lock your doors, and leave the night to us."

My jaw threatened to drop. His eyes actually *glowed*, holes punched through darkness to a sterile place full of fox fire. And when he smiled, baring teeth whiter than the fresh snow already beginning to cover up evidence of the fight, I saw fangs that should have looked like a cheap set of Halloween falsies. But they didn't, because they were growing out of his jaws, upper and lower canines too long, front teeth subtly modified to hold flesh down or tear it free so the animal could get at hot blood.

"Ohshit," I whispered, and my voice seemed very small. My entire body shivered, drawing up against itself. Have you ever been so scared your flesh starts literally crawling on your bones? Yeah. Like that. "You're a . . . You're one of *them.*"

"I am Kouros. A *djamphir.*" His chin lifted a little when he said it, like it was a title or something. His hair ran with wet gleams, like it was oiled. "And you're nothing more than helpless right now. Go away."

Helpless my ass. I swallowed bitter iron. *He's a sucker, Dru. Get out of here. OhGod get out of here.* "Tell me what happened to my father." It was hard, but I kept my eyes on him. I wanted to look at the buildings behind him. Somewhere in there was a long concrete corridor I'd seen before, and a door that still might have something behind it.

Only, would that something be anything I wanted to see?

His smile widened, the teeth prominently displayed like an animal's warning grimace. "Some other time. Soon, since you'll be seeing me again. Now go home, little girl. And lock your doors."

There was a sound like ripping paper, and he simply *winked out*, snow spraying up in an impressive fantail. I let out a scream and squeezed off a shot, tracking the smear of *something wrong* bulleting through the air. It passed close enough to touch my cheek, flipping a few stray curls, and a flat, eerie little laugh echoed before falling dead against the snow. A breath of scent slid by my face, like warm apple pies.

I lost sight of it slipping away down what was certainly the way in or out of here, a long channel, probably a dirt driveway under a blanket of snow. I swallowed sourness, tasted a bitter citrus rind against my tongue, and knew I had to get out of there too.

I didn't want to. I wanted to find that corridor and see if anything of Dad was left down there. There just wasn't *time*.

Instead, I clumped past the truck, the way the smear had fled. The scent of apples and cinnamon trailed slightly before the wind whisked it briskly away. And about fifteen feet past the back bumper, my boots sinking through and hitting gravel—a good sign—there was something else. A spray of crimson drops sinking into the white.

I'd hit him. Whatever he was.

I got the hell out of there.

CHAPTER 18

Five or ten miles an hour through blowing snow, chains rasping against ice and packed, sanded muck as well as a fresh, fast-falling layer of slippery whiteness that spun like feathers in the cone of my headlights. The drive home was no fun. I was shaking all over despite the heater blasting away, and when I finally made it into the driveway past 9 p.m., I parked at an angle that could only be described as drunken.

The lights were all on, solid gold shining warmly through thin windows. The blinds in the living room were finally down, though. My teeth were chattering by the time I got to the front porch, and I saw the shadow of something moving in the living room.

I hoped it was Graves, but my right hand went reflexively into my pocket and curled around the switchblade. I stood staring at the front door for a second—*probably right where something else stood a day ago,* I thought, and shivered harder. The memory seemed to belong to someone else, a long time ago and far away.

The locks chucked, and the door yanked open. "Jesus Christ," Graves said. "Where the hell have you *been*? Whose car is that? Are you okay?"

I let go of the switchblade, finger by finger. All of a sudden I was so glad to see him it wasn't even funny. He'd come back and waited for me so I didn't have to come home to an empty house. He was right—nobody had twisted his arm into approaching me at the mall *or* taking care of me. And he really sounded worried.

I didn't blame him. I probably looked like hell.

The porch creaked as I looked at him, blinking back something weird and hot. It overflowed, and one tear tracked its way down my cheek.

"Oh, shit." He was in his sock feet, and stepped out onto the porch, grabbed my arm, and dragged me into welcome warmth. I leaned against the wall inside the door as he closed and locked it, and just closed my eyes.

"We need to talk," I managed around the lump in my throat.

"No. Really?" If the words had been loaded with any more sarcasm they would have staggered. As it was, they only fell flat. "What the hell happened?"

"That's my dad's truck." The shivers were coming in waves now. "I found it. I found the guy attached to the phone number. He kn-kn-knows something."

He took it calmly. "Huh. You should get out of those clothes. You're dripping on the carpet."

Then again, Graves didn't know—and I couldn't explain—about the streak-headed werwulf and the boy who stood on snow as if it was a dance floor. It's not the sort of thing you can explain to someone who's only touched the Real World once.

I wasn't able to tell him that the boy was probably something more inhuman than the wulf who had ended up shredding his shoulder. That the boy wasn't a *boy*, was probably older than any adult I ever knew. And that he'd probably turned my dad into a zombie, and I was next unless I could come up with a plan, and a good one.

Why would he turn Dad into a zombie, though? I mean, suckers aren't the only thing that can turn people into hungry walking corpses. It happens all the time. Voodoo, burial in contaminated ground, black sorcery, working at big chain retail stores—there were endless ways someone could end up reanimated.

Still, they like to play with their prey, the suckers. Zombification is only one of their tricks.

They call themselves all sorts of tribal names, but hunters call them only a few things—suckers, *nosferatu*, "those undead bastards." And they're one of the few things everyone, no matter their personal feuds or dislike, will band together and try to kill. There were even whispers of werwulfen sometimes working with groups of human hunters to take a nest out. Wulfen and suckers don't get along; nobody knows why.

But why would a wulf and a burning dog *and* a sucker be after Dad *or* me?

It was the same mental ground I'd been retreading for hours, not getting anywhere. Now that I wasn't concentrating on driving, it was worse. *But why did Dad have his number? What was Dad doing out here? He didn't mention anything to me. He* always *had me help him find out what we were hunting.*

If Dad was hunting a sucker and he wanted me out of the way, why wouldn't he warn me or leave me somewhere safe? Why would he take me along and not talk about it?

I stared at the boxes stacked in the hall. It smelled red in here, like tomatoes and spice, and Graves put an awkward arm over my shoulder. "Look, I made some spaghetti. I also stopped by the mall and got some of my clothes and stuff. So, um, why don't you just get cleaned up and dried off, and you can tell me what's going on? You look cold."

I *was* cold, a chill that had nothing to do with the weather running through the center of my bones. Ice in the marrow, a buzzing in my head. The circular mental motion started again, my brain struggling over the same rut it had been in since I turned the key and the truck ground into life.

Go over it again, Dru. Think it through.

Suckers *could* make zombies. I knew that much. As a matter of fact, it was one of the questions you asked first when you ran across the reanimated—was it voodoo, burial somewhere weird and bad, suckers, or something else responsible for controlling the shambling corpse? If it was just someone buried in contaminated ground, you could fix it easily enough. If it was voodoo, you could find out who had access to corpses *and* a nasty habit of raising them.

If it was a sucker bringing the rotting bodies up from the ground or making their own corpses, though, you were pretty dead unless you had luck or backup. I was running low on both.

"Dru." Graves shook me a little, peeled me away from the wall. Peered down into my face, his unibrow puckering. "Come on. You look like you've seen a ghost." He caught himself and gave his peculiar, barking laugh. "That's pretty possible, isn't it?"

You have no idea, kid. I found my voice. "Pretty possible. Yeah." It took an effort to step away from him. I barked my shin on a box and winced a little. "I'll go get cleaned up. Spaghetti sounds good."

"Ragu." He shrugged. "It was all that was around. You want me to reheat some?"

I know it was all that was around; Dad loved Ragu sauce. With tons of garlic. My heart gave a squeezing twist. "Sure. Thanks." My stomach grumbled a little, despite being closed up tighter than a bank after hours.

His face eased. He let go of me and tried a tentative smile. "No problem. I was worried about you."

You know what? So was I. I'm already as good as dead. There's no way I can fight a sucker. He's just playing with me. There it was, the stark truth. "Yeah. Me too." I made it down the hall and up the stairs, stripped out of my wet clothes—my back twingeing every so often, reminding me that I'd wrenched it again—and crawled into some sweats and a T-shirt. The side of my head, where I'd clipped it on the fountain, stung softly. My ribs ached, and I had to wriggle around in the bed gingerly until I found a position that didn't hurt. I lay still, trying to make the no-pain last as long as possible, hearing Graves humming a little, off-key, downstairs. I stayed awake only long enough to pull the blankets a little higher up and feel a moment's worth of regret at not eating when he was going to all the trouble.

Then I blinked out.

* * *

I don't often dream of my mother.

When I do, it's always the same. She is leaning over my crib, her face bigger than the moon and more beautiful than sunlight, or maybe it's just that way because I'm so young. Her hair tumbles down in glossy ringlets, smelling of her special shampoo, and the silver locket at her throat glimmers.

But there is a shadow in her pretty dark eyes; it matches the darkness over the left half of her face. It's like the shadow of rain seen through a window, light broken in rivulets.

"Dru," she says, softly but urgently. "Get up."

I rub my eyes and yawn. "Mommy?" My voice is muffled. Sometimes it's the voice of a two-year-old, sometimes it's older. But always, it's wondering and quiet, sleepy.

"Come on, Dru." She puts her hands down and picks me up with a slight oof! *as if she can't believe how much I've grown. I'm a big girl now, and I don't need her to carry me, but I'm so tired I don't protest. I cuddle into her warmth and feel the hummingbird beat of her heart. "I love you, baby," she whispers into my hair. She smells of fresh cookies and warm perfume, and it is here the dream starts to fray. Because I hear something like footsteps, or a pulse. It is quiet at first, but it gets louder and more rapid with each beat. "I love you so much."*

"Mommy . . ." I put my head on her shoulder. I know I am heavy, but she is carrying me, and when she sets me down to open a door, I protest only a little.

It is the closet downstairs. Just how I know it's downstairs I'm not sure. There is something in the floor she pulls up, and some of my stuffed animals have been jammed into the square hole, along with blankets and a pillow from her and Daddy's bed. She scoops me up again and settles me in the hole, and I begin to feel a faint alarm. "Mommy?"

"We're going to play the game, Dru. You hide here and wait for Daddy to come home from work."

This is all wrong. Sometimes I hide in the closet to scare Daddy, but never in the middle of the night. And never in a hole in the floor—a hole I didn't even know was there. "I don't wanna," I say, and try to get up.

"Dru." She grabs my arm, and it hurts for a second before her grip gentles. "It's important, baby. This is a special game. Hide in the closet, and when Daddy comes home he'll find you. Lie down now. Be a good girl."

I protest, I whine a little. "I don't wanna." But I am a good girl. I snuggle down into the hole, because it's dark and warm and I'm tired, and the shadow on Mommy's face gets deeper. Only her eyes glitter, glowing summer blue instead of their usual soft laughing brown. She covers me up with a blanket and smiles at me until I close my eyes. Sleep isn't far behind, but as I go down I hear something and I understand she's fitted the cover over the hole, and I am in the dark. But it smells like her, and I am so tired.

I hear, very faint and far away, the closet door close, and a scratching. And just before the dream ends, I hear a long, low, chilling laugh, like someone trying to speak with a mouthful of razor blades, and I know my mother is somewhere close, and she is desperate, and something very bad is about to happen.

CHAPTER 19

School started right up again the day after, and the day after *that* Graves talked me into going. I think he didn't know what else to do, and I gave in after only a token shouting match.

What the hell, right? I was already dead. All I had to do was wait for the blue-eyed boy to find me again. I mean, Jesus, I was just sixteen, right? Dad's truck was back in the driveway, but if I blew town I'd just die on some highway, probably at night, seeing something loom in the rearview mirror, or I'd get run off the road and ripped up in a ditch somewhere.

It was only a matter of time.

So, why not? Why not just do what he said?

At least it got me out of the house, where I was only prowling the rooms, getting more and more jumpy, looking at the stain on the living-room carpet, snarling at Graves when he tried to get me to eat. I'd managed to get the engine-block heater on the truck plugged in so it wouldn't freeze, even though the garage door was still broken and useless. That was about all I could do other than roam through the house like a madwoman, staring at everyday objects as if I'd never see them again.

I spent the nights crouched in the living room with the blinds up, my back against the wall, looking out at the wasteland of snow that was the front yard and jerking myself into wakefulness every time I dozed off. After the first night I figured I'd better put the gun down, and when Graves nagged me about going to school—probably because he thought I was getting a little weird—I told him I would to shut him up.

I didn't have the heart to tell him he was sharing a house with someone marked by a sucker. I mean, why rain on his parade? I tried to get him to go back to the mall, somewhere, *anywhere* away from me. It wasn't safe around me, but he stubbornly refused, and what could I do? Beat him up? I *could*, but why expend the effort?

I was so tired. So, so deathly tired. At least during the safe hours of sunlight at school I was surrounded by other people, and I was fairly sure I could sleep.

Bletchley, however, had other ideas. "Are you *with* us, Miss Anderson?"

I stared at the whiteboard at the front of the classroom. It was a valid question. *Was* I with them? I didn't think I'd ever been with them. Not the normal people, at least. Maybe there were one or two of them who had what Gran called "the touch." Maybe there were even a few of them who'd seen something weird or inexplicable, but they'd probably forgotten it as soon as they—

"Miss Anderson?" Bletchley was delighted. Her egglike eyes swam behind her spectacles, and she picked at the bottom of her sweater—the blue one with knitted roses, this time.

I just kept seeing Dad's face, half-chewed, the bony twitching of his fingertips. Blood on snow, and feet in heavy boots resting lightly on the unmarred top crust. The streak-headed werwulf snarling, its top lip lifting. And the hiss of the burning dog as it landed in the fountain, sulfur and stink and—

"No," I said finally. "I don't think I'm with you, Bletch."

In front of me, Graves slid down in his seat as if making himself smaller. I almost thought I heard him whisper, *shit*.

I heartily agreed. But I was too tired to deal with Bletch's crap. My eyes were full of sand and my entire body hurt.

A ripple went through the classroom. Bletchley stiffened and opened her mouth, but I was awake now. A nice nap ruined, not like first and second period, where I'd just put my head down on the desk and tuned the entire world out.

"As a matter of fact," I continued flatly, "I was just wondering why I was sitting here listening to you, when you obviously don't like anyone under twenty-one very much. It's like you only think real life starts when you can legally buy a beer or something. But then I realized another thing. You're scared of us."

"*Miss* Anderson— " Bletch began, but the words just kept spilling out. *Despite* the thin little voice in my head telling me that I shouldn't be saying the things I was thinking. Even if they were true.

Adults probably listen to that voice a lot. Did Dad ever stop telling me what he was thinking? What *hadn't* he told me?

I opened my mouth and had no idea what would come out next. "You probably thought teaching would be easy. A whole classful of helpless little snots for you to bully." I grabbed for my bag, made it to my feet, and almost knocked the whole desk over. Barked my hip a good one, and it added to the garden of bruises and scrapes all over my body. Pretty soon the sucker-boy would find me and I wouldn't feel anything ever again. "More every year, and they're always so easy to push around. Because you've got the power, right?"

"Sit *down*!" she hissed. Bright spots stood out on her withered cheeks, just as if someone had stamped her with one of those ink things they pop on your hand at clubs to prove you've paid the door fee.

I wasn't going to sit down. She probably didn't think I would, either, but maybe she figured it was worth a try.

"You've got all the power, and nobody would listen to us anyway. Because we're just kids. Who cares about *us*?" I ducked through my bag strap. It was too heavy, but that was because of what was in it. Graves made a restless movement, his hair and coat rustling.

Bletch inhaled and opened her mouth again to tell me to sit down or shut up. If I gave a damn, it might have even stopped me—that's what they count on, the hard teachers. They count on the weight of authority to get to you before a protest can even get halfway out of your mouth.

Fury ignited behind my breastbone, a hot glow like coals blooming into something sharp and dangerous. It was the same old crap—someone thinking they can push you around because you're young, because you're helpless. You had to just sit there and take it because you were under a certain number, because you weren't a real person yet; you could be picked up and dropped like a toy, left behind or thrown away—

"I don't think so," I continued, right over the top of her. "I think every goddamn kid you ever bullied is going to haunt you one day. And *I hope you choke on it!*" I didn't realize I was yelling until I had to fill my lungs with a gasping sound that would have been funny if not for what happened next.

Bletch's eyes bugged out of her head. She buckled, grabbing at her desk with one claw, the other clutching vainly at her throat, and made a hoarse, inhuman cawing noise.

The first one to start screaming was a pretty little brunette in the front row. I thought her name was Heather; she was wearing, of all things, a cheerleader's uniform. Why she bothered with umpteen feet of snow on the ground was beyond me. But right now her face was distorted with shock, and she let out a shriek that might have done a train justice. The sound made a few kids jump, and another one—a brunet boy with a thick neck and a jock's varsity jacket—let out a high-pitched squeal that harmonized oddly.

I finished gasping for air and stared at the teacher, who folded down like a piece of wet laundry let loose from the line. She thudded to her knees, and her face turned a weird plummy color. The bugging of her eyes began to seem natural and inevitable, but a faint alarm sounded in the back of my head. Other kids were screaming now too.

My gaze snapped away to the whiteboard. It was chattering madly against the wall, held on only by brackets. The instant I looked at it, there was a hollow cracking sound, and it fell, slamming onto the floor and actually *breaking*, a gigantic rip zigzagging horizontally across it.

A sensation like steam escaping through a valve slid through me, a sense of exquisite release.

Bletchley gasped and fell on her side, but regular color started to return to her face. She was breathing now. Someone retched in the back row, and my head snapped aside as if I'd been slapped, my cheek stinging. The air was thick with crawling electricity, suddenly hot as summer and humid like a thunderstorm was approaching.

Graves sat utterly still in the middle of kids who were getting up out of their chairs or screaming. His eyes were green flame, and his earring winked, a single silver star. His mouth was slightly open, as if he'd just had a hell of a good idea and was giving it such deep consideration the rest of his face had declared a vacation.

I turned around, my legs shaking like I'd just finished a hard five-mile run, and made it to the door. A new noise cut through the bedlam—the chimes for class ending, ringing in the middle of the hour. Now *that* was weird.

I let out a jagged sound that might have been a laugh, and fled.

***

I was four blocks away and still moving at a pretty good clip when his hand tangled in my coat, getting a good handful of my hair too, and he yanked me backward. I'd've gone down in a heap if he hadn't shoved me upright, but as it was I overcorrected and we both fell over into a small mountain of dirty scudge-snow shoved aside from the street. I wasn't wearing my gloves or a scarf. Snow burned my hands as I tried to struggle to my feet. My bag got tangled up, and Graves cussed me a blue streak, finishing up with, "—the hell did you do *that* for?"

"Boy," he continued, bouncing up off the frozen-solid drift like he was one of those weighted-at-the-bottom dolls, "you sure know how to throw a party. I've been bitten, beat up, tied to a bed, James Bonded out, and now you finish off by choking a goddamn *teacher*!"

I didn't try to say I hadn't been touching her. There was no point. I'd been ill-wishing her—*hexing*, Gran called it, and to those with the touch it wasn't small potatoes. I was pretty good at untangling hexes and curses, but not so good at throwing them at people, mostly because Gran wouldn't hear of it. *Cain't hex, cain't heal*, she would always mutter, especially when the men from the county were out assessing property tax. *But hexin's a strong medicine, Dru. You mind me now.*

To Gran, "strong medicine" could be good or bad, just like the laxatives she was forever talking about. *Good for makin' the mail move smooth, but too much and you shit yer brains out. Mind me now, Dru.*

I'd once set out to ask her how exactly such an operation as the moving of the brain out through the digestive system was accomplished, but I'd lost my nerve.

Graves reached down, grabbed the front of my coat, and yanked hard enough to rip fabric, succeeding in hauling me to my feet again. "You'd better tell me what's going on. Or I swear to God, I'll—" He peered down at me. "Jesus Christ. You're leaking."

If by "leaking" he meant "sobbing like a girl," I guess so. I wiped at my nose with my sleeve, snorted out a bray of a laugh, and went back to sobbing. Tears slicked my face, and I shoved him away. "Fuck *off*! I don't *need* you complicating things! I'm *dead*, goddammit! Don't you get it? I'm *fucking dead*!"

He shook dirty snow out of his hair. "You're not dead. You're too goddamn annoying to be dead. Now come on. They called 911 for Bletch—I don't think you want to be here when that starts happening."

Jesus, why won't you just leave me alone? I was about to yell again, but sirens started in the distance. It was like a slap of cold water across the face, and I realized I was indeed crying completely and messily, and I was covered in dirty snow, I was pretty sure my socks didn't match, I was a song of different aches and pains, and I hadn't washed my hair in two days. I felt greasy and cruddy, my back felt like it was on fire, and the heavy weight in my bag was definitely not my smartest move.

I was being utterly idiotic. The realization woke me up out of whatever stupor I'd been wandering in for days now.

I hitched in a shuddering breath, trying to get some kind of calm back, failed miserably, and didn't protest when Graves grabbed my arm and started off down the sidewalk.

"Why can't I have a normal girlfriend?" he asked the air over his head. "I finally meet someone I like and she turns out to be crazy. Oh, well."

"*Girlfriend*?" I half-choked, almost spraying snot out of my nose. *Good one, Dru. You didn't brush your teeth today, either. Sloppy, very sloppy.* I was going to break out in a huge way after all this. It was going to be Zit City on the Anderson face. But right now my cheeks were so flaming hot it didn't matter.

He gave me a sideways glance, and I really saw the guy he was going to be in a few years lurking under his baby face and the wild hair. His cheekbones were going to come out and he was going to be one of those pretty half-Asians. He already had good skin, even if it was reddened by the cold. "Well, jeez, you know."

Was he *blushing*? So was I, if the lava flow covering my face and spilling down my throat was any indication. He kept glancing at me, and I couldn't look away.

For Christ's sake. The lunacy just would not end.

I wiped at my nose again, wished for a Kleenex. "I don't—" I began. *I don't date. I don't have time, even if you are one of the better kids I've met. And—*

He shrugged, his cheeks going a deeper tomato red that had nothing to do with the snow. The flush spread down his neck, even. We were about even in that department. "It was a joke, Dru. God. Just relax, will you? Come on." He kept dragging me. Admittedly, I didn't put up much of a fight. But still . . . "A whole day at school ruined. You're gonna wreck my GPA."

"I thought you were going to take your GED anyway." My lips were numb. My hands were too; I stuffed them in my coat pockets. The sirens whooped and brayed, getting closer.

"I want to get into a *college* so I don't have to be *poor*. GPA still *matters*," he informed me in the tone reserved for gormless idiots. "But hey, I've been good all year. Might as well take a couple days off. Now, you wanna tell me what's going on? I've been thinking you probably don't want some stupid kid messing up whatever you've got going, but I told you, I'm *in* it now. I might as well know what I'm facing, right?"

I looked down at the sidewalk. My face was still sweat-hot, prickling in the cold. Feet had worn some of the snow down; deicer, rock salt, and sand had done the rest. Ice rimed the concrete, but it was pretty passable, all things considered. It was a nice clear day, clouds lowering around the rim of the horizon but not closing the lens of the sky just yet. The only problem was the cold, knifing straight through every article of clothing.

"That stain in your living room is about the size of a body." Graves let go of my arm, but I kept walking next to him, powerless to stop. "And your dad . . . I'm not stupid, Dru."

I know you're not. "You wouldn't believe me." I was mumbling like a kid caught out after curfew.

He didn't look at me, but his shoulders hunched. He turned the corner just as the ambulance roared by, and I followed. Once we were a block away, the siren shut off abruptly and it was possible to talk again.

Graves gave me a sidelong glance. He wasn't red anymore, but the new weight in his gaze was uncomfortable. "Yeah? Try me." Two steps further, and he hunched even more, an oddly fluid movement.

"I keep seeing it. In my dreams. That thing that bit me."

I hadn't told him I'd seen the streak-headed wulf again. It just didn't seem like good news to give him. "That's normal. It's like, post-traumatic stress or something." I swallowed drily. The last of the sobs hitched to a halt. After crying that messily your head gets clear, whatever chemical it dumps into your blood giving you a lightheaded buzz.

"Is it normal that I can smell people now? *Really* smell them, and *really* smell what they had for lunch? And is it normal to be able to see in the dark? Like, as if it was day? And what about being able to move quicker than I should be? It's like I'm dialed to superhero now. Is *that* goddamn normal?"

I stopped, staring at him. He kept walking, paused a few steps away, and looked over his shoulder. "Come on, keep up. It's cold out here."

"You really . . ." *This is what comes of not shooting someone when you have the chance. Dad would have shot him. But he didn't turn into a fur rug!* "You didn't change. You shouldn't be having effects like that."

"I thought you said I was safe."

"I thought you *were*." My cheeks were now cold, stinging wet. I shivered. Once I started I couldn't seem to stop. The high-octane trembling ran through me like ice water. "Where are we going?"

"Nuh-uh." He shook his head, dark hair swinging. Most of the snow had been stripped free, the rest melting, water clinging to the strands. He was a blot of black on the gray and dirty-snow day, hardly the most inconspicuous kid. "Your turn. What the hell happened to you? You've been set on 'weird' ever since you left me in that coffee shop. Not that you have to stretch very far for it."

"I . . ." I held my breath, let it out in a sharp sigh, and decided to take the plunge. What was he going to do, laugh at me? "I saw someone. I have this . . . thing. . . . Anyway, I found my dad's truck by following this thing I have. It tells me stuff sometimes. There was a—the wulf that bit you, it was there." *I don't know anything about this, and that's wrong. I should be hitting the books to find out all I can, and hitting them* hard. "And a sucker showed up."

"The thing that bit me?" His face squinched up, hard, as if he'd tasted something bitter. "And a sucker?"

How the hell am I supposed to explain? "As in, *blood* sucker. We call them all sorts of names—*nosferatu*, undead, sucker, you know—"

"You're a *vampire hunter*? Jeez. Really? Or do they call it something different?" He sounded amused and thoughtful, rather than uncomfortable, at the thought.

"They just call it hunting. And not just vampires." *You're taking this really well.* "Other stuff, too. Whatever's dangerous and messing with people. My dad did it; I helped. Something killed him and turned him into a zombie. Probably this sucker—they can do it. Anyway, the sucker ran the wulf off and told me to go home. He's going to come kill me."

"Why? I mean, doesn't it make more sense for him to kill you there? Not that I'm in a hurry for you to bite it, you know." He actually hopped from foot to foot like a bird, impatient. "Come on. Keep moving. Your lips are turning blue."

"Leave my lips out of this." But it was awfully cold, and as soon as I started moving I was reminded that I hadn't put on a sweater, either. How *had* I gotten out of the house this morning? I suddenly wanted a hot shower more than anything else in the world. "They like to play with their victims. They get bored, I guess."

"Doesn't make much sense," he repeated.

Haven't you ever had a cat? "Like so much about this does?"

"It does, actually." He slid out a pack of Winstons, offered it to me, and frowned when I shook my head. "I mean, look at all the shit on TV. It's all over—witches and werewolves and all that sort of stuff. No smoke without fire, right? My stepdad used to say that."

It was by far the most information he'd ever given about his family. We were just sharing all over the place, Graves and I. The houses around us watched with their prissy little doors shut tight, blinds drawn down, driveways empty. "It's not like it is on television. You need to get that through your head right now. It's dangerous and dirty and smells bad and—"

He tapped out a coffin nail and lit up, stuffing the pack back in his pocket. His breath was already a cloud of smoke. "Yeah, well, so is sex and drugs and everything else worth doing. So what's our next move? You're the expert here."

I'm no expert. I'm just a kid. "I don't . . . I mean . . . my dad did all the planning." I couldn't believe I'd just said something so mealy-mouthed.

"So? What would he do?" Graves's coat flapped. He exhaled a stream of tobacco smoke. His nose wrinkled. "Gah. This doesn't even taste good now."

"Then why do you do it?" *He would get everything together and go back to those warehouses, looking for the "scene" so I could tell him what happened. He would take me to canvass the occult stores and the bars where they know about the Real World and find out who this Christophe is and where he sleeps—if he could cajole the information out of someone. He'd barricade the house or move somewhere else.*

But there was no way I could find a lease on my own without some serious work, and a hotel would be expensive and full of nosy adults unless it was a flophouse, which would be expensive and full of nasty people looking to take a bite out of a teenage girl.

I could make sure all the windows and doors at home were barred to evil—Gran had taught me that. It wouldn't stop a zombie—but I had someone with me now, right?

And I had guns. And grenades.

Great, Dru. So you could blow both yourself and your new friend up? Dad told you never to mess with the grenades!

But Dad wasn't here. I was on my own. Except, well, for Graves.

Who shrugged, taking another drag and screwing his face up hard. "Habit. I'm an addict, okay? Can we get back on topic? What would your dad do?" He didn't look like he was going anywhere. He looked, in fact, determined to stay put.

It was probably a bad thing. It might get him killed. But I couldn't help feeling relieved.

I couldn't help being glad he was around.

"He'd make a daylight run." I was shivering so hard the words almost got chopped into bits. "Where I found the truck. He'd go back and start digging where that streak-headed wulf scuttled away to. Track it if he could."

"Streak-headed?" He waved it away as soon as I opened my mouth, his cigarette trailing a line of smoke. "No, don't tell me. I've got a better question. Was that you? Did you do that to ol' Bletch?"

I swallowed the lie I meant to tell. "I guess so. It's called a hex. I've never thrown one before." *And that's something to worry about too. Where the hell did that come from? I've never been able to do that.*

But I'd never been so angry before, had I? Or so hopeless. And I was doing new things all the time now. The *touch* was getting stronger.

"Then how do you know it was you?" He looked down at his feet, obediently carrying him over the sidewalk. Stopped and motioned me around an icy patch; there was only room for one person to walk. "Looked to me like she had a heart attack once someone called her a bully to her face."

"Did I call her a bully? I don't remember that bit." I shuffled, picking my way around the ice. The glare of sunlight off snow pierced straight through my head, and I was suddenly very aware of my empty stomach.

There was a sound of moving cloth. "It was great, Dru. You said what everyone's been thinking for *years*."

"I'm glad you approve." *Still, I hexed her. Dammit. Gran would have a cow. Dad would take one look at my face when I got home and give me the Lecture About Using Gifts Responsibly.* My bag was too heavy. I fussed with the strap, trying to get it to not cut into my shoulder.

Graves's half-yipping laugh came again. "I was about to stand up and applaud, but people started screaming."

When his coat came down on my shoulders I gave a half-startled, nervous sidling step or two, almost dumping myself on the bank of road-snow. Again. "Are you crazy? It's fifty below out here!"

He shrugged, his thin shoulders moving under a ragged red wool sweater that had seen better days. He *had* brought a lot of his clothes over, and it was a relief to see him in something new. "You're making me cold, you're shivering so hard. I'm used to this, Florida girl. Just say thank you, okay?"

I winced half-guiltily, remembered I *had* told him about Florida. "You're nuts." But the coat was warm, and I pushed my arms through the sleeves. My bag bumped my hip, and as soon as we got home I'd have to clean it out. "Let's go home. I want some lunch and we can plan."

"Sounds good."

We walked in silence for a little while, crunching under each footstep like little bones clicking and breaking. I smelled him on his coat—healthy boy, deodorant, testosterone, cigarette smoke, and the faint tang of fried food. My cheeks tingled, but I didn't blush. Instead, I stared down at my feet, moving independently of me like good little soldiers, and hunched my shoulders so I could take a deep breath. Funny, but you don't really realize how personal it is to smell someone. He wasn't Dad, but he was right here with me.

I bit my lip, then I opened my mouth. "Graves?"

"What?" He sounded wary. I would too, if I was dealing with a crazy girl who had just hexed a stupid history teacher and told me all about suckers and wulfen.

"Thank you." The coat was really warm; I could see why he wore it. The shivers began to ease. The clearheaded sense of being cried out and ready to get to work dawned over me like a blessing.

I could tell he was grinning by the sudden feeling of warm sunshine on my back. "No problem, Dru. First one's free."

CHAPTER 20

The truck was still parked cockeyed in the driveway, and the phone was ringing when we let ourselves in. Graves went straight to turn the heat up, and I reached the phone just as the tinny repeated shriek ceased. "Probably the school calling to tell on you," he said, with his bitter little bark of a laugh.

There were a lot of missed calls lately, but the thought of *that* one sent a chill up my spine. "Jesus. I suppose you could pretend to be my dad." I struggled out of his coat, now wet with slushy ice near the hem since he was so tall it dragged when I wore it. My shirt held a faint ghost of cigarette smoke now, too, as well as an even fainter ghost of deodorant.

"You've got some kinky ideas, Miss Anderson." The heater wumped into life. I passed him in the hall and headed straight for the first weapons crate.

The gun came out of my bag, and I discovered I was sweating. What had I been *thinking*? It was loaded, one in the chamber, and the safety (thank God) on. Going to nice suburban schools meant I didn't have to worry about metal detectors, but it was still stupid to pack heat to Foley High.

Dad called it "the rabbits"—when a hunter got stupid, blunted by fear or the walloping unreality of the Real World. I suppose a better term would be shell shock, or even monster shock.

I was about to strip the gun and set it back in the box when my head jerked up. A half-second later, the doorbell rang. I jerked around, my nostrils filling with the smell of coppery rust. It mixed uneasily with the sudden wax-citrus tang in my saliva.

Ohshit. And something occurred to me—it was broad daylight, sun splashing off the snow.

Suckers don't go out during the day. So it was *something else.*

But *what*?

There was a fast, light flurry of taps on the door. And the shimmer of something weird behind it, clearly visible. The blue lines of warding weren't visible, but I could *feel* them, thread-thin, running together and humming. Gathering themselves like blue lightning.

If whatever-it-was took two steps to the side, it could peer in the huge, uncovered window and see me crouching near a weapons crate, my frozen hands locked around a nine-millimeter and my legs suddenly cramping.

OhGod. Not right now.

But you don't get to choose what comes after you, and when. If you did, life would be a lot simpler, wouldn't it?

Graves appeared in the doorway to the living room. His eyes were wide, white-ringed, and he looked almost as scared as I felt. His cheeks were cottage-cheese pale under their even goldenness. For an ethnic boy, he certainly got pretty white.

"What do we do?" he mouthed, and I didn't even try to pretend there wasn't serious bad news standing on the porch.

I snapped a glance at the front window and the wasteland of snow that was the front yard. *Jesus. I've got him to protect, too. He's not trained for this.*

I motioned him back with one hand, eased myself down to the floor, and began to crawl-slink along the carpet, gun in one hand. I checked and rechecked to make sure the safety was on, and was careful to point it away from my fool head.

More light taps. The sense of breathing, amused impatience welling up behind the door sent chills down my spine. Crawling over the discoloration on the carpet gave the chills more weight. There was a faint, rotting tang of zombie, not enough to make me gag but enough to make me wish I didn't have to slither over it.

I made it to some halfass cover—a row of boxes to one side of the television. The angle was bad, but I could at least see a slice of the porch and, hopefully, whatever was at the door.

Dust got in my nose as I shimmied behind the boxes. The urge to sneeze filled my nose, trickled down my throat, and damn near made my eyes water. *Do this right, Dru. You'll only get one shot.* I got my legs up under me as another flurry of taps hit the door.

I rose, carefully, slowly. Peered over the top of a box holding spare clothes and blankets.

The angle was indeed bad. But through the glass, I could see a moving shadow as whatever was out there shifted weight, probably from one foot to the other.

Assuming it had only two feet.

But weird stuff usually only came out at *night*. This was wrong, all wrong. I pointed the gun carefully, braced myself. The top of my head felt very, very exposed, poking above the boxes.

"Dru—" Graves half-whispered. There was a queer sliding noise, ending with a click.

What the hell was that? The shadow moved slightly.

"Dru—" Graves, again. Like we were in class and he was trying to pass a note or get someone to copy from.

Yeah, sure, like this kid's ever copied. Puh-leeze. "Shut up," I whispered, as quietly as I could. *Should I take a shot through the wall? I thought the angle was better over here. Dammit.*

"The door," Graves whispered. "The locks are moving."

Oh shit. I scrambled to my feet and launched myself over the boxes. It was an amazing leap—I don't even remember my wet boots touching the floor on the other side. I piled into the hall past Graves, shoving him down and aside. The door, its locks rotating and clicking into the open position, the knob turning slowly and paradoxically too fast for me to stop it; I barely got the safety off, raised the gun as the door blew open, a wave of intense cold streaking down the hall.

The lightning-crackle of the warding didn't even slow him down.

The blue-eyed boy's fingers closed around my wrist, and he casually twisted the gun free. It clattered on the floor, thankfully not going off.

There's one thing to be said for your dad leaving you a fifty and a reminder to do your katas. When a bad guy busts into your house and grabs you, you can punch him in the face hard enough to make him stagger back, blood pouring from his patrician nose.

Red blood. Not black, and not sheened with the opalescent slug-trail of sucker blood. Memory clicked inside my head—the drips on the snow that night had been red blood too.

Suckers bleed black; there is no hemoglobin left in them. It was why they needed fresh transfusions all the time. I hadn't thought of it before, too tired and scared to think anything *like* straight.

Too late now.

What the hell?

He stumbled back, his hair no longer dark-wet and sleek but light brown and shaggy, and I took a step, foot coming down solid and other leg bending, knee jackhammering up, and I got him a good one in the nuts—or would have if his arm hadn't swept down and smashed right above my knee, harder than anything human had a right to hit, deflecting my knee just a little bit. A burst of apple-pie scent came out of somewhere and hit me in the face.

Graves finally let out a yell. The blue eyes flickered past me, but I was already moving. Dad always said that the nut shot was great if it went through, but a girl always had to have a backup—because a guy won't expect you to go for the nuts *and* for something else.

I guess since the groin is the center of a guy's world, he rarely guesses it isn't the center of *yours*.

My fist, already folded up, headed for his throat like an express train. Next came the open palm, the heel of the hand striking just under the nose and driving up so the nasal promontory broke and slid into the brain. If I could just move fast enough.

Work it, Dru! Harder! Harder! Dad's voice, yelling—but there was no time for that, because there was a shattering roar behind me and something bulleted past, something long and lean, moving faster than it had any right to, hard to look at because it was blurring like clay under fast-running water. It hit the blue-eyed boy and threw him back at least six feet, and they were still going when the boy's head clipped the lintel and they tumbled out the door, onto the porch, and out of sight.

What the—? But I was already moving, forgetting the gun and tearing for the front door. The noise was immense, a growling roar mixed in with high-pitched but unmistakably male laughter, along with thumping that shook the whole house.

That was Graves. Hairy and moving like a bullet on speed.

He wasn't supposed to change! It seemed to take forever to reach the door, and by that time they had shattered the porch railing and dumped off into the front yard. There was a sickening *crack!* and an amazing fountain of snow jetted up.

"*Stop it!*" I screamed, but they weren't paying any attention. There was so much snow it was hard to see what was happening, but it looked like the blue-eyed boy had Graves—or what had been Graves—by the scruff and was flinging him around.

I took three steps, launched myself off the porch, and flew just like Supergirl, fists outstretched. I tackled the blue-eyed boy *hard*, all the breath driven out of me and my shoulder giving a huge burst of pain, and knocked him ass-over-teakettle. We went down in a tangle of arms and legs, and I gave the kid a good sock in the stomach before I realized what he was yelling.

"*I'm here to help you, fucking morons!*"

I rolled free, snow stinging my hands and face, and leaped to my feet just as Graves launched himself again. Time slowed down; my hand shot out and grabbed a fistful of his wild, curly hair—wilder and curlier now. He wasn't furry all over, but he was *changed*, something inhuman shining out through his burning-green eyes and the air hardening and shimmering around him like heat off a black sidewalk.

I gave a huge yank, only mildly concerned at the fact that I shouldn't have been able to move fast enough to catch him. The world had gotten very, well, basic, and the fact that this new kid was bleeding red had just truly made its way through a haze of adrenaline.

Better not rabbit anymore, Dru. Come on. Control the situation.

My abused shoulder gave a howl, but I held on grimly; Graves's legs flipped out from under him, and he let out a sound like that dog in the cartoons reaching the end of his chain and getting roinked but good. I let out a hurt little cry, my fingers cramping, and Graves hit the ground, his hair—vital, curly, springing with harsh life—slipping free of my hand.

"Where the hell did you get *that*?" the blue-eyed boy snarled. His face was a mask of blood, the right half already puffing up and discolored from my first punch. He was, again, not dressed for the weather—a black V-neck sweater about as thick as a piece of paper, jeans, and black sneakers caked with snow. I caught another breath of a good, spicy apple smell, and wondered if one of the neighbors was baking.

Sunlight gilded his hair, bringing out blond highlights in the brown. It looked like a new, expensive shaggy cut, and when Graves snarled at him he snarled back, lips peeling back and exposing teeth that were only bluntly human. They both made rumbling sounds—Graves like a huge-ass, very pissed-off dog, and Blue Eyes like metal rubbing against itself.

"Just hold on a minute." I reached down. Graves had struggled up to sit on his haunches in the snow. He was still actually growling, a low deep thrumming sound that rattled my teeth. Just to be safe, I put a hand on his head—not that I'd be able to stop him if he launched himself now, but it was worth a try. "Graves? Hold on a second, please."

"He can't hear you," Blue Eyes said. "The beast has him."

"Screw *you*," Graves snarled, and I was really happy to hear that.

Werwulfen don't talk. Not in their animal form, anyway—the streak-headed one hadn't been able to do much more than make weird noises. Their mouths aren't made right for talking once they shift into their other form.

Talking was a good sign, and it meant *not-werwulf*. But that was *definitely* what he'd been bitten by, he hadn't changed in twelve hours, and he'd been a virgin, right?

It should have meant he was safe. But Graves was doing all sorts of things he wasn't *supposed* to. I wished again I knew more about all this, instead of just what Dad and I could piece together with the help of some moldering leather-bound books passed from hunter to hunter and kept behind the counters of *real* occult stores, not brought out until a hunter presents his bona fides.

Books I should have been spending some serious time with instead of moping, by the way.

"Just everyone hold on. Hang on for one red-hot second." I dug around in my memory, pointed at Blue Eyes with my free hand. "You. Christophe, right?"

He actually gave me a correct little half-bow, spreading his arms, and I began to feel a little faint. Because even though he didn't have fangs now and his hair was sticking up, powdered with snow, he *still* rested on the top crust of a drift like a feather. My eyes struggled with what my brain was seeing, gave up, attacked the problem again, and decided since he was standing in a flood of bright sunlight, he was Something Else.

But you saw the fangs, Dru!

"What the hell *are* you?" I wished I hadn't ditched the gun, but told myself again that it had been a good idea—one of the few good ideas I'd had in the last couple days. What was I going to do, start shooting in broad daylight? That would have been a fine how-do-you-do. The wind shifted, and I smelled apples again. My mouth watered.

His smile stretched, became a model of lunatic good cheer. "I could ask you the same thing, little girl. Why didn't you tell me who you really were?"

"You knew my name." I struggled with the lunatic urge to pat Graves's head. *Just stay still for a second; let me question him.*

"The name is *not* the thing," Christophe said, tipping his head back a little and addressing the cold blue sky. The sky that was, in fact, the exact shade of his eyes.

Go figure.

His gaze swung back down to me, and he shrugged. "Should we move this conversation inside? That is, if you can keep a leash on your little lapdog there."

Graves stiffened, but he didn't move. The thrumming growl coming from him petered out, and he rose, slowly, his heels coming down and the rest of him unfolding fluidly. "What is he, Dru?" Thank God, he sounded at least reasonably calm. "He doesn't smell right."

"Look who's talking." Christophe folded his arms. He should have looked ridiculous with snow plastered all over him, but somehow he didn't. "I told you, I am *djamphir*. I am of the *Kouroi*. I hunt the beasts that fill the night. And you, Miss Anderson, are like and unlike. Why didn't you tell me what you were?"

"You killed my father." But I didn't sound so sure. I wasn't so sure, now. "What, I was supposed to trade baseball cards with you?"

"I didn't kill your dear Papá. I warned him away, but he was determined. He had a bone to pick with Sergej." His face twitched, a shadow rolling over it as I watched, fascinated. "Don't we all."

"Sergej?" The name sent a thin glass spike of pain through my skull. My skin chilled, and I realized we were all standing out in the goddamn snow. "Who's that?"

Christophe stared at me like I'd just asked what oxygen was. Then he bent over, wheezing, and I realized he was laughing.

You know, I thought I'd gotten used to weird, but this is something else. I'd dropped my arm. Now I grabbed Graves's sweater and pulled him back. He came without resisting, his head dropping forward like a little boy's. "I don't feel so hot," he said, very softly, and coughed.

"I'm not surprised." My teeth were gritted so hard the words had to struggle free. "I think we have some reading to do." I didn't want to turn my back on Laughing Boy, so I had to walk backward, high-stepping to get my feet out of the snow. The front yard looked like a tornado had hit it. Thank God nobody was home in the middle of the day to see this.

I almost went down hard on the porch steps; Graves grabbed the railing and we swayed drunkenly. Step by step, we retreated up, Graves leaning on me heavier and heavier. The vitality was running out of him like water out of a broken cup. Laughing Boy stopped wheezing and watched this with interest.

"I don't suppose you'll invite me in." He grinned, the same feral grimace that had bared his teeth earlier. They were so white, pristine.

But they weren't fangs. Not now.

"Nope." I beat Graves to the punch, just in case he didn't know that was a really bad idea and decided to say something.

"I'm not like a *nosferat*, you know." Christophe moved forward smoothly, his feet still not denting the snow. *How did it get all over him if he can do that?* "I don't need an invitation to step over your threshold."

Yeah, you came right in past the wards and *the threshold.* "I bet you say that to all the girls," my mouth replied, with no real direction from me. Graves sniggered weakly. I got him up on the porch and kept moving back. It felt uncomfortably like Christophe was herding us.

Blue Eyes grinned, still examining us both. He moved like he had all the time in the world, gliding like oil over the snow. "He's going to fall asleep soon. That *was* his first change, wasn't it? How long ago was he bitten? And by what strain?"

My breath made a cloud in front of me. Graves slumped against my shoulder. It was hard to believe he had just been running around growling like an Alsatian moments ago. "I'll ask the questions, *Chris*. You just give answers. What the hell are you? And if you didn't kill my father, who did?"

"You really don't listen, do you? I'm *djamphir*. Called a half-breed, but technically more like a sixteenth. We're the product of unions between women and *nosferatu*. Surely you've heard of *that*."

My stomach turned over hard. *Holy shit.* "Actually, no. Not really." *Only in movies. Really bad movies.*

"Well, where have you been hiding, Miss Dru?" He was up the steps in one bound, his feet touching lightly, like ballet slippers. It was like watching a cat levitate. "I suppose you don't know what *you* are, either."

I could not get the thought of apple pie out of my head. Gran always served hers with a slab of cheese; Dad liked it that way. "I know what I am. I'm cold and hungry and pissed off. Thanks." I reached blindly for the knob, meaning to sweep the door closed and shut him out on the front porch, and hesitated.

The door hadn't done a fat lot of good five minutes ago. Still, the way he was grinning through his mask of blood wasn't encouraging.

I backed up. The gun was on the floor, too far back for me to kick the door closed and get to it. "If you're evil, you're barred from my house." My throat was dry. Graves picked that moment to go completely limp against me, and instead of being ready to kick ass, I was suddenly in danger of going down into yet another inglorious heap. My back ran with hot pain, and my shoulder wasn't too happy.

Christophe stepped over the threshold, swept the door closed, and caught Graves's other arm. In one efficient trice, he had taken all of the weight and was maneuvering Graves with dancerlike grace. It looked like Gene Kelly hauling around a doll full of sand. "Where do you want him?"

"Upstairs." I scooped the gun up. "And move slowly."

One blue eye sparkled at me. The blood was already drying. The heater was on—God, the bill was going to be sky-high this month. "If I wanted either of you dead, I'd just leave you to the wolves. 'Tis their season, after all."

Yeah. Sure. Whatever. "I'll keep the gun just in case. What are you doing here?"

"I thought I'd pay you a visit, my dear. Since you're so interesting."

My mouth shifted into high gear, leaving my brain behind. "You know, you're the second guy in a few days to call me that. You should be more creative."

Good one, Dru.

"I do hate to be imitated." He was hauling Graves up the stairs like the kid weighed nothing. "He'll be fine, if you're wondering. He'll sleep for a couple hours and wake up disoriented and hungry. I hope you have meat in the house."

Does bologna count? "Um, okay. Are you a hunter?" I trailed along behind him, suddenly wishing I could see Graves's face. And unless I was going nuts—which was a distinct possibility—this kid smelled just exactly like a fresh-baked pie. It was a good smell, and it made me hungry.

"Among other things." He reached the top of the stairs, sniffed, and carried Graves into my room. "My, isn't this cozy. I'll bet he sleeps *here*." He dumped the kid on the cot and covered him up with a few quick yanks on an Army blanket. Scratchy but warm, and it would forgive the snow melting from Graves's clothes.

His face looked less wary when he was asleep, and the unibrow wasn't that noticeable. His mouth gapped open a little, like a toddler's, and I pointed the gun at Christophe.

"Okay. Slowly. Back away from him."

He spread his hands, a flash of irritation crossing his blood-smeared face. "Why do you make me repeat myself? I just told you I don't want to hurt either of you. You're a babe in the woods. Who is this kid, your pet?"

I could barely believe it, but I outright bristled. If I had hackles, they would have gone straight up. "He's my *friend*." *And you're not.* "I think we need to have a little chat."

"I agree." His shoulders slumped a little, as if he was tired. "Do you have a washcloth? I'd like to get the blood off my face."

It was a pretty reasonable request, I decided. "Downstairs. Kitchen." But I covered him with the gun the entire way.

I'd hit him once, after all. And here in the house I'd already shot a zombie. Maybe this smartmouth blue-eyed apple-pie boy would be next.

CHAPTER 21

W**ithout the blood** on his face, and in full light, Christophe turned out to be not just sharp-nosed but sharply handsome, too. The sweater, snowmelt weighing it down, clung to his torso. He was in good shape, and strong—I was going to have a bruise above my knee where he'd plugged me.

I kept him covered with the gun from one side of the breakfast bar while he wiped himself off, rubbing at his hands and passing the washcloth over his face. His chin was a little sharp, but he had great cheekbones. "That isn't necessary," he said, his back to me, glancing up out the window to the backyard. He didn't say a damn thing about the plywood-and-blanket baffle over the destroyed door. I wondered if he could smell the zombie.

"You'd better start talking," I informed him the third time he rinsed his hands. "I don't have all day."

"You might have all day, but you certainly don't have all night." He turned and leaned against the counter, his hair lying down a bit more now but still artistically mussed. Those blue eyes scored holes of brilliance in his face, and his elegant mouth made a small movement as if he tasted something on the borderline of bad. "Are you expecting visitors?"

What? "No." *I was going to re-ward the doors and windows, and I think I'd better as soon as I get you out of here.* "But you're not asking the questions, bucko. *I* am. Why don't you explain how you know my father and what *exactly* you are?"

He shrugged, and the heater shut off. I almost jumped out of my skin. "I'm *djamphir*. I hunt *nosferatu*. I suppose human hunters don't know much about us—at least, the amateurs probably don't." He grinned, and I found myself disliking him intensely. "And I know your father because he set me back months. I had almost finished preparing a trap for Sergej, but then your father had to come blundering in with his vendetta and ruin the whole thing. He's dead, then? I thought as much when I saw them take him."

"You saw it? What happened? And who the hell is Sergej?" I couldn't pronounce the name the way he could, like it was in another language. It sent the same glass dagger through my head, and the house creaked sharply as it settled on itself.

He rolled his eyes, a very teenage movement, but oddly strained. "Sergej, the Princeps. He's old, and nasty. He's the *nosferat* Dwight Anderson's been hunting these twelve years."

Hearing him say Dad's name was bad. Hearing him say *that* was . . . well, it was worse.

Dad was hunting a sucker? No way. He always told me that was bad, bad news. That you couldn't pay him enough. "Dad's been hunting other things." My heart gave a single hurting leap, like a spike driven through my chest. "I don't think he ever went after a sucker." *But . . . I could be wrong. There was that town north of*

Miami. Dad got the heebies really bad on that one.

And then there was that month I spent with August. I had a thought about that, something I should really do, but what Christophe said next knocked it right out of my head.

"Your father was a gifted amateur. It was your mother who was the real hunter." He was still looking at me steadily, as if weighing my reaction. A slant of winter light through the window brought out all the sharp detail on his face, the nap of his sweater, the glow in his eyes. "What do you remember about her?"

We're going to play the game, Dru.

I swallowed drily. My mouth was watering. The cinnamon and spice smell was downright distracting, especially since it covered up the faint omnipresent tang of zombie." Not much. She died when I was five."

"She was *murdered* when you were five." He folded his arms and watched my face like something was growing there. "You didn't know?"

My palms were sweating, my heart going a mile a minute. *What the hell do you think you know about me?* "How the hell do *you* know? You're as old as I am."

He seemed to find that funny. At any rate, a pained little smile crossed his sharp face. "I've got my own ways and methods, Miss Dru. And I'm going to be hanging around for a little bit. I'm your guardian angel. You *really* don't know what you are, do you?"

Irrational, nameless anger welled up behind my breastbone. Who did this guy think he was, anyway? *I said I'd be asking the questions here. Why do I feel more like he's questioning me?* "Yeah, guardian angel. Riiiight." I didn't think I could get any more sarcastic, but I gave it a try. "I told you, I'm hungry, tired, and pissed off. That about covers it. I don't get what you're hinting at."

"Do you know what *svetocha* is? No, of course not." His hand turned into a fist around the bloody washcloth. It was weird to see the difference between the white-knuckle clutch and his interested, bland expression. "I'd give a lot to know how your father thought he was going to handle you once you reached maturity. Or how he hid you. But if I know what you are, chances are someone else does too. They'll want to capture you—or kill you. Either way, you won't be running around loose for long. And if Sergej catches you, you might wish you were dead."

Oooh, was that supposed to be a threat? I summoned up my best *I don't give a shit* attitude, the one I used when in a Real World bar with Dad. "Why, because I know about the Real World? Whatever." I was getting tired of standing behind the breakfast bar. I wanted something to eat and I wanted to take a very hot shower, and I wanted my skin to stop running with chill prickles of foreboding. "I think it's time you left."

Not to mention I wanted a chance to sit down and think about this. He could just be shining me on, true. But . . .

Yeah, *but*. The most horrible little word in the English language. I hate that word. It just means something else is going to go wrong, or the shit is going to get deeper.

And it was deep enough already.

"You don't listen very well. You're in danger, Dru. Whatever you've seen up to now is a cakewalk compared to what's just around the bend. Word is out that Anderson's dead, and Sergej's looking for anyone he left behind—which means they're starting to suspect there *was* someone left behind. A secret your mother kept." His knuckles were still white around the bloody washcloth, and he was staring somewhere over my left shoulder so intently I almost looked to see what was looming behind me. "And here you are, running around with a *loup-garou* and ignoring all kinds of good advice."

Loup-garou, another word for werwulf. I stored the term away. I could find something out about that; it was time to hit the books like it was going out of style. "So this Sergej guy. He's a sucker, and he killed my father?" It was kind of hard to talk through all the rushing noise in my head.

The same noise I heard when I woke up a few mornings ago and found the world had twisted off its course and deposited me in a nightmare. The noise that was behind the word *gone*. Another little word I hate.

"I don't know if *killed* is the precise term. He likes to break them before he sends them into the afterlife. Your father might even be alive, for all we know." A millimeter's worth of change went through his face, those perfectly carved lips compressing slightly, and I was suddenly, instinctively aware he didn't even believe it himself.

So you don't know. You're guessing just as much as I am. It was a relief to start thinking logically again. I blinked hard, twice, trying to put everything together inside my head. "So what the hell are you doing here?"

"I suppose you could say I represent those who think you're precious. I told you, I'm your new guardian angel. Aren't you glad?" A wide, sunny smile broke out over his face. It would have been attractive if it hadn't been so downright freakish. Like a Halloween mask.

Some angel. Yeah, I'm just warm all the way through. "Precious? For what?"

"*Djamphir* are always male. If they breed with human women, they rarely have female offspring. When they do, those females are *svetocha*. The *svetocha* are fertile sometimes; their sons are strong, but their daughters—doubly rare as they are—are stronger. They always breed true when they throw a female." He paused, cocked his head, and took a good deep sniff. I wondered if he could smell pies too. "I'm good, yes. I'm strong by virtue of my blood. But with the proper training, Dru, you can become toxic to *nosferat*. You can become capable of killing them just by breathing in their vicinity. Once you bloom."

Yeah, and I'll put on a cape and spandex, and fly to the moon, too. "Wait. Hold on just one cotton-pickin' minute. You're telling me I'm part *sucker*?" I shook my head hard, my hair actually flying. "Sure. Tell me another fairy tale." *My mom was my mom. She wasn't a sucker, goddamn you. I know she wasn't.*

"You know better than most how true some fairy tales are." He scanned the kitchen slowly. His eyes were so blue, and they roved over every surface like he owned the place. "Can I have a glass of water? Rolling in the snow with a new *loup-garou* is thirsty work."

Yeah, it's water you want? I saw your fangs, buddy boy. I pointed with my free hand, kept the gun trained on him. "Glasses are up there. How do I know you're what you say you are?" *Or that anything you're telling me is anything close to the truth?*

See, that was the thing. None of this could be true.

So why was I still listening to him?

He half-shrugged, a single graceful lift of one shoulder. "I'm out during the day. You shot me the other night—that hurt, by the way—and I bleed red, as you verified not ten minutes ago. I can smell the difference on you and on your pet upstairs—and I saved your life. Aren't those enough reasons, or do you need more?" He got a glass down, moving silently except for the squeak of the cupboard. "I could have killed you both, you know. You're laughably untrained."

I've been doing this all my life. Still, it might be worth it to find out how he did a few things. Like standing on snow without leaving footprints. That would be a good skill to have.

What if his spiel about *djamphir* was true? I strained my memory, but couldn't drag up anything. Nothing but the movies, and while they might be better training than you'd think, they're also not as specific or thorough as a good book.

But what really happened to Mom?—I shut that thought down in a hurry. I didn't want to think it.

I didn't want to think about it *at all*. There was too much else to get out of the way before I could even begin.

It sounded like this Christophe knew more about the Real World than I did. His number had been in Dad's book—but without the mark that meant he was safe. He was still a contact, and—here was the magic thing—he might actually be useful.

I hated thinking about it that way. Just like I hated thinking about how useless Graves was, though to give him credit, he'd tried.

What did I want? Was it worth keeping this guy around?

Did I even have a choice? I had the gun now, but I had the sneaking suspicion Christophe was *letting* me keep it. I had another suspicion, too—if he could smell something on Graves, or something on me, he could probably smell the zombie stain in the living room. Why wasn't he saying anything about *that*, friends and neighbors?

The rushing in my head was really bad. It covered up other sounds I didn't want to hear—tapping on a window, the soft *wump!* of flames sprouting along a broad hairy back, or the terrible howls of a streak-headed werwulf. This was getting to be too much for me.

I was pretty much at the mercy of whatever this guy decided to do anyway. Wasn't it just this morning I'd been resigning myself to him killing me?

"So what's it going to be?" Christophe asked, as if he could read my mind. The spaces between his words were odd, as if he had some sort of weird American accent. I've heard just about everything on the continent, but I couldn't place it. "You're going to have to trust someone, Dru."

I'm thinking I trust Graves, even if he is seriously wigging me out with this growling and leaping around thing. I'm thinking you're lying about my mother.

Why bring her up at all, though? Dad didn't talk about her, even to August. He just never mentioned it. How could this guy know anything about her?

I had other things to worry about. *I'm thinking I* don't *trust you until I know why you want to be so helpful.*

But it was, I had to admit it, comforting. He was a professional. He'd taken care of the streak-headed werwulf and chased it off, and could obviously handle himself. Having someone else in my corner, someone more experienced who knew more than I did, wasn't something to be sneezed at.

Wasn't that what I'd been wishing for? And now here he was in my kitchen. Smelling like apple pies and looking at me with a direct seriousness that made him even cuter. The bruising spreading up the side of his face had halted, and under it he was very pretty. Not jock-pretty, or the hurtful kind of pretty that tells you a guy is too busy taking care of his royal self to think about you.

No, his face just worked. Everything in proportion, the artist in me noted. Except the sharpness of his chin and that shadow in his eyes. Like he knew more than he was telling.

Way to judge him on his looks, Dru. Come on. The rushing noise in my head drained away. I swallowed drily. "All right." I clicked the safety on and set the gun aside. "What do you suggest?"

"That's a good girl." He grinned. It wasn't the feral grimace he'd used before, but a genuine smile that lit up his cold eyes. There was blood drying in his hair, and he was dripping on the kitchen floor, but that smile more than made up for it. "First, Miss Dru, we take stock of your weapons and I bring some of my own. Then, before dark, we ward your house again. We may well have visitors tonight."

* * *

"I don't like it," Graves whispered. All in all, he was taking this pretty calmly. He touched the cookie jar, running his finger over the cow's belly, and took his hand back when I gave him a raised-eyebrow Look.

I closed the dishwasher, twisted the knob to turn it on. My hair was drying into frizz, but I felt a lot more human after a hot shower and some honest-to-God lunch. "I don't either. But he knows things. Like about you." I caught myself whispering too, as if Christophe hadn't left to go "pick up a few things, be back before dark."

"I thought *you* knew things." Graves picked up an empty pizza box—I'd sprung for delivery, since the road was clear and we'd pretty much eaten the house clean. Groceries were in order. If there was no more snow tomorrow I'd go to the store.

It was like having Dad in the house again. Only not really. Dad would have been watching cable or quizzing me on tactics. Graves was just following me around and half-jumping nervously every time something creaked.

"I do know things. He knows *more* things." I eyed the stack of plates left over and popped the drain stopper in, reached for the dish soap. "You're taking this awfully calmly."

His face twisted up wryly. "It was amazing. It was like I could smell everything. Like the world was slow but I was moving at regular speed." He set the empty box aside, opened up one that still held two pieces of pepperoni with extra cheese. "God. I never thought I could be this hungry."

"There's cereal, too, when you're finished with that." I stared at the bubbles rising in the sink, white froth. Stole a sideways glance at him from under my lashes, looked hurriedly back at the soap foam. "Graves? Thank you."

He hastily swallowed. "For what?" Took another ginormous bite. His hair was a mess and his eyes glowed feverishly. The brighter green looked really nice on him.

"For everything. I mean . . . you didn't have to." *You didn't have to get me a cheeseburger. You didn't have to hide me. You didn't have to stick around or get me out of school today. You didn't have to be . . . trustworthy.*

"Hey." He shrugged and grinned, cheese hanging from the corner of his mouth before he hooked it in with his tongue. "It's not like I have anyone else, Dru. I figure we're both in the same boat."

Yeah. And it's sinking fast. I paddled my fingers in the water. "So what happened to your parents?"

He tossed the half-eaten slice back into the box. "They didn't want me. I bounced around in foster homes for a while, had some bad times. Almost got stuck in juvie because they didn't know what to do with me. Then I figured, I'm smart enough to take care of myself. So I did some lying and some moving around, and made myself a plan for getting all grown up and never being helpless again. *Ever.*" His eyes narrowed and he shrugged, as if there wasn't a world of pain hiding behind the words. "I've done pretty good, too. Mostly it's arranging things so people just assume someone's responsible for me."

"Yeah." I knew all about *that*.

There's a fifty on the counter, Dru. And do your katas. But Dad loved me, and there was never any question that he wanted me. He would never have just dropped me off somewhere and abandoned me, would he? He'd always come back.

But I'd always worried. *Always*. And this time he hadn't come back at all, had he?

"So what are we going to do before he comes back?" Graves eyed me, and I put the first three plates in the soapy water. Flipped the water off.

We. It sounded so simple when he said it like that. "We do the dishes. Then I show you how to ward the house—" I caught his wide-eyed almost-panic, and an unwilling laugh bubbled up in my throat. "Don't worry. All it takes is imagining—it's simple. We'll go over it before Christophe comes back. He helped close up the house before he left, but it doesn't hurt to do it again—and it doesn't hurt to have you know how to. My grandmother said you should do it every couple of days anyway to keep it fresh." It hurt a little to talk about Gran. Not nearly as much as it hurt to think about Dad, but close.

My brain returned to Mom, playing with the idea like a cat pawing a mouse. It couldn't be true. Mom wasn't a sucker, and neither was I. It was impossible. I went out in the sun like everyone else.

Including Christophe. He was out by day, too. Jesus.

"And then?" Graves asked, picking up a towel. I rinsed off the first plate and handed it to him. It was nice having him around; Dad couldn't be bothered to dry dishes.

"Then we look in a few books and figure out if everything Christophe told me before he left is true." *Especially about loup-garou.*

"Okay." He stared at the plate, polished it in circles with the towel. "Dru?" He opened up the right cabinet, set the plate gently away.

"Hm?" I swirled my fingers in slippery soap-water. The patterns almost made sense if I unfocused my eyes. The touch was getting stronger. Gran had told me it might happen, but she hadn't been too specific, and I hadn't really thought much about what that might mean.

The lump in my throat wasn't quite disgust and it wasn't quite fear. I couldn't figure out *what* it was. Svetocha. *Part* nosferat. *Is he serious?*

Well, we were going to find out. Funny how having something solid to work on gave me the sense of things being on track again. Not *right*—it wouldn't be right again, not ever. But on track. Better.

Right enough.

"Am I still human?" Graves took the next plate after I rinsed it off, swiped at it with the towel. Scrubbed at it a little harder as color mounted in his golden cheeks.

Am I? "Yeah, sure. Of course you are."

He shrugged. "I dunno. I felt like I wanted to kill him."

You're not the only one. I suppressed a shudder. "I'm not surprised. If he is what he says he is, you guys are pretty much enemies. Wulfen don't like suckers. Or even anything that smells like suckers."

That managed to prick his interest. "Is it like a big war between them?"

"Not exactly. They're just . . . well, they're like jocks and nerds. Or hyenas and lions. They coexist, right, but they're different breeds and they don't mix. And they're always on the lookout for each other." I paused. "A group of wulfen might help another group of wulfen or something else they don't like against a sucker, and suckers sometimes kill stray wulfen, of whatever type. There are lots of types, like tribes, and the suckers are organized into tribes, too. Their allegiances shift, but the suckers never band together to take out wulfen, and the wulfen don't really go after suckers unless it's to avenge one of their own. So they have this kind of agreement:

Each group doesn't really hang out with the other." I handed him a dripping glass and was kind of surprised. *Guess I knew a little more than I thought. That's a relief.*

"Okay." He nodded, dried the glass with finicky care, and put it up. "So. Warding the house. That some sort of witchcraft?"

What do you know about witchcraft? "More like folk magic. My Gran was a tooth-curer and hex-lifter out in the sticks back East. A wisewoman. You start throwing the W-word around and people get a little tense." *They still burn people in some places. Even here in the good ol' US of A. There was that one town—*

"I guess so. So what's involved in this?" He looked far more interested than I'd ever seen him in school, and it did wonders for him. His face looked leaner, more defined and less babyish. Maybe it was the light through the kitchen window, since Christophe had looked pretty nice under it, too.

God help me, I'd just dumbed down everything Gran taught me into folk cures. She would have just said, *A little bit o' this and a little bit o' that, and never you mind what I call it if'n it works,* while fixing him with that beady-eyed stare that had made more than one grown adult quail.

They hadn't called Gran a witch, but nobody wanted to cross her. And they would come to her door at dusk or in the middle of the night, for cures or other things. Payment was in eggs or salt pork, or herbs, or a bolt of material Gran would make dresses or quilts from. Those quilts sold for a good price, too, since rumor had it that Gran Anderson's quilts would keep lightning from the house or help make for an easy pregnancy.

I'd thought that was normal until she sent me down to the schoolhouse in the valley. And then later, after she died and Dad came to collect me, I'd found out other people didn't take spitting in someone's shadow as a deadly insult, didn't wash their floors with yarrow, and had no idea how dark and inimical the night could be.

"Dru?" Graves looked a little worried. I came back to myself with a jolt and finished washing the spaghetti pot from a couple nights ago. All shiny-clean. "Some salt water. I've got my Gran's rowan wand, too. And we've got a bunch of white candles. One of those should do fine."

CHAPTER 22

They smell like dust, paper, old leather, and each one of them costs a pretty penny. There's Aberforth's *Creatures of Shadow*, Belt-Norsen's *Demoniaca*, Pretton's *Encyclopedia of the Darkness*, and Coilfer's weird but totally readable *Collection of True Folktales*. Which I've scared myself with a number of times, because Patton Coilfer could *write*. Dad told me that he came to a bad end, something involving an African curse and a bunch of masks, one of which had belonged to the semi-famous Sir Edwin Colin Wilson.

That's enough to give anyone who's read *True Folktales* nightmares, let me tell you.

We had other books, but those were the first I pulled out. After a few seconds of thought, I pulled out another prize possession—Haly Yolden's *Ars Lupica*, with its tooled leather cover and worn gilt-edged pages. Graves was making coffee—probably too weak, of course—while I spread them out in the living room and started flipping through indexes.

It's funny, a lot of books that would be otherwise useful don't have indexes. You have to kind of shoot by guess, and that's never fun. Especially when you start sneezing uncontrollably at the dust, or when you have to find something in a hurry. The only thing more annoying is having to go through microfiche. *Real* microfiche, not just the electronic captures of 'fiche they've been doing whenever they have funding lately. Nothing like scanning ancient newspapers on a 'fiche reader to make you feel old and dry. And give you a headache like a mule kicking in your skull.

I had to go through a couple of different spellings (*dhampire, dhamphir, dhampyr*) before I found *djamphir* and figured out they were all basically the same thing, and when I did, I settled down for some scanning. True to form, Coilfer was the best written and most useful of the four.

The *djamphir*—he spelled it the way Christophe had pronounced it—was a half-human vampire killer. Some had a thirst for blood; most were rumored to have bone problems. Lots of them were twins, but girl twins were never mentioned. Just boys, like a lot of other things in the books about the Real World. It's like girls are invisible.

Anyway, they were supposed to be often born without bones, and most of the legends were from the Balkans. If *djamphir* survived to adolescence or adulthood, they hunted *wampyr* or *upir*—suckers. Suckers had the hots for human women in a big way, and often bred with them. The result of those unions were *djamphir*, and once there was a taint of sucker in the bloodline, there were always *djamphir*, no matter how many generations passed.

The half or quarter or whatever bit of *wampyr* in them made *djamphir* good vampire hunters. They were always paid whatever they asked for, in cattle, clothes, or "even women."

Yeah. The Real World isn't big on feminism.

Djamphir were long-lived, possibly immortal—*if* the suckers didn't hunt back. But a lot of the suckers did. A lot of them killed their own part-human progeny, too. With a vengeance.

I had to sit back and think about that for a moment. *Ugh. That's* awful.

"Coffee," Graves said, and stopped in the door, looking at me a little weird. "You okay?"

We're going to play a game, Dru.

I shook my head, pushing the memory away. "This is gruesome stuff."

"Figures. So, is he telling the truth?" He handed me my cow mug, the one that matched the cookie jar.

"Haven't figured that out yet." I pushed the Aberforth and the Pretton over to him. "Look in those for *loup-garou*, but don't lose the pages I've marked, okay? And that one right there, *Ars Lupica.* Check that too."

"*Loup-garou.*" He looked down at the scrap of paper I'd written it on. "Okay. You got it."

"You're probably really good at this research thing." I blew across the top of my coffee, took a small sip, and was pleasantly surprised. It was getting better.

"This doesn't seem like math." He spread his free hand, looked at it. Tendons stood out on the back, his fingers blunt and nail-bitten, his knuckles chapped a bit but getting better. "And a lot of this is a direct violation of physics. Conservation of energy should make some of this stuff impossible."

"I don't know about that. I just know what I see." I took another sip. I'm not one for a lot of caffeine, but I felt fuzzy-headed. Slow and stupid.

"Yeah. That's the trouble with theories; the real world is always kicking the shit out of them." He settled down, stripping his hair back from his face. "Doesn't this sort of shit, well, *bother* you?"

I thought about it. "You mean, like it shouldn't exist?" I couldn't express it better than that.

But he understood, or I'd understood him. "Yeah. Exactly. It's . . . well, it's kind of obscene."

That's one way of putting it. "So's a lot of other stuff we take for granted. Burning down rain forests. Serial killers. Rush-hour traffic. Life is pretty obscene whatever way you slice it, Graves." I looked back down at the Coilfer. *Having your dad turned into a zombie kind of takes a cake, though. I'm not sure which cake it takes, but it definitely takes one of them.* "This sort of stuff is just icing, you know. On the cake."

"Some icing." He flipped immediately to the indexes, I noticed. "Wow."

"Yeah." I took a deep breath, another sip, and pulled my attention back to the page.

The djamphir *can use a variety of means to kill a* wampyr, *of which the most popular in folklore is a hawthorn stake. . . .*

* * *

It was a productive afternoon, even though I took down enough coffee to feel jittery by four o'clock. I closed the last book with a sigh. We were as ready as our small collection of texts could make us.

"So we're fairly sure?" Graves kept repeating "fairly" as if it were an exotic foreign word. "I'm not going to get all hairy, like that thing we saw?"

"Nope. According to this, the *loup-garou*'s a skinchanger, not actually a werwulf. Congratulations, you bucked the odds. About all you'll have is a hunger for raw meat." I shuddered. "Which you might even be able to eat, with the boost to your immune system."

The way he squinched up his face made me smile.

"Yeah, I'll get right on that dietary change. But nothing about girl . . . *djamphir*?" He tasted the word, rolling it around on his tongue, and bolted the last swallow of his coffee. It had to be cold by now.

I looked out the front window at the mess of the front yard, bits of brown grass showing through like mange wherever he and Christophe had scuffed the snow all the way down. The sky was lowering, threatening still more as sundown approached, and the radio gave faint squawks about a weather advisory. Why they would bother *now*, after days of this stuff, was beyond me.

Bits of wood were thrown in an arc, the porch railing completely shattered and flung out in an oddly perfect line. They'd hit it *hard*.

"Nope. Nothing on that." I didn't mention anything about my mother. It was nobody's business, even with Christophe's dark hints. I always thought I'd got the touch from Gran, along the Anderson side.

Now that I thought about it, nobody ever mentioned Mom's family. It just wasn't talked about. I didn't even know her maiden name, though I could probably dig up their marriage certificate. It was probably in the fireproof box.

But I wondered, and it wasn't a comfortable wondering. It was like having one of the legs your world rests on whomped away, and I wasn't too steady already.

All the legs of the table were getting chopped out from under me. Mom. *Whomp*. Gran. *Whomp*. Dad. *Whomp*.

If this was a cartoon, I'd be teetering on just one leg with my face twisted up in a picture of dismay.

It was late. Evening was gathering in the bluish shadows, even the reflection of light off the snow fading. Under the coffee jitter, exhaustion and sleeplessness plucked at my eyelids. My arms and legs were heavy, my shoulder hurt, and I knew I should probably take something for the way my back was twitching and sore.

"You hungry?" Graves asked, and I came back from staring at the front yard and realized I was. But given the choice between going to the store and getting some information under my belt, the information was probably the better bet. You had to be alive to eat, after all. I could always go tomorrow.

Which reminded me, there was the money situation to think about. And—

There was a flurry of taps at the door. Light, mocking taps.

I jumped, letting out a thin little cry, and Graves flinched, knocking over his empty coffee cup. The door swept open, and I dove for a gun, my right leg prickling because it had gone to sleep. I rolled, my aching back fetching up against the ammo crate, and clicked the safety off.

I didn't even think about it. Graves stupidly crouched right where he was, his eyes as big and green as a kid's, flicking nervously between me and the doorway. The air around him shimmered faintly, stilled.

"Easy, little birdie," Christophe called down the hall. "I can smell your adrenaline, you know. Come help me carry this in. I hope there's some coffee left."

Graves looked at me. We hadn't even seen him approach, I'd just been staring out at the front yard. You could see the walk and the driveway, for Christ's sake. Did he just show up out of thin air? Even in the *daytime*?

Yeah. Pretty obscene. I clicked the safety back on and let out a breath I hadn't been aware of holding. Dad would have kicked my ass for it, of course—holding your breath while under fire is a bad idea. You can pass out or just not think clearly if you're starving your brain of oxygen. There were even stories about people passing out because they were holding their breath in combat.

I was lying there on the floor, feeling a cold draft tiptoe down the hall and into the living room, and all of a sudden I felt very, very lonely.

"Come on out, little rabbits," Christophe called cheerfully. I could just see him grinning. "Come see what *Dyado Koleda* brought you, eh?"

What the hell is he talking about?

Graves pushed himself up. "Jesus," he whispered. He edged through the doorway into the hall, and I realized that he was trying to stay out of my field of fire.

Smart kid.

"There you are." There was the crinkle of plastic bags. "Help me with this. I stopped at the grocery store. The air smells of snow again, and not just a little bit, either."

"How'd you come up to the door without us seeing you?" Graves wanted to know. I swallowed drily and put the gun back on top of the ammo crate, pushed myself to my feet. My leg ran with waking-up tingles, like fork tines jammed into the muscles.

"I'm very sly." Christophe sounded in a hell of a jolly mood. "Now come on, beast of burden. Carry some of this. Where's *Księżniczka*? The princess?"

"Dru's finishing her coffee," Graves informed him, sarcasm dripping from every word. He came stumping down the hall with his hands loaded with shopping bags. I saw something green poking out of one. "We've been doing research."

"Oh, good. Stretching your minds like good little children. Your guardian angel is pleased." The front door closed, and there was more plastic rustling. "And?"

Graves didn't reply, just stamped past the stairs and into the kitchen. I stepped out into the hall and was greeted with the sight of Christophe in a fresh sweater, navy blue this time, with white stripes on the sleeves. It made his shoulders look a little broader, and his jeans were clean and dry. His hair all but glowed with blond streaks, and his eyes burned with sheer good cheer.

The smell of fresh apple pies filled the hall. I felt even more frizzy and hopeless.

"I brought weapons. But you can help carry these." He indicated the six shopping bags clustered around his booted feet. A backpack dangled off his shoulder, and a wide leather band crossed his chest. The blunt end of a shotgun poked up over his shoulder.

"You went grocery shopping with a shotgun?" I folded my arms, my stomach twisting with hunger.

He spread his hands, still grinning, teeth white in the shadow of the hall. "People see what they want to see, Dru. You know that. I brought canned soup. Bread. Some of the things I saw in your kitchen, and some others."

What do you want in return? I stayed where I was. "What do I owe you?"

That made his smile even wider, if it were possible. "Nothing at all, little bird. Nothing at all. May I come in?"

What is it with these boys buying me food? I shrugged. "Doesn't look like I can stop you. There's nothing in the books about girl *djamphir*."

"Books." He shrugged. "And anyway, the books your father was likely to find wouldn't have such secrets in them."

I don't like the way he talks about Dad. But I just took a few steps forward, grabbed three of the bags, and turned on my heels.

"Dru." Short and sharp, he said my name like a challenge. All the good humor had drained from Christophe's voice.

I looked back over my shoulder. He stood with his back to the door, his teeth and hair glimmering. He looked impossibly finished for a seventeen-year-old.

God. Kids with guns. I had enough hardware to start an insurrection in my living room, and this kid was wandering around with a shotgun, for Chrissake. And Graves could probably wreak some serious havoc if he was angry enough and the change had him. Where were the adults who were supposed to handle this thing?

All dead like Dad, maybe? It was a nasty thought. "What?"

After a short, searching pause, he shrugged. "Nothing. I hope I brought what you needed."

I hope so, too. But I don't have any clue what I need now. Although that shotgun is a good start. "Thanks for stopping by the store. I don't know how much longer I can stay in this house, though."

"Oh?"

You're not my first visitor, Blue Eyes. I just swept on down the hall and let him chew on that.

CHAPTER 23

I woke up out of a sound, dead sleep, a dream I couldn't quite remember about the dark hole in the closet receding as soon as I opened my eyes. The window was full of the weird directionless nighttime shine of streetlamps reflecting off fresh snow, and Gran's white owl fluffed its feathers and stared at me.

I was nice and warm, and Graves was breathing quietly on his cot. There was a faint sound—the television, downstairs. The soundless sound of someone breathing there, too.

Comforting. And a little bit scary.

I'd thought I wouldn't sleep with Christophe in the house. But as soon as my head touched the pillow, I'd gone out like a light.

The owl stared back at me. The smell of moonlight chased the fading tang of oranges across my tongue.

I slid out of bed, quietly, hissing in a soft breath as the temperature differential touched my skin. Even with the heater on, it was colder outside the warm nest of my bed. I stepped into sweatpants and pulled them up over the thermal bottoms I'd been sleeping in, yanked my tank top down, and fisted crusties out of my eyes with the other hand. I slipped past Graves, who made a slight sound as if he was dreaming, and ghosted down the hall, avoiding the squeaks. The stairs unreeled under my feet, and I was a shadow in the hall. Blue television flickers painted the wall; as I passed the door to the living room, I saw Christophe in Dad's camp chair, a shotgun—probably the same one I'd seen before—across his knees, his head dipped forward as if he slept. The television was turned way down, a black-and-white war movie I was sure I'd seen before unreeling between bursts of static.

That's not right. It shouldn't be static. We have cable. The thought was slow, moving through pudding.

Carpet, the boxes still piled in the hall, and a bullet hole shining with television light. They all looked very sad and quiet, refugees from a former life.

The front door was glowing. Thin threads of bright, cheery, summer-sky blue outlined it and scribed a complex pattern across its face, like tribal tattoos. I watched, fascinated, as they swirled like oil on water. Everything was dead silent now, the world wrapped in cotton.

I eased forward. Step by step, bare feet floating an inch above the cheap carpeting. There was a little slip-slide to each footstep, as if I was in a cartoon and someone had tied pats of butter to my feet. The door loomed larger and larger. I was on a conveyor belt sliding toward it, and my hand came up without my volition, stroked the locks. The two deadbolts moved silently, and my hand closed around the knob.

Don't do it, Dru. Don't go out there.

I wasn't planning on going anywhere, was I? Oranges ran in

rivulets across my tongue, fresh instead of waxed, and the shock of tasting them made my head hurt faintly, as if something had slid a thin metal tube through my skull. The knob hissed and slid like water on a hot griddle under my touch, and the blue lines on the door drew together, swirling uneasily.

The door opened silently, swinging wide, curtains of blue parting just slightly to let me through. I stepped out gingerly, still floating. Funny, but it didn't seem so cold anymore. The porch was bare, a section of railing torn loose, dead plants in plastic pots under a light scrim of frost, icicles clustered from one end near a gutter's drainpipe. They shivered, those swords of water, as my gaze blew across them.

The stairs unreeled under my feet. It was snowing again, big fat flakes whirling down in patterns I didn't have time to study; they looked like the tribal tattoos on the door, rivers of frozen stars. A humming had begun in my middle, like an electrical cord plugged into my belly button. The line of force was almost visible, snaking away across the humped drifts in the front yard, beginning to lose their peaks and valleys under a blanket of fresh white.

Where am I going?

There was a soft explosion of sound overhead, wings flapping frantically, and Gran's owl glided past, the eerie snowlight picking out faint dappling on its feathers. It circled, cutting a tight little figure eight with its wingtips, and slowed, floating down the street.

The line attached to my belly snapped taut and began to pull me faster. I leaned back, my heels lower than my toes as if I was waterskiing, and the sense of motion was weird—but not weirder than my hair hanging down, no breeze touching my cheeks or skin.

I'm the Girl in the Bubble. Wow. A dreamy giggle boiled up inside my throat, died away. The world twisted like dribbles of paint on a spinning paper plate, darkness and snow-reflection whirling together, and the owl banked again, wings outstretched and the pattern of eyes on its underside glaring through me for a moment. It dipped, then brushed past my head. I felt the wind of its passing kiss my cheeks and forehead, my hair stirring slightly before dead air returned.

It was weird, skating through the streets, the line at my belly unreeling, sometimes snapping me left or right, dragging me up over hillocks of piled snow and dropping me on their slopes, each landing curiously cushioned so it didn't jar me. Across streets, through alleys, once up and over the curve of a snowed-in car—the thought of someone waking up in the morning to find footprints running up over their car was hilarious, in a slow, disconnected way.

But I'm not walking. I'm surfing. Snow-surfing. Wow.

The owl made a soft passionless *who? who?* sound, and the tugging at my belly slackened. The line kept humming, but it didn't pull me. Instead, I found myself looking at a two-story frame house. Old and dilapidated, it had once been yellow. A massive, naked, gnarled oak tree stood in front, its twisted limbs reaching for the sky.

Why does that look familiar? I studied it for a long moment, cocked my head. The owl settled on the tiny strip of broken roof over the porch. The snow was deep, drifting up against the steps and swallowing them.

But I knew what those steps would look like. I knew what the porch would say if I stepped on its old groaning wood, and the screen door—busted off its hinges, plastic yellow crime-scene tape old and faded and fluttering over the yawning cavern leading into a front hall—I knew what sound it would make if it had still been whole. The hinges had squeaked one long, long note, a *heehaw!* Like an amused donkey.

There would be stairs inside, right off the narrow foyer. Up those stairs and to the left, there would be four doors: a bathroom, probably mildewed by now since the door was all busted open, a main bedroom and a smaller bedroom, and a closet.

I know this house. Somehow I know this house. I stared as the owl mantled, then tilted its head and made its soft call again. Its yellow eyes were old and terribly, terribly sad.

I moved forward, each footstep slip-sliding worse than before, as if butter was melting under my feet. It was hard—the air grew darker and darker the closer I got. And there, at the bottom of the oak tree, was a scorched place where the snow lay discolored and sunken. A moon-silvered figure lay under the darkness, terribly still, crushed under the running shadow.

What is that?

The owl called a third time, a new note of urgency in the soft tones. I put out my hands as the buzzing in my belly got worse, a hornet's nest in my gut, rattling and scraping.

Wait. I know something. I know this house—

The world shivered. I looked down at my hands and realized I could see right through them. Faint snowlight shone through my translucence, the curve of my forearm like glass full of solid smoke.

I was a ghost.

The owl spoke one final time, only that wasn't right, because it wasn't a soft hoot. It was a bell. A loud, rasping, heavy sound; the hornets had broken out of my belly and were swarming. Stinging needles rammed through my fingers as I reached the shadow of the oak tree, its branches buzzing like a rattlesnake's tail right before it decides *to hell with this* and launches itself to bite.

"What the *hell*?" someone said, and I thrashed up out of unconsciousness, snapped free of wherever I'd been like a rubber band popped off expert fingers, and came out swinging.

* * *

The window was open. Cold air drenched the room. Christophe twisted my wrist, deflecting the punch; Graves let out a high-pitched cry and the room was full of the sound of beating wings for a moment. But not soft, feather-baffled wings—no, this sound was leathery, rasping against the air.

Christophe and I tumbled to the floor while Graves wrenched the window closed. "Jesus *Christ*!" Graves kept repeating, in that same high-squeaky voice. It would have been funny if my entire body hadn't been pinned-and-needled, every square inch of skin stinging. "What the *hell* was that? What was that thing?"

I froze. Here I was in my own room, it was cold, and I was still in my thermal bottoms and tank top. My bed was thrashed out of all recognition, Graves's cot was overturned, and the room was full of a dry rotting scent, like molding feathers.

"*Revelle*," Christophe said, grimly. His eyes burned blue, and he kept his hands clamped around my wrists, lying on top of me as if it was the most natural thing in the world. His skin was warm, and he was heavier than he should have been. All the breath left my lungs in a huff. "Dreamstealer. Hush, little bird, just a snake in the nest." This was whispered into my hair, a hot circle of breath against my shivering scalp before he raised his head. "Is it clear or snowing?"

"Snowing." Graves locked the window and shuddered again, wrapping his arms around himself so his elbows and shoulder blades made sharp-shadowed angles. "Jesus. It just came in, and Dru—"

The hollow between Christophe's throat and shoulder moved slightly, and the tingling heat coming off him drowned me. "Shush. Dru? Talk to me. Are you all right?"

I suppose he was asking because his face was in my hair, his legs twisted with mine, and he was holding onto my wrists so hard it hurt, like he had steel bands in his fingers. "Get *off* me!" I managed, before I was well on my way to suffocating.

"Yeah, she's okay." Graves cocked his head, looking at us both.

"Perhaps." Christophe let go of me—not fast enough, I might add. The pins and needles running through my skin peaked, and I curled into a ball on the floor, whooping in a gigantic, never-ending breath flavored with the ghost of apples fighting through the moldy feather-scent. The hall light was on, a rectangle of warm yellow on the floor, and I began to dry-retch.

It didn't feel good.

"*Damn* it." Christophe made it to his feet in a single curling, fluid motion. His hair was slicked down against his head, dark and sleek. "God and Hell both *damn* it. I didn't think he'd send *that*."

"Who? Who would send—someone *sent* that?" Graves's knees were all but knocking together. It sounded like his teeth were chattering, too, but his eyes burned feverish-green. "Holy shit. What the hell was it?"

"A wingéd serpent, come to rob the nest." Christophe shouldered him aside and checked the window. "She must have let it in, thinking it was someone else. Or . . . What I wouldn't give to know—" He halted, staring at the glass and the river of snow whirling down, some of it brushing the pane with little spidery sounds. "He must think she's close to blooming. But I didn't know he had access to a dreamstealer—only the Maharaja breed them." Frustration pulled his tone taut, edged each word with steel.

Can I die now? I dry-retched again. It felt like all my innards were trying to crawl out the hard way. *I thought I was outside. I know that house. That was where we lived Before.*

Before the world changed. Before Mom—

Could I find it again? I probably could. The memory wasn't fading like other dreams. Instead, it was sharp-etched, each individual owl feather shaded just so, every twist of the oak's branches easily remembered, burned into the space behind my eyelids. But my body folded up on itself in revolt, each muscle locking down. *God, what's happening to me?*

Christophe drummed his fingers on the window. The sound went straight through my head and I curled into a tighter ball. "If it was clear, I could track it. Especially now that it's wounded." He cast one bright glance over his shoulder. "That was a smart move, skinchanger, to hit between them."

"Thanks." Graves didn't sound like he accepted the compliment.

I coughed, swallowed, and hoped I wouldn't throw up for real. *Would someone mind cluing me in?* But it seemed pretty obvious—something hinky had come up to the window, and I'd mistaken it for Granmama's owl.

Or had I? I'd been gone, not here at all. I *knew* Gran's owl, and I knew that house. "It was from Before," I managed, through teeth tight-locking together. I was cold as if I'd been wandering out in the snow.

Hadn't I been?

"Get water." Christophe grabbed Graves, shoved him toward the door, and shook his hands like they had something icky on them as soon as he let go. "Get a glass of water. *Hurry.*"

Graves bolted, his curlywild hair all but standing up. I heard him bouncing down the stairs far too quickly, careering off the walls.

Christophe turned away from the window and dropped to his knees beside me. "Stupid," he hissed. His eyes were burning, and when I managed to tilt my head and look up there were dimples in his lower lip—where the fangs slid out from under the top lip and touched, ever so gently.

I couldn't even care. I was too busy.

What, me? What did I do? My heart gave an amazing leap and settled into pounding in my chest. It was getting harder to get air in through the retching, little sips of apples mixing with the fading cloy of rotting feathers. It was funny, it didn't seem like my body was rejecting dinner. It was more like a full-body spasm forcing a dry little sound up through the pipe of my throat and out of my mouth.

Christophe leaned down. His hands cupped my face, twisting my neck awkwardly. "You will breathe," he said calmly. Those eyes glared blue at me, colder than a thin winter sky. Snow hissed against the window, and Graves cursed downstairs. A cupboard slammed shut. "You will breathe, and you will *live*. I'm not having it any other way, *milna*. Breathe."

I tried. My eyes rolled back into my head. Darkness descended, a deep star-spangled night. My head pounded, excruciating pressure building behind my nose and eyeballs. Little spackles of light squeezed down as even my eyelids spasmed. Pain like a silver spike went through me, from the crown of my head to my soles, running down each branching nerve channel.

Graves galloped back into the room, cursing under his breath. Christophe's hands left my face, and my head thumped onto the floor a second before he shouted and threw the glass of water straight into my face.

The seizure stopped. Spluttering and choking, I twitched like a landed fish on the floor and drew in another deep heaving breath, hitched, and let it out with a torrent of cussing that would have done Dad proud, even during truck-fixing sessions.

"Yeah," Graves said, breathing heavily, when I ran out of air enough to curse and just sputtered. "I'd say she's okay."

"Idiot." Christophe handed him the glass as I tried to wipe water off myself. My muscles were weak as overcooked noodles. "That was too close. Get a towel."

"How about *you* get one? I already ran downstairs, and you're the one who threw water all over her." Graves leaned forward, eyeing me. "Hey, Dru. You were French-kissing a winged snake. Creeptastic."

"It was *stealing* her *breath*, imbecile. Go get a towel." Christophe shoved him, and Graves shoved back. The floor groaned sharply as their weight shifted. If I could have gotten in a smell through my nose it would have been the slightly oily dryness of pure macho.

Graves's lip lifted, and his teeth were just as white as Christophe's. "Don't order me around, asshole. I was here before you."

Jesus. Boys. I found my voice. "Goddammit, fuck you *both*. Get out of here." It was hard to sound forceful with my tank top soaked and every muscle in my body loose as wet spaghetti, but I tried my damnedest. "Go downstairs and make me some hot chocolate. Unload the dishwasher. Do something useful instead of getting in a testosterone match in *my* bedroom."

For a long, exotic moment they both stared at me, green eyes and blue burning. I managed to push myself up on weak arms, got my behind under me, and leaned against my mattresses, shivering. The heater puffed into life, but the not-sound of snow against the windowpane made me feel cold all over. *I was gone. I was out of here, and someone did something to my body. Oh, Gran, I wish you were here for real and not just sending your owl. You could tell me what the hell to do now.*

Tension snapped in the room, the air relaxing as they stepped away from each other. Christophe glanced at the window again, his profile still sharp and fanged, his hair sticking close to his head as if he'd gotten water dumped on him, too. His lips firmed up, sharp teeth retreating, and he looked like a new idea had struck him.

Graves, holding an empty glass from the kitchen, finally grinned at me. His eyes glowed, too, but green instead of blue. He looked as relieved as it was possible to get under his hair and beaky nose. "Sure you're okay?"

No, I'm not. I'm freaked out, and you guys aren't making it any easier. But my voice was steady. I was a master at putting on a steady voice. "Make me some hot chocolate. I'm cold. And both of you get out of here." I hugged myself as hard as I could. *I could be an actress. A talent for creative lying just has so many applications.* "Or I'll shoot you."

Christophe didn't look convinced. He blinked, as if just returning to the room, folding his arms and giving me a sideways glance. I expected his eyes to send little blue flashlight beams through the dimness. "What do you think—"

"Chris. Shut up." Much to my surprise, he did. "Go unload the dishwasher. Graves can show you where everything goes. When I get downstairs, you can tell me what that *thing* was."

They trooped obediently out of my room, and I rested my forehead on my knees. Regular aches and pains—my back twinging, my shoulder unhappy—returned like old friends, crawling back under my skin. This just kept getting more and more complex, and I wasn't sure what was real and what was the Real World anymore. Where were the grown-ups who could handle this?

An idea quivered on the tip of my brain, but I was too weirded out to follow it. Instead, I breathed deep the way Gran had taught me, and tried not to think. It was pretty useless, though, because the same thought kept coming back, circling like Gran's owl on soft soundless wings.

I could find that house again. I know I could. It's from Before. And it's in this city.

Why didn't Dad tell me we used to live here?

CHAPTER 24

"**Sergej." Christophe handed** me a mug of Swiss Miss. We didn't have any marshmallows, and I couldn't seem to warm up, even with a wool sweater on and Mom's quilt around my shoulders. "He's very old. You could call him the oldest we know of in North America and probably South America, too. He came from Europe after the war."

"Which war?" Graves wanted to know. He leaned against the breakfast bar next to me. Christophe set another mug down on the counter and gave him a withering look.

"The *Great* War, of course. Not the genocide masquerading as war from that horrid little Austrian corporal. Sergej drank his fill on the battlefields of Łódź and Gorlice-Tarnów. Before, he was merely one of the petty lordlings among the blood-drinkers. Something in the War changed him, and he came to America. Since then, he's been spreading the disease here. Killing for fun and food, and contaminating the proud and the petty to swell the ranks of his legions. We've been trying to kill him for so long."

That perked my ears right up. "We? We *who*?"

"The Order. Your mother was one of us." He said it like he would say, *That television show is on tonight*, or, *I'm going to pick up some milk at the store.*

"The *what*?" I stared at him. "What the hell?" *First she was a vampire hunter, now this. What does he really know about Mom?* "She's dead."

"Indeed. The only *svetocha* in sixty years. Sergej himself came out of hiding to kill her. She was rusty and weak, and she must have hurt him badly, but he managed."

Something horrible and buried rose briefly. *We're going to play the game, Dru.* And that ticking, like a heartbeat, faster and faster, closer and closer. I shoved it down—it was only a dream, wasn't it? I had other problems now.

Hold on just one red-hot second. First questions first, then we'll get into this "order" thing. "So why would Dad be calling *you*?"

Christophe's face changed. For the life of me I couldn't say how. "I think he had finally found out he needed the Order. He blamed us for your mother's death, thought a mere human could do what we couldn't. He went out to hunt alone."

I stared into the hot chocolate. It made a type of sense. Dad went wack after Mom died, and I never thought that much about it. It was just *there*. I didn't remember Mom dying.

Did I?

I remembered Dad's face, set and white, and him fighting with Gran. It was the only time I ever heard them disagree. Most of the time Gran just said *mmmh* or did whatever the hell she wanted to without bothering to give Dad the benefit of her opinion.

But that one time, when we'd arrived at the cabin in the middle of the night, they'd fought. We'd been driving with the windows down, the sharp cold smell of the mountains at night flooding through the car along with the purr and rattle of the engine. When we stopped, it had smelled like dust and new-cut grass, cold clear air and nighttime. I'd been so tired, curled up and sucking my thumb even though I was a big girl.

It was my sharpest memory of childhood, the first rock to loom up solidly in a fog of conflicting impressions before the time I actually started paying attention to everything around me. I guess you could say that's when I started growing up, smelling the sharpness of winter leaves, hearing the ticking of Gran's stove, the smell of frying eggs because Gran was cooking them just as we rolled up the rutted, potholed dirt road dipping and swinging up to her place.

Gran had actually *yelled.*

What you gwun do, Dwight? That chile ain't old enough to know what's happenin'!

Dad's voice, hoarse with something that might have been tears, though it was funny to think of Dad ever crying. *Damn straight she's not. Which is why we're here. Nothing can get to her here. You may hate me, old woman, but I'm doing the best I can.*

And every time I would beg and plead to go with Dad, he would just smile and ruffle my hair. *Not now, princess. When you're older.*

Gran would snort and set her false teeth together, and after Dad left she would keep me busy for days. There was no shortage of work up at her cabin, and maybe she thought it wouldn't give me time to think.

But a lot of waiting for your dad to come back and collect you gives you plenty of time to think, whether you're pitchforking hay or gathering berries or helping make salt pork.

None of that was going to help me now. I had to concentrate on what was in front of me. *Think, Dru. What would Dad ask?* "Who is this Order?"

"*The* Order," Christophe said, like I would say, *Duh, breathing!* "Professional hunters, mostly *djamphir*—the *Kouroi*. Though there are some of *his* kind." He waved a languid hand over his shoulder at Graves, whose face was set and almost white. "They do help."

"He's *loup-garou*," I supplied helpfully. "A half-imprinted werwulf. Stronger and faster than human, but not as strong as the furry type. We know that. We're not totally stupid."

Graves gave me a single, extraordinary glance. I don't know whether he understood that I didn't like Christophe's dismissive tone. But we'd been over it in the books just that afternoon, for God's sake, and we had a better idea of what had happened to him.

Graves was luckier than either of us had guessed. Not every kid who gets bit is a virgin—or gets bit by a wulf old enough and *strong* enough to half-imprint through that.

And more importantly, I didn't want Sucker Boy here thinking Graves was a second-class citizen or something because I'd gotten him bit.

"Exactly. There are full werwulfen as well as *loup-garou* in the Order." Christophe poured more milk into the saucepan and kept it moving. His own mug stood at attention right next to the stove. "The skinchangers are the princes of their type."

Well, isn't that special. "So you're saying I'm part sucker." I touched my mug with a finger. It was scorching hot.

"The *upir* can't stay away from human women. Sergej is . . . Well, the more powerful they are, the more mating allures them. He's always been careful to kill the offspring as well as the mother, though, lest they become a threat. All *djamphir* are survivors, or descendants of survivors." He took a deep breath, his shoulders stiffening. "They would kill us on sight if they could. And we return the favor. Just one big happy family."

And I thought Dad and me put the "fun" in "dysfunctional." "So this Order, they've been trying to kill this Sergej guy?" *The one you say killed my mother?*

It wasn't that I didn't believe him. It was just that my dad didn't raise an idiot. Sure, this guy had a good story and had saved my life, but good stories are as common as sneezes in the Real World. So he was *djamphir*, so what? It didn't mean he had my best interests at heart.

Or that everything he told me was the strictest truth.

On the other hand, what reason did he have to lie to me? *Or* keep me alive?

"Since 1918. He's canny, and he doesn't come out of hiding. Instead, he sends his minions, and he's old and glutted enough to have plenty of *those*. Like the wulf you saw the other night, the one with the pale patch on his temple? That's Ash."

Graves shivered, and so did I. I pulled the quilt closer around my shoulders, leaned into the counter. "How did a werwulf end up working for a sucker? Aren't they enemies?"

"Sergej," Christophe said quietly, "is an expert at breaking things to his will. Even wulfen. Ash has been his for a long, long time." The silence following this was only broken by the sound of the saucepan moving, and the chuckling hiss of snow against the window, until Christophe shook his head and continued. "If we could catch Sergej in the open, we could probably kill him. Especially if we had a *svetocha*. A fully trained daughter of one of our best." The milk sloshed back and forth in the pan. "I don't think you realize just how rare you are, Dru."

Sends his minions. Would they happen to include a burning dog, too? Or was that something else? "What about the burning dog?"

"Burning dog?" Christophe sounded thoughtful. "Tall and black, before it ignited?"

I thought of its glassy darkness before it inhaled and lit up like a burning Christmas tree. "Yeah. Big teeth. And it was huge."

"Big as a horse," Graves said.

"Ah." Christophe said nothing more.

"That's where the streak-headed wulf—Ash—first showed up. Following the burning thing."

Christophe nodded thoughtfully. "Ash and a tracker. How did you—"

"We drowned it in a fountain," Graves supplied helpfully. He actually sounded proud. "Then Dru shot that wulf-guy. After he bit me."

Christophe was very still for a long moment. "Ash and his trackers have been the death of many a good soldier of the Order. And two raw, untrained—"

"Yeah, we kicked his ass." *And nearly died.* But I kept that part of it to myself. My ribs twinged a little as I moved. "Wait a minute. How many of you guys—Order guys—are there?"

Christophe drew himself up, unconsciously straightening. "A few thousand *Kouroi* here in the States. More in Europe. Quite a few in Asia. We're all over."

You are, huh? "How come I've never heard of you? Dad and I have been pretty much all over the continent and I've never heard a single thing about you guys."

"If you know how to listen, you probably have. Your father's friend August Dobroslaw in New York, for example. He's one of us." A dismissive half-wave with his hand, and Christophe went back to keeping the milk moving as if it was the most interesting thing in the world.

I felt like I'd been pinched somewhere numb. *August. I've been thinking about him lately, too.* I nodded. "Then I can call him and he'll verify your story." My hair fell in my face. I lifted the hot chocolate and sipped it gingerly. My tongue got burned. I had to suck in a long breath. Snow spattered against the windows, and I shivered. I was *still* cold. The wind had a hungry sound again tonight, and I wasn't feeling safe even with Graves next to me.

Even with Christophe standing in the kitchen fiddling with the saucepan. "Do it and find out." His shoulders dropped. "If he does verify my story, as you put it, you think you could be a little nicer?"

"I'll try." It was my turn to sound sarcastic. Graves made a restless movement next to me, and I bumped him with my shoulder. Letting him know I was with him.

It helped me, too. The pressure of his arm against mine was comforting.

Graves drew in a deep, dissatisfied breath. "I want to know something. How are these things finding Dru?"

Silence, broken only by the sound of small snow pellets hitting the window. It was a hell of a good question.

The zombie found me because Dad knew where I lived. The streak-headed werwulf might have been watching the truck, and in any case he'd gotten a good noseful of me at the mall—which didn't explain how he'd arrived *at* the mall. If the burning dog was a tracker, as Christophe said, that explained some things—but not where it had picked up my trail in the first place.

And what about whoever was knocking on the door before dawn? I hated to admit it, but that bothered me the most. Why hadn't whatever-it-was tried to get in? Unless the warding had kept it out, which meant it *could* have been a sucker. Maybe even this Sergej.

The name sent cold little fingers sliding up my back. I had more to think about. Like how exactly had Christophe found me?

And the thing, whatever it was, that had opened up my bedroom window and sucked my breath out? A *snake with wings*, Graves had said.

Dreamstealer, Christophe called it. *Revelle.*

I was still cold, gooseflesh spilling up my arms and down my back. Had it been a dream, or had I been outside my own *body*? That was a creeptastic idea, and something all too likely—it was just the way the touch could work. Gran would have known what to say about it. Hell, even Dad might have had a clue. I could have asked him some questions.

"Have strange things been happening to you lately, Dru?" Christophe poured hot milk into his mug, picked up the spoon, and stirred it. The saucepan was set aside, every drop of fluid gone. He'd gauged the amount just right. "Things you didn't know you could do? Strange things, strong things, things you shouldn't know suddenly clear as day to you?" He turned and leaned against the counter, his eyes glowing slightly. The kitchen was dark but the dining room light was on, and his hair still looked sleeker, lying close to his head without all the highlights reflecting.

"Other than hexing my teacher and having the world stop like a movie on pause?" I shrugged. "I've always been weird. My grandmother called it "the touch". It's gotten stronger. But all of this is weird, even for me."

"*That's* saying something." Graves took a huge slurp, made a low half-swallowed belching sound, and I was surprised into laughing. He gave his own peculiar painful laugh, too, and I felt a lot better.

Christophe studied us, his face shut like a book. "Then you're close to blooming, Dru. Becoming a full *svetocha*." He blew across the top of his mug. "I wish I knew. . . ."

Blooming? I let Mom's quilt slip down a little. My hands were warmer now. "You wish you knew what? We're in a sharing space right now; you might as well ask." Graves bumped me back with his thin shoulder, and the urge to laugh hit me again. You know how it can just suddenly bubble up at the most inappropriate times? Like you're just sitting there, and a thought hits you sideways, or the absurdity of the world just smacks you out of nowhere and you have to swallow a giggle?

Yeah. Like that. I swallowed the sound; it stuck in my throat and threatened to turn into a belch. My shoulder burned dully, and my back was stiff. Getting knocked around and having someone lying on top of you doesn't do much for back pain.

"I wish I knew how your father thought he was going to train you *or* hide you long enough for you to survive into adulthood. Among other things." Christophe sighed, and set down his mug with a click. "I'll be in the living room."

And just like that, he walked away. He moved down the hall like he knew the house better than I did, and a few seconds later the formless mutter of the television blurred through the hiss of snow.

"I don't like him," Graves half-whispered.

"You already said that." I took another scalding gulp of hot milk and sugar. *There isn't even any real cocoa in this. It's all just artificial flavor.* For a moment I thought about Gran's hot chocolate and I wished, suddenly and fiercely, that I was five years old and safe again. And then I thought of Gran always washing the floors with herb mixes meant to keep evil away, and I wondered how safe I'd really been. "I'll call August tomorrow."

"Then what?"

How the hell should I know? But I did. I finished swallowing and leaned against the counter, watching the pattern of whirling white outside the window. "Then I'm going to find out everything I can about this Sergej guy. If Chris is right, and he killed my dad . . ." I swallowed the sudden lump in my throat.

Graves didn't think much of the notion, even half-formed and unstated. "Then what? If he's right and they've been chasing him for so long, what the hell are *we* going to do?"

We? But I suppose it never occurred to Graves that he might want to sit out whatever was going to happen next.

No. Of *course* it hadn't occurred to him. I'd thought of ditching him more times than I could count, and I suddenly felt like a complete asshole for it.

My chest felt funny, tight and warm at the same time. "My dad wasn't a dumbass. He taught me a lot. Maybe he taught me something these guys don't know." *Dru, you're lying.*

But what else could I do? If Christophe was telling the truth, this Sergej guy—those cold insect feet walked up my back again—turned my dad into a zombie. You don't just *forgive* something like that, do you?

But I was just a kid, and I was seriously out of my depth here. I'd shot a werwulf, yeah, and done a lot of running away. And I'd found the truck, but that was more Gran's owl than me.

If this was a game, I was losing pretty badly. I should probably get the hell out of the stadium while I was still alive.

"Oh." Graves's shoulder bumped mine again, hot milk slopping inside my cup. Warmth stole back into my fingers and toes, finally.

Still . . . "But maybe these Order guys could teach me something too. And you. There's got to be something good in being stuck on superhero, right?"

He sighed heavily. "If it makes me fall asleep and then wake up craving two whole greasy pepperoni pizzas, man, I don't know."

I actually laughed, cupping my mouth in my hand to keep it down.

"I noticed something, too." Graves didn't even crack a smile, and motioned toward the living room. "He's not answering your questions, really. I mean, not completely. Not like he doesn't have something to hide, you dig?"

I guess not. "If he is who he says he is, he's got reasons not to." But I met Graves's eyes, and we stared at each other for ten seconds or so, the meaningful type of stare that can happen when you know someone and eye-talk is more efficient than spending a half-hour stumbling with words. Snow slid against the window, and a thread of cool draft touched my cheek. I was going to have to put a real back door on soon, even with the almost-enclosed porch out there.

Graves shrugged. "If you say so." *I still don't trust him,* his green eyes said. There was hardly any hazel left, and the contrast was startling against caramel skin. Seen in profile, his nose looked proud instead of just too damn big for his face. When he shivered a little and hunched his shoulders, I had the sudden urge to put my arm and Mom's quilt around him, and just stay there for a while.

The thought made me feel warmer, but I didn't do it. Instead, I finished my hot chocolate. It was still too hot, but it didn't feel like liquid lava going down. "I'm going back to bed."

"Why don't you call this August guy now?" Graves hunched his shoulders even further.

"Because it's nighttime in New York, and if it's night, he's out hunting." I shuffled around the breakfast bar and put my mug in the sink. "Hey, Graves?"

"What?" Cautious, his shoulders still hunched.

He must be used to people trying to get rid of him, I thought, and the sharp jab of pain that ran through me twisted all the way down.

"Thanks. You got that thing off me, right?"

He stared into his hot chocolate like it held the secret to the universe. "Yeah, well, the window was open and it was really cold."

What does that have to do with the price of tea in China? But then I realized what he meant. It even called a creaking, half-painful smile to my face, and the last of the cold and goose bumps flushed away on a wave of welcome heat.

No problem, Dru. First one's free.

CHAPTER 25

As soon as I woke up the next morning, grainy-eyed and feeling like I'd been beaten with a lead pipe, I stumbled downstairs and ate some cereal standing up. Graves got up while I was doing that, took one long look at me, and headed for the living room. I heard him say something to Christophe, and they both went out the front door.

The smell of apple pies didn't quite fill the house, but it was there, a thread under everything else. It was kind of hard to take Christophe seriously when he smelled like baked goods. I wondered if other *djamphir* smelled like Hostess Twinkies and sniggered to myself.

Then I remembered Christophe kneeling in the snow with a shotgun to his shoulder, facing down a streak-headed wulf and all but laughing, and the sniggers dried up.

I yawned and padded to the chipped yellow plastic phone attached to the wall. There was one number, at least, that I had memorized, because it was so easy. And, well, you don't forget a guy who can snap a flame off his fingers while other guys could only flick boogers. Especially not when you spend a month in his apartment while he's out with your dad, dealing with a demonic rat infestation.

And another month while your dad is off doing who-knows-what, coming back all beat-up and scary looking. August liked my omelets, and I must've cooked hundreds of them for him.

The phone rang five times before he picked up and cursed. August's voice was nasal through the line, laden with Brooklyn wheeze, every vowel cut short like it personally offended him. "This better be good."

"Hi, Augie." I tried to sound cheerful. "It's Dru."

"Holy . . ." There was a sound of sliding cloth, paper, and a clatter like he'd just dropped a knife. It didn't take him long to recover. "Hi, sweetheart. I miss your omelets."

I'll bet you do. You ate two of them a day because you wouldn't bring home anything but eggs and vodka. It was an adventure getting you to buy some bread. "I miss your coffee. Hey, August—"

He was quick on the uptake. Something probably didn't sound right to him. *I* probably didn't sound right to him. I didn't even sound right to myself, with a dry stone trying to lodge itself in the back of my throat.

"Dru, honey, where's your dad?" *And why isn't he the one on the phone,* was probably what he wanted to say.

"He came down with a bad case of reanimation." I tried to sound flip and offhand, but I think I succeeded only in sounding scared. And tired. And like I just got up.

August actually choked, and I heard a metallic sound as if he'd dropped something else. "*What?* Holy fu—uh, I mean, *damn*. Where are you now, kid?"

Oh, no you don't. "I want to ask you a few questions. First, are you part of the Order?"

A long ticking silence crackled in my ear. Finally, I heard the click of a lighter and a long inhale. I could see his apartment, the full ashtray on the spindly kitchen table, the window that looked at a blank brick wall, the walls loaded with protective items from different cultures—African masks, *ojos de Dios*, a heavy silver crucifix. I could almost hear the traffic outside his building, but that could have been because it was clearly audible through the phone. "Holy shit. Where are you?"

Like I'm going to tell you until I know what's really going on. "Are you a part of the Order, August? Yes or no." *My dad didn't raise an idiot. You know that.*

"Of course I am, what did you think? Where are you, honey?"

I told him, and he sucked in a long harsh breath.

I knew that sound. It was an adult getting ready to Deal With Me. I never in a zillion years thought I'd be relieved to hear it.

August didn't mess around. "Where's Reynard? He should be there. Put him on the line."

Oh wow. "Christophe? He's out on the porch having a cigarette and bonding with my friends." *In other words, Graves is keeping him occupied so I can make this little phone call.* "You know him?"

"He's only one of the best the Order has. Dru, you have to get *out* of there. Tell Christophe it's a red zone and you *have* to be gotten out of there."

I'd never heard August sound frightened before. "Because of Sergej?" The name stung my tongue, and I wondered if it was because of the touch or because I knew it was a sucker.

It was the first sucker's name I'd ever known. Some people who know about the Real World won't say them. They'll use initials or code words.

August almost choked. "Goddammit, Dru, this is serious business. Get Reynard and *put him on the line*."

Finally, someone was going to deal with this. An *adult*. A real adult. "Fine, you don't have to yell. Hang on." I dropped the phone on the counter and stamped down the hall to the front door, jerked it open.

Graves's head swung around—he had a cigarette halfway to his mouth and looked pale under his perpetual tan. He was wearing *my* gloves, though they were a little too small for him, and the edge of his long black coat flapped as the wind cut across the porch, rattling the bits of dead plants that hadn't been iced down. His hair was a wind-lifted mess, but Christophe, calm and immaculate, wore the same sweater and jeans. He stood near the hole in the porch railing, his head up as if he was testing the wind. Blond highlights streaked through his hair again, and they almost seemed to move.

The cold cut right through me, and I wondered if he could teach me how to walk around in the middle of it so easily. "August wants to talk to you." It was like carrying messages for Dad, and I didn't have to name the feeling swelling behind my heart.

It was relief, getting stronger with every second. Here was someone more experienced than I was, even if he was my age. Just what I'd wanted, right? Someone who could tell me what to do now that the lines that kept my life on track had vanished. Between August and this guy, things would get Under Control. It would be Handled. It would be Dealt With.

Chris gave me an odd look as he passed, his blue eyes darkening and apple spice drifting in his wake, and I shivered. Graves pitched his butt out into the snow, the glow of the cherry vanishing in a gray glare caught between cloud-hazed sky and white-shrouded ground. "He checks out?"

I nodded. Something dry and hot caught in my throat. "Yeah, he checks out all right. Come in, it's freezing."

Graves pushed past me, and I glanced out over the street. It was so quiet, a blanket of white over everything. The snow had come down hard and pebbled, a moaning wind flinging it everywhere, and the radio said ice was coming. The morning had dawned clear and sunny, but now the sky was overcast and lowering, striations of darker cloud like ink just dropped into water billowing under the higher cloud-cover.

Huh. I stepped out onto the porch, cupping my elbows in my palms. Hugging myself. It was dead quiet except for the uneasy sound of air moving, the porch posts and the corner of the house like a ship's prow, slicing the waves and producing a low hum of torn air.

We could have been on the moon, I realized. The house set away from the other houses like that one kid at school who's always dressed just a little bit wrong.

No wonder nobody'd come to greet us when we moved in, or heard the gunshots and screaming.

The street was an evenly frosted expanse of white. The two driveways that didn't lead into a garage had car-sized lumps of unbroken snow, the paint jobs peeping out from underneath—the blue minivan at the corner, the green, wallowing Ford across the street. And in front of the garages were wide, pristine ribbons of snow leading down to the street.

Why doesn't this feel right? I had to look a little harder before the assumptions I made started crumbling and the wrong note in the orchestra jangled hard enough for me to catch it.

No tire tracks. There wasn't a single break in the snow. The street looked as deserted as a Western town right before the bad guy rides in for the ultimate battle.

The sunlight dimmed, and a chill fiercer than the wind walked down my back. I was shivering, though I didn't feel it, and Graves's curly head popped out of the doorway. "What the hell are you doing, trying to freeze to death? You're not even wearing a coat."

I took my time, watching the street. Nothing felt hinky at all.

It just felt quiet. Empty.

Dead.

The snow must've cleared up sometime this morning when the sun rose, because we were all up having our hot chocolate and funny snakes with wings before dawn, and it was coming down hard then. What, everyone just decided to stay home today? Maybe. But. . .

The last piece of the puzzle slotted into place as Graves made a spitting sound of annoyance. "What the hell? Dru?"

I stepped back, shifting my weight uneasily, as if the porch might decide to fall apart at any second. "The porch lights." I sounded queer even to myself. "They're all on, and it's the middle of the day." *It's eleven, and it gets dark early this time of year. Real dark, real early.*

"Yeah," he said. "Christophe said that, too. What are you—"

"We have to go." My teeth chopped the words into little bits, and I made it inside, pushing him down the hall and sweeping the door shut. Warmth closed around me. I locked the deadbolts and leaned against the door. *How long until sundown? I don't know, have to check.* "Pack your stuff, okay? And help me with the ammo boxes, and—"

"Dru?" Christophe, from the kitchen. I didn't know him at all, but I knew that tone.

The *Oh shit there is serious trouble, honey, pack everything up again and let's get movin'* tone. He appeared at the end of the hall, his sharp face suddenly graven with frowning lines that made him look a lot older.

"I know," I said. "I've got to get the ammo packed." He halted, regarding me, and I swallowed crow and a few lumps of my pride, too. "Will you . . . I mean, would you help us get the truck loaded?"

I had to keep leaning against the door because my knees were deciding again that they weren't knees, they were actually noodles. Fully cooked noodles at that. And what I was really asking was something more like, *Will you help me? Please?*

Christophe's blue, blue eyes flicked to Graves, and I was suddenly positive he was going to say, *Sure I can, but we can't take him. He'll drag us down.*

Oh, Christ. What was I going to do if he said that? Graves tensed, a movement I could feel even though all the starch had gone out of me, as Gran would have said. And I reached over, grabbed Goth Boy's thin shoulder, and dug my fingers in.

Dad would never have left me behind. Not willingly. I was damned if I would leave someone else in the dust.

He bought me a cheeseburger. It was a ludicrous, laughable thought. But it was just the surface over a truckload of other things. I hadn't heard a single word of complaint from Graves, not even over getting bit or having a gun held to his head. He'd done the best he could to help me, and that was something strangers rarely ever do. I was shipwrecked, and he'd been the only thing I could hang on to.

And he hadn't let me down. Not once.

He was all I had. I wasn't going to leave him here.

Christophe's eyes fastened on my hand. He really did look old before his face smoothed out and he nodded, as if finishing a long conversation with himself. His shoulders went back and his chin came up. "You probably have a system," he said, folding his arms. "What goes in first?"

"My bed—the mattresses. Everything else gets folded up and—" I stopped dead, as the next problem rose up and crashed into me.

"Where are we going?"

"Don't worry." Christophe dropped his hands. "I'll handle that. Start your packing, Dru. You, wulf-boy. Come with me."

***

What does it say about your life when two hours of three teenagers working folds all of it up in the back of a Chevy half-ton's camper?

I put Mom's cookie jar in the top of the bathroom box and bit the packing tape, tore it deftly, and taped it down. "This one's important," I told Graves. "Pack the blankets around it." *Next to the fireproof box. The one with the ashes in it. God, Daddy, I wish you were here.*

If wishes were fishes, even beggars would eat. Gran was fond of that saying, too.

"Got it." Graves tramped out of the kitchen and toed open the door to the garage. Christophe had manhandled the garage door open, metal squealing in protest—the broken spring rubbing against itself with a sound like a lost tortured soul.

Well, maybe not *exactly* like that, but pretty damn close. Dad and I had both tried to get the garage open, knowing it was going to get cold, but in the end it was a lost cause.

But not, I guess, for a half-sucker. *Djamphir.*

Would I be as strong as that once I did that thing Christophe was talking about? Blooming? Would I smell like a bakery item? Or was that just him? Did he use pie filling for cologne?

But Mom had only smelled of fresh perfume and goodness.

Mom.

Too many questions. Not enough time to answer any of them.

"I *know*," Christophe said into the phone. "Just send a pickup;

I'll get her to the rendezvous. Don't worry about that." A long pause while someone yakked on the other end. It sounded dire, especially with the way the wind was moaning a counterpoint; he'd been on the phone for ten minutes while I finished the last boxes and Graves carried them out to the truck.

He laughed, a sound twice as bitter as Graves's little unamused bark. "Do you have to repeat yourself? She's no good to us dead, and I'm the one who found her." Another pause. "They can court-martial me later. Right now I need a pickup. I don't care what the weather report— All right. Fine. *Ciao*." He hung up, stared at the phone for a few moments, and turned sharply on his heel.

I was still on my knees, a roll of packing tape in my hands, watching him.

He took two steps to the sink, peered out the window. Eerie yellow-gray light slid through, touched his hair, and made the highlights livid. "Daylight's going to fail before we're out of town."

I could only see a slice of sky through the window, cut off by an overhang and icicle-festooned gutters. It looked like the thunderstorm weather I'd seen a million times, only without the gasping-thick humidity you get below the Mason-Dixon. "It's only—"

"Do you think this is natural weather, even for here?" He shrugged. "I should have made contact earlier. I was banking on being able to distract him. And I was banking on Sergej being certain your father wouldn't be stupid enough to bring you here."

You just shut up about my father. "Dad wasn't stupid." It came out a lot wearier and less sharp than I thought it would. "He had reasons for everything."

"I don't suppose you'd know how good those reasons were, would you? Never mind." He waved his hand as if brushing away a fly. "We've got to get you out of here. I've got an extraction point.

They'll dock me for it later." A tight, feral smile pulled up the corners of his lips, his blue eyes burning, and I watched an ink stain of sleek darkness slide through his hair and vanish, the highlights popping out like shafts of sun on a faraway horizon. "But bringing in a *svetocha* might balance that out." He shrugged. "I'll drive."

Oh you will, will you? "Do you have your license?" *I don't know if I like the idea of you driving Dad's truck. Or if I like how I'm suddenly some sort of good grade for you.*

"What are you, a cop?" He held out his hand, and I automatically went to give him the packing tape.

Instead, Christophe's fingers closed around my wrist, warm and hard. His eyes met mine, and I didn't know what to think about what I saw burning in their depths. His smell *shifted*, somehow. Like the wind veering and bringing you a breath of honeysuckle on a summer's day.

I stared up at him.

The garage door opened and Graves hopped in. "It's getting colder," he announced. "And I've got the last boxes in. Have to hand it to you, Dru, it's packed tighter than Bletch's . . ." The words died.

Christophe pulled. I came up in a rush—he was *strong*. Not regular wiry-strong, or even as thoughtlessly twitchy-strong as Graves had been with the werwulf imprint burning in him. He pulled me up as if I was a piece of paper, and the only thing scarier than the strength was the sense of restraint, like he could crush my wrist if he chose to. I ended up too close to him, and he pulled again, as if he wanted me even closer.

I stepped away and twisted my hand, breaking toward his thumb. That's the weakest part of any grip. My shoulder protested, and so did my back. I was going to have to find some aspirin or something.

He did let me go—but I wasn't sure, suddenly, that I could have pulled away if he hadn't let me.

He wasn't that strong before. Or was he, and just not showing it?

Graves stood stock-still, watching us both.

"Keys, Dru." Christophe's teeth gleamed in the weird stormlight, one of his wide feral smiles. "The sun's fading, and if I can feel it, we can bet Sergej can too."

I struggled with this, briefly. I drove when Dad got tired, so I knew the truck better than anyone else right now. I knew how it shimmied when it hit a certain number of miles per hour and how to tap the brakes in snow; I knew how it was likely to wriggle its butt when it was packed to the gills and a whole host of other little things. I also *really* didn't like the idea of handing over my keys to this kid, no matter how much August vouched for him.

But August *had*. And I'd wanted someone to take care of me, hadn't I?

I just hadn't thought it would be some kid my own age, no matter how mature he seemed. If this was the "best" the Order had . . .

And I didn't trust him enough. He was just too . . . *dangerous*. "Where are we going?" I finally said.

"The extraction point's in the southeast section of town. Burke and 72nd. If you'd have come down there when I invited you, before Sergej knew for certain you even existed, I could have gotten you out of town and safe in the Schola in a trice." Another easy shrug. "But we have to work with what we've got, now. Give me the keys, Dru."

My bag lay on the counter. I dug in it for a moment, and my keychain jangled as I finally fished it out. "It handles weird when it's loaded. I should drive."

"Dru." Christophe's tone was icy. "If you want to get out of this alive, you'd best do as I say."

Well, gee, when you put it like that . . .

"Wait a second." Graves took two long swinging steps forward. His hair all but snapped and crackled with electricity. "She's driven the thing before, all the way across town in a whiteout. And it's *her* truck."

"I didn't ask you to yap, dog-boy." Christophe made a sudden swift movement, but I saw him coming and yanked the keys back.

It was a close thing—his fingers grazed mine and I skipped nervously to the side, clearing the breakfast bar and dragging my bag with me. It fell, the strap fetching up against my free hand, and everything inside it shifted. That put me between the two of them, and right in the cold draft from the garage.

Get the situation under control, Dru. "Let's get this straight." I had to clear my throat, because the look on Christophe's face—eyebrows drawn together a fraction, eyes burning, mouth in a tight line with no hint of a smile—made him look twice as dangerous.

And, I had to admit, very pretty, especially with his hair shifting back and forth. That smell of his should have been ludicrous, but it just made me hungry.

I wet my lips with my tongue, a quick nervous flick. "It's *my* truck, *I'll* drive. You'll stop making nasty comments to my friend. We'll all get along until we get out of town, and when we do that you can go back to your Order and Graves and I will be on our way." The wind shifted again outside, its moan veering toward a crescendo. The yellow-green light made everything look bruised, and a queer ringing under the sound of the wind threatened to fill my ears.

I tasted wax oranges, and my vision wavered for a bare half-second.

Not now, dammit. This is important. I pushed it aside and kept my gaze locked with Christophe's, daring him.

Once, in this little podunk outside St. Petersburg, we'd run across a huge beast of a dog guarding a place we *really needed* to get into. Dad didn't have the touch, but he showed me something else that day. He called it "starin' down, before the *throwin'* down, honey." It meant just looking at the thing in your way as if it was no bigger than a pea, making up your mind that it wasn't going to scare you or move you.

Dogs can smell fear, and sometimes people—or things from the Real World—are the same way. But ninety-nine times out of a hundred, a dog can also smell when you're the alpha. It takes the same kind of flat look and decision to be fearless as facing down a bunch of jocks bent on harassing someone.

Shoulders square. Heart thumping, but not too hard. Eyes glazed with dust and buzzing with what I hoped was power. I gave him the look I'd practiced in the mirror so many times, and pretended I was Dad, grinning easily in a bar frequented by the Real World, hands loose and easy, one of them resting on a gun butt and the other just touching a shot glass, while I sipped at a Coke and pretended not to notice.

It should have been Dad there. He would have sorted Christophe right out.

"Where do you think you're going to go that Sergej can't find you?" He made another grab for the keys, but the world slowed down and I was quicker again—just by a fraction, but still. Graves sucked in a breath and I skipped backward again, hoping he had the sense to move.

"I'm not so sure he's the problem, Chris." I ducked through my bag's strap and backed up again. Another few steps would get me to the door to the garage, and if I took my eyes off him I wasn't so sure he would stay put, either.

There were a whole lot of things I wasn't sure of anymore.

The *djamphir*'s hand made another swift move; my eyes darted instinctively, and things got very confused. I heard a snarl and a clatter, my feet shot out from under me, and the keys were ripped out of my hand. Something very warm and hard clamped around my throat, and Graves let out a high, yipping yell. Glass shattered.

Christophe's hand tightened just a little, and I choked, staring up at his three-quarter profile as he looked toward the other window, the one that looked at the bit of greenbelt running at an angle beside the house.

The window he'd just thrown Graves against. Right over the spindly little kitchen table that had been here when we moved in.

He looked down at me, fangs sliding beneath his upper lip, his eyes burning. The highlights had bled out of his hair, slicking it back against his head, and his eyes were actually *glowing* in the bruised, ugly light slanting through the kitchen.

"I'm being patient," he hissed, the *t*'s lisping slightly because of the fangs. "I'll get you and your pet through this alive, but you have to do *what I say*. Got me?"

How did he do that? And the other thought, so loud I could have sworn I said it out loud. *Could he teach me that?*

"Sonofa*bitch*," Graves growled, and the obscenity shaded into a low sound that rattled broken glass as cold wind spilled into the room, laden with the flat iron tang of snow and violence. "Dru? *Dru?*"

He didn't even sound human, though it was recognizably my name.

"As soon as the sun fails out here, all your neighbors will wake up." Christophe's fingers weren't cutting off my air, but there wasn't any space to wriggle, either. "I only wounded the dreamstealer; it probably crept through every window on the block and laid eggs in their sleeping bodies before dawn rose. When those young hatch, they'll be hungry, and here you are. Such a nice little morsel." He cocked his head slightly. "On the good side, Sergej probably doesn't know you're alive, but he's suspecting, since his expensive little assassin didn't come back, and as soon as the sun fails he'll— *Stay* where you are, dog-boy!" He lifted his free hand and pointed, probably at Graves. The growling subsided a little, but it was the sound of a wolf getting ready to spring, not a teenage kid who had just been thrown into a window. "Are you going to behave, little bird?"

I might have even agreed with him, at least long enough to get his hands off my throat, but the wind rose to a shriek and I realized two things.

The light was really bleeding away fast, no longer bruised but dying, my ears popping under a sudden shift in air pressure.

And the growling wasn't just coming from Graves.

The werwulf barreled through the door like a freight train and hit Christophe squarely in the chest.

There was a horrible crushing half-second as his fingers tightened on my windpipe before they were ripped away. I only found out I was screaming after I'd scrambled backward on palms and sneakered feet like an enthusiastic crab-walker at a drunken frat party, and spilled down the two steps onto chill garage concrete. I barked my elbow a good one on the doorframe, didn't care, hit so hard my teeth clicked together and I almost lost a piece of my tongue.

Another furry leaping shape sailed over me, melting and reforming as it flew, and I flinched, running out of breath and hitching in more to scream again.

"*DRU!*" someone yelled, and Graves leaped out the door, narrowly missing landing on me by twisting in midair, with a kind of breathtaking, unthinking grace. He had something glittering in his right hand—my keychain, I realized, just as he skidded to a stop and the noise from inside the house began to crash instead of just roar. Wood splintered, something thrown against the wall hard enough to punch the drywall out toward me, splinters from the studs ramming through, and there was a massive wrecked yowl of pain.

I made it to my feet and hesitated for a split second, long enough to hear other crashes and howls. It sounded like more of them had arrived—shadows flitted across the open mouth of the garage, and the howling began.

If you've ever heard that sound, you don't need it described, but here goes. It's like a spiral of glass on the coldest night you've ever known, naked outside in the deep woods. Just *hearing* it is enough to give you nightmares about hunching near a fire and praying the wood holds out until dawn.

But what's even worse—what makes it *so* much worse—is how the howling drills into your head and starts pulling on deep, secret things in the brain.

The blind, hungry thing on four legs that lives in all of us.

I clapped my hands over my ears. Graves grabbed my arm, his fingers sinking in so hard it almost went numb, and hauled me toward the truck—still parked crosswise, but it had started up just fine earlier. Thank God for the engine-block heater.

Maybe I shouldn't have stopped to pack.

Another long lean bullet-streak of fur bolted into the garage, its padded feet slithering on smooth concrete starred with oil droplets from a car long since vanished. Graves let out a smothered yell. I clutched at him like a girl at a scary movie hanging onto her jock boyfriend, and the thing actually lifted its lip and snarled at us before plunging past.

"They're going to *kill* him!" I yelled.

"Better him than us!" Graves screamed back, and yanked me

toward the truck.

The sky had gone livid. Little pinpricks of ice were showering down, lifting and massing on random eddies and swirls as the wind, confused, keened and turned in circles. Graves yanked the driver's-side door open and clambered in, and I followed.

It's not right to leave him there. It wasn't. But Jesus, what else were we supposed to do? Because the werwulfen were even climbing on the *roof*, lean humanoid shapes running with fur, orange-yellow eyes like lamps. There were at least six of them, and one landed with a thump right in front of the truck and spread its lean, muscle-ropy arms, its black-gummed upper lip lifting and the thrum of its growl making the dashboard groan sharply.

Graves and I both screamed, high, oddly harmonized cries that would have been funny if the situation hadn't been so deadly serious.

I jammed the key in the ignition and twisted so hard I almost bent it. The Chevy roused, its engine sound pale compared to the thunder rumbling around my house.

OhGodohGod—I smacked the lever into reverse and didn't want to turn around to see where I was going. As if I could have anyway with the camper stuffed full of my life. The truck slewed and jolted back as the werwulf loped forward, tongue lolling and teeth gleaming. The cord for the engine-block heater popped free like a cable in a high wind.

Graves grabbed the dash as we plowed through the weak spot in the mountain of snowplow-piled ick. It was a lucky thing I hit right where I'd run into it coming home a few nights ago. The back end bore down, chains rasping, and I cut the wheel a little too hard. The truck groaned, shook itself like a dog coming out of water, and decided to settle.

I jammed it into "drive" and hesitated again. Christophe was in there. August had said he was all right, and—

"DRU!" Graves yelled, and I hit the gas. The chains bit and we lurched forward, but he was pointing out the windshield, as something long and sinuous, with thin membrane wings, landed on the hood and bonked itself a good one on the glass.

I screamed again, a short little bark because I'd lost all the air I ever breathed, and for one blinding second I remembered what had happened last night after my unconscious, sleepwalking body opened the window. How the thing's tongue had pressed against mine, cold and nauseatingly slimy, tasting of spice and dead rotten ooze, like a Thanksgiving candle gone horribly wrong.

Like Christophe's good smell, turned to badness.

Christophe, back in the house with the werwulfen. I was too busy to think about it.

I hit the windshield wipers. They smacked the mini-dreamstealer's small wet snout, and for good measure I pushed the lever back and hoped the washer fluid wasn't frozen. For some reason, it wasn't, and it gushed up, spraying the thing.

It screeched, the sound scraping against the inside of my brain, and was flung aside as the wind crested again, the truck's springs groaning as fingers of cold air pushed against its side. My breath came in short sharp puffs of white.

"Holy shit," Graves whispered. "It had babies."

That's what Christophe said. Christophe. "OhGod," I whispered back. "They're going to kill him."

"I thought he was going to kill *you*." His teeth were chattering. Tiny round pellets of ice caught in his curls sparkled in the dimness; I flicked the headlights on. The street unreeled, and I saw the stop sign on the corner. Houses clustered around us, each of them with their porch lights on. Windows broke with sweet, sharp tinkling sounds, darkness crawling out from behind the blinds and oozing over jagged glass. The wind was suddenly full of thin wriggling things, diaphanous wings ragged and beating frantically as they dove for the truck.

"Hold on—" Snow slipped and slid under the wheels. I gave it some more gas. We were achieving a scorching twenty miles an hour—faster than it sounds with the wind howling like a lost soul, a sky the color of rotten grapes overhead, and winged snakes with dull gummy poisoned fangs trying to splat themselves through the windows.

I'm glad we're not trying this in summer. The lunacy of the thought jerked a giggle out of me, a high-pitched, crazy little sound.

I goosed the gas pedal again; the stop sign was coming up fast, and I had to pick a direction.

Right or left?

Not much time. I racked my brain for geography, but the goddamn things wouldn't stop splatting against the glass so I could *think*. Right or left? *Rightorleftrightorleftrightorleft—*

I jerked the wheel to the left, tapped the brake a little, and we started to slide. There was a smaller pile of snow, a hillock where the plow had scraped the slightly bigger road and blocked off the entrance to this one, and I had a mad moment of wondering if someone would get a stern talking-to once the neighbors called in and complained about not being able to get off their own street.

One of the winged snakes hissed, a sound clearly audible through the windshield, and I suddenly knew without a doubt, the knowledge springing whole and complete and awful into my head, that there wouldn't be any irate calls from anyone on my street. Ever. All the pretty houses that turned the cold shoulder to my house were only full of death and broken bodies, the little winged snakes tearing at flesh as they hatched. The mama snake might be dead or dying somewhere, but the babies were very much alive—and they were hungry.

Dru. What have you done?

Graves yelled something, but I had my hands full. The truck, unhappy with what I was asking it to do, fishtailed to see if I was paying attention. I got it back on track, bumping through the piled-high drift and feeling the front end bounce a bit. The chains bit again, the back end wallowing, and we pulled through onto the sanded road, traction suddenly giving me a whole new set of problems.

There was no traffic. The winged things shriek-hissed, battering themselves against metal and glass—I wondered if their gummy little teeth would do any damage to a tire and had to let off the brake as a skid developed, steered *into* it, the wheel twisting like a live thing in my hands.

Good one, Dru! Dad's voice echoed in my head, as if he was sitting right next to me, teaching me what he called defensive driving. *Physics is a bitch, ennit!*

"It is." I barely recognized my own voice, high and breathy. The skid eased, and the crunching sound was the bodies of the winged snakes. They were falling rapidly now, flopping on the icy road surface before we rolled right over them, at a whopping twenty-five miles an hour now. "It certainly is."

"What?" Graves had both hands braced on the dash. The back was packed too solid to move much, but something rolled under the bench seat and I hoped it wasn't the first aid kit. *Or* the field box. All we needed now was random gunfire.

Oh, please God, no. Christophe. Why was I worrying about him? Why was it okay to leave him behind, but not okay to leave Graves?

That's not the right question, Dru. A slight hill sloped downward and the truck picked up speed, the horrible crunching noises reaching a peak as the wind moaned. I turned the wipers off—they weren't doing anything and the snakes were falling like dead flies now. Tiny pellets of ice hit the windshield and bounced away.

The right question is where the werwulfen came from, and why they're after Christophe. Work on that. But I had too much to deal with already.

Then, amazingly, a stoplight reared up ahead of us, and there was actual traffic on the cross-street. Not much, just a couple of cars, but the people inside probably didn't know what to make of the things festooning the truck as we rolled through the green light. I let out a choked sound, realizing my cheeks were wet, and the streets snapped into a recognizable pattern behind my eyes. I was taking the bus route to school, probably because it was familiar.

Holy shit. Goddamn.

"Graves." I had to cough to get my throat clear. The crunching under the wheels began to fade, serpent bodies running with thin black moisture as they melted off the car, decaying rapidly. "There's a city map in here somewhere. It was on the seat. Find it and navigate me."

"Yeah." His voice broke. He sniffed, and I realized we were both crying—me steadily and messily, and him as quietly as he could. "Sure. Right. Fantastic. Where the hell are we *going*?"

Oh Lord, I don't know. "Burke and 72nd, out near the suburbs."

"Okay. Sure. Why are we going there?" But he peeled his fingers off the dash and swiped at his eyes with his coat sleeve. I couldn't take my white-knuckled hands off the wheel, but I wanted to. I wanted to reach over and comfort him.

I wanted someone to comfort me, too. "Because we won't get out of town alive at this rate. Not on our own." *During the day. It's still supposed to be day.* The headlights cut a cone of brightness, and the streetlamps were on. The taste of oranges bloomed again in my mouth, terribly, wax coating my tongue. "That's where we'll find Christophe's backup and an extraction point. We need backup. Backup is good. Getting out of town is even better." *God. Christophe.* My throat hurt and my arm pulsed. I'd probably have finger marks all over me by tomorrow—if I saw tomorrow, that was.

"Great." Paper crackled. Graves let out a hoarse sound, and I pretended not to notice. My own sobs shook everything about me but my eyes and my hands, stiffly clutching the wheel as if it was a life preserver. "What the hell was that all about?"

"I don't know." *I can't even guess.*

CHAPTER 26

As if to add yet another layer of unreality, halfway there the sky lightened to depthless iron-gray in the space of a mile, as if we'd driven through some sort of porous wall and into normality again. Instead of little pinpricks of ice, dime-size snowflakes started whirling down, dancing to their own beat. The heater began to blow something other than freezer-draft, slowly warming up. My fingers were numb and I wished one of us had thought to throw a box of tissues in the car—wiping my nose was getting to be a necessity instead of just a nice thing to do.

Graves had finished crying and slumped against the seat, his hands loose and open in his lap. Driving actually wasn't so bad if we stuck to the main streets, everything scraped and sanded, slippery but passable. I deliberately didn't look at him.

I know that much about boys. They don't like it when you watch them cry. Even if you're still leaking yourself.

"What's going on?" he said, finally. "Why didn't they try to kill us? Those were the same things that bit me. Werwulf things."

But the one that bit you belonged to a sucker, and we don't know if these did. I nodded slightly, kept my eyes on the road. We still had three-quarters of a tank and the engine was warm now. "It was like they were driving us away." I coasted to a stop at a red light, my fingers gripping the wheel so hard they ached. My head was still ringing, full of the peculiar clarity that follows a crying fit. "We're going to get to the extraction point. Someone will be there. We'll have to tell them what happened to Christophe. And they'll be able to tell us what to do and get us out of here." I *hope*.

The light turned green. I checked—the cross-street was deserted. There was a coffee shop on the corner, warm yellow shining through its windows but nobody moving inside. Streetlights burned, even though it was daylight. The snow was beginning to pick up. Our tire tracks stretched black behind us. I eased down on the gas.

"This is weird," Graves said softly. "It's like we're the last people left on earth."

I could have done without that thought. But it wasn't like I hadn't been thinking it myself. "Is it usually busier around here?"

"Yeah. That's Marshall Street right there; it's *always* hopping. Maybe . . ."

"Maybe what?"

"Maybe we should stop there. Where I've got friends." He wiped at his face. "I don't trust whatever Christophe told you. Even if he checked out through your friend."

I weighed the options. My head hurt with all the thinking I was asking it to do, and the tears clotting up my throat and threatening my eyes weren't helping. "Anyone we find is just going to be in danger. We're going to *put* them in danger. I might not trust Chris, but I trust August. He wouldn't steer me wrong."

"So what were the werwulfs doing?

"Werwulfen," I corrected. *How the hell should I know?*

"Whatever. What were they *doing*? And those snake-things—"

"The snake-things were trying to get at us. But the werwulfen . . . I just don't know. Maybe they were after Christophe, but the one that bit you, he wasn't—I just don't know, Graves. I'm sorry." *I got you into this. I'm sorrier than you'll ever know.*

"I thought he was going to kill you." He stared out the windshield as I stole a corner-of-the-eye glance at him. "I wanted to tear his throat out."

I don't think he was going to kill me. But he certainly wasn't playing nice. Graves sounded like he was having a hard time with the idea of anyone killing anything—I knew exactly how that felt. So I decided to change the subject. "How did you get my keys?"

"He dropped them." Silence wrapped around us both. Empty streets in the middle of the day, not a soul to be seen—even wrapped up and picking their way along the sidewalks. "God, this is weird."

You bet it is. Can a sucker do this? Change the outside world? Is that possible? Or are people just feeling the bad outside and wanting to stay in? The tires crunched. Snow kept falling, getting thicker by the minute. "Dig under the seat. There're a few metal boxes. One's blue, that's first aid. The second one's red, you don't want that either. The one under me is gray, and it's got a gun. We want that one."

He waited for a few seconds. "I suppose that would be a good idea. I don't want to mess with it, though."

"Just get it out." I probably didn't want him messing with it either, if he wasn't used to firearms. "I'll handle the shooting, I guess. You just turn up the superhero."

He didn't find it at all funny. "I'm serious, Dru. I saw him hurting you, and I just—"

I know. "Did he hurt you?"

"Nah. I broke the window, though." A jagged, bitter little laugh. He fiddled with the seat belt, and I thought of telling him to buckle up. "I was really worried about that, too. Go figure. I saw him hurting you and it was like . . . something inside me woke up, and I wanted to kill him. Really kill him, not just like saying you want to kill someone. You know? Like I wasn't even myself anymore."

"Oh." What did you say to something like that? My heart gave a funny little skip. "I'm glad you're here. This would he horrible on my own."

I expected a flip answer and a flash of humor, but he just slumped further into the seat, bent down, and started digging underneath. "Yeah, well."

Well, you can't expect him to be very happy about this, Dru. My eyes flicked to the driver's-side mirror for a second, catching . . . something. I kept looking, but it was gone and didn't come back. Just a shadow. The ringing in my head wouldn't go away. My shoulder hurt, and my arm wasn't too happy either. "Are we close?"

"Turn south on 72nd; it's two streets up. Then just follow that until we hit the suburbs." He curled himself up to half-lay on the seat, peering underneath and digging for the field box. "How often does something like this happen to you?"

"Not very," I admitted. I swiped at my burning cheek with the back of my hand. Tears rose again. I pushed them down, wished I had a hankie or something. Dad always had a hankie. Most of them had his initials embroidered on them in Gran's neat, careful stitches. "More like never. Dad was always around."

"I'm sorry about your dad, Dru." He peered up awkwardly, his head almost in my lap. His eyes were very green, and since he wasn't a white boy, he missed out on the blotchy part of crying.

I attempted a half-smile, ended up with a weird grimace. "I'm sorry you got bit." I rubbed at my eyes again. The snow hissed under the tires, clumped on the windshield wipers.

"We're sure I'm not going to get all hairy like those other things, right?" He tried a smile that looked like it hurt and fished out the field box.

Another shadow flickered in the mirror. Was it nerves, or was there really something back there? I risked going a little faster. "Absolutely. Even Christophe said so, and it was in the *Ars Lupica*, too." *Dad paid good money for that book and never found a chance to use it. I wish he was here to see it useful now.*

I flinched. Dad. Christophe. Both gone. There had to have been at least a dozen werwulfen.

Why hadn't they attacked *us*?

Graves sat back up. "Jesus," he said quietly.

I heartily agreed. And the snow began to fall in rivers.

CHAPTER 27

Way out in suburbia, the streets had naked trees clutching at the sky, their cold limbs grasping at soft white ribbons and sometimes festooned with icicles. Some actually had Christmas lights up, though it wasn't even Thanksgiving yet. Or maybe they just hadn't taken them down from last year.

The streets were scraped and sanded out here too, but they were fast blurring under the onslaught of snow. 72nd Street had turned into McGill Road briefly, then jagged and become 72nd Avenue, narrowing, winding, and branching off like an artery getting further and further from the heart. The houses got a little bigger, the sidewalks broad and scraped clean. I saw flashes of fields, too—weird blank expanses of flatland, scarred only by the lines of ditches and more naked, shivering trees. The wind howled. Graves played with his half-empty pack of Winstons, glancing longingly at the window every now and again. If the wind wouldn't have torn a cigarette out of his hand, he could have had all the smokes he wanted. I might have even joined him, no matter how bad it smelled.

And, you know, if I could have forgotten the slithering, thumping sounds of the little winged snakes hitting the truck. I suspected that might make me nervous about rolling the windows down for a good long while.

The shadows kept flitting behind us. Whatever it was could have overtaken us if it was really serious about it. We were barely crawling, and I'd started to shake, hungry and sick from adrenaline all at once.

I would have given a lot for another cheeseburger just about then. Or a strawberry shake. Or anything, really. Even some stale granola.

But not apple pie. The thought made me feel even sicker.

"There's Compass Avenue." Graves shivered, though it was warm enough with the heater blasting. "Next comes Wendell Road, and then Burke. If the map's right."

I eased off the gas, ready for the truck to misbehave at any moment. The dashboard clock was still set to Florida time, an hour ahead. I was getting sick of this polar bear shit. "How do people live up here? This is insane."

"They dress up a lot. Do their hair. And drink. Beat their kids." Graves shifted nervously. "They beat their kids a *lot*." We rolled through two more intersections, then slowed to a creepy-crawl, the engine turning over smoothly, wipers muffled. "Why the hell are we coming out here again?"

"Because we won't make it out of town before dark on our own. It's already two in the afternoon." I peered at the sky, squinted out the windshield again.

"We could make it. I've got money. We could just get the hell out of here. We could take a bus if the truck won't—"

"A bus. Like we wouldn't get caught at the station waiting for the next one when the sun goes down. For God's sake, Graves, we need *help*." I wondered if I should tell him that I was seeing little darting things in the mirror. He didn't need that to worry about. "Huh."

We slowed down.

Burke and 72nd was actually a three-way intersection. Directly in front of us, where the two roads split to make a Y, a stone wall rose. There was nothing else around; the houses had petered out half a block ago and open space—weedy lots or fields, who could tell—ran away on both sides. Just over the wall on the right, a red-tiled roof peeked, little bits of color peeping out under the snow.

"Burke and 72nd. It's got to be that place." I goosed the gas, pointed us toward the right fork. "Jesus. Talk about conspicuous."

"I've never been out this way." Graves drummed his fingers on the door. "It smells bad."

Well, you're the one with the super nose now. "Bad how?"

"Rust again. And something rotting. Like a dumpster in summer."

I sniffed deeply but didn't smell anything. The ringing in my head was a constant; I was used to thinking through it now. I didn't taste anything other than hunger and the thin metal tang of exhaustion. My back hurt, my throat hurt, my arm wasn't too happy—I was just bad all over, and ready to hand over this whole problem to someone older and more experienced.

Why hadn't I just given the keys to Christophe? He might still be alive if I had.

"I wish I'd just given him the keys." My voice broke on the last word. I snuffled up another sob, pushed it down. It was time to stop being a whiner and focus on getting us out of town.

"I don't." Graves's fingers drummed, paused. "What are we going to do, drive up to the house and walk in, announce we're vampire hunters, and ask them pretty-please to—"

"We're going in to find whoever Christophe had coming to pick us up. If I'm valuable to them, they'll help us get out of town." *Then I'm going to sleep for a week, and after that . . .*

After that, what?

"What if they . . ." He didn't go any further, but I knew what he was thinking.

"Graves." I swallowed, tried to sound hard and sure. "We're leaving town *together*. Period. End of story. You got that?"

He didn't say anything else. I didn't dare look at him.

We crept along, snow now coming sideways and the truck's springs making little sounds as the wind tried to push us into the wall. In a little while there was a driveway—obviously recently cleared—and the truck struggled through the turn as if I wasn't controlling it. An ornate iron gate was open, swept back to either side, its curlicues heavily frosted with ice. In the middle of a vast expanse of circular driveway, a fountain lifted—some kind of shell shape with a big spike coming out of the middle. Drifts piled against the wall and the edges, but the driveway itself was clean.

The house was three stories of massive overdoneness, a pile of pseudo-adobe. Why anyone would build a hacienda up here among the Eskimos was beyond me.

The truck obediently turned, following the unrolling driveway. I eased it to a stop and let out a sigh. "Okay. Let's—"

"Holy shit." Graves was staring past my nose, out the driver's-side window. "Um, Dru?"

My neck protested when I turned my head. All of a sudden every bone and muscle I owned was tired, and I had to pee like nobody's business. Driving in a snowstorm is like pulling a sled; you work muscles you never knew you had.

The big black gate had shaken itself free and was closing, little driblets of snow falling off like flaking skin. Ice crackled, and the sky overhead was a sheet of painted aluminum. The gate latched itself with a muffled clang, and a fresh wave of cold wind rattled it, moaning through the metal gingerbread.

That's either very good or very bad. I peered up at the slice of the house I could see. Warm electric lights through every window, no shadow of movement, no sense of someone home.

It *couldn't* be empty.

"Dru?" Graves sounded very young. It occurred to me that as much as I wanted someone older and more experienced, he must want it twice as much. And I was all he had.

The weight settled on me, heavier than ever. "I guess we go in." *If this is Christophe's extraction point. It kind of makes sense, close to the edge of town and everything, but still . . .*

It felt hinky. Super extra hinky with a side of bad sauce.

The engine kept running along. I could probably take out the gate with this piece of heavy metal. But if I killed the truck, we'd be out in the snow with no way to escape.

This is where Christophe said. So why are you stalling? I put the car in park, eyed the front of the house again. The front door was a huge thing of wet black wood. *They certainly like everything super-sized out here. All hail Middle America.*

I made up my mind and reached for the field box. "Stay in here. I'm going to check it out."

"No way. Are you *crazy*?" Graves shook his head like he was dislodging a bad thought. "Don't leave me out *here*!"

"Look, if I don't come out, you drive the truck through those gates and get the hell out of here. I'll go inside and make sure it's safe. No reason for us both—" *To get killed,* I was about to say, because it was what Dad often said. "—to go in," I amended hastily, "because someone needs to stay out here and keep the truck running in case we need to leave in a hurry. I'm trained for this." *At least, I'm better trained than you are.* "I'll do it."

"Jesus." Graves stared at me. His eyes were very, very green. "You've got a death wish."

Right now I have a bathroom-and-sleep-somewhere-safe wish, kid. "No, I don't. I want to get out of this alive and I want to get *you* out of this alive. Look, just stay here and keep the motor running. You know how to drive?"

"Are you kidding?" The look he gave me qualified as shocked. "I ride the *bus*."

Oh yeah, this just keeps getting better. "Don't worry. It's a piece of cake." I opened the field box, checked the gun. The clicks of the clip sliding out and back in, the safety checked, were very loud in the snowy silence, the wind suddenly hushing to a damp not-sound.

"Oh yeah? What if the door's locked, Dru?"

I actually smiled. At least, the corners of my mouth pulled up. "Places like this are never locked," I said quietly, and unlocked my door.

As soon as I slammed the door shut the wind came back, random curls flying into my eyes, driving snow against my cheeks, white flakes sticking to them. I went around the front, not looking through the windshield—if I did, I would only see Graves looking pale and scared, and I didn't need that.

I was scared enough for both of us.

There were only three steps leading up to the door. Big concrete urns that might have held plants were now only mounded with snow.

There's nothing growing in here. It's all concrete. I shivered—it wasn't as cold as you'd think, but snow tickled me with little wet fingers, clinging to my eyelashes and soaking through my sneakers.

I touched the door, closed my hand around the knob. It turned easily, and I heard a soft, passionless sound—an owl's throaty *who? who?*

I looked back over my shoulder. No sign of Gran's owl, but the call came again, muffled like feathered wings. The truck kept running, smooth as silk. The door opened silently, snow blowing in past me.

Through the door, then, into a foyer floored with little pieces of varnished wood all smushed together and waxed to a high gloss. I stood shivering and looking at a flight of stairs going up, a chandelier dripping warm waxen light. The gun was a heavy weight pointed at the floor. I snicked the safety lever off and wished miserably that Dad was here.

How do you know he wasn't? a little voice said in the very back of my head, and a cool bath of dread began at the base of my skull, sliding down my back with soft wet flabby fingers.

I know, I told that horrible little voice. *I saw where he died, I think. He left the truck right outside, and he went down a hall in an abandoned warehouse. And someone was waiting for him.*

The lights were on, but it was cold in here. Cold as a crypt. I took another two steps into the foyer, saw a hallway, and the light changed imperceptibly.

I whirled. The door slid closed, the slight sound of its catch just like the sound of the safety clicking off. The taste of rust ran over my tongue in a river, followed by the wet rotten smell of oranges gone bad, fuzzy and leaking in a blind wet corner. The ringing got worse, filling my head with cotton wool.

Something glinted on the floor, past a little square of rounded darkness that my eyes refused to see properly for a moment.

Oh shit. My sneakers made small wet sounds. Little tracers of steam lifted off my skin, it was so cold. My breath made a cloud, vanishing as soon as I inhaled. I moved as if in a dream, or as if it was last night, something pulling my unresisting body forward. It hurt to bend myself over to pick up the familiar black leather billfold.

It was thick with cash, and I flipped it open, saw Dad's ID, him staring into the camera like he dared it to take a bad shot of him. The picture of Mom was gone, but the mark where my thumb rubbed the plastic every time was still there, like an old friend. I straightened, automatically stuffing the billfold in my pocket, and was compelled to step forward, looking at the other little thing, glittering patiently on the waxed floor.

It was silver, and as I bent my aching knees to take a look at it my body knew, chilling all over, gooseflesh prickling across my back and down my arms.

It was a heavy locket, almost as long as my thumb. Scrollwork on its front I knew better than my own name, even, and a silver chain, now broken, that I'd seen all my life. The scrollwork made a heart with a cross inside it, and on the back there would be little foreign symbols sketched, where they could rest against the skin.

I touched it with my index finger, letting out a clouded breath that ended on a short sound as if I'd been punched and lost all my air. My fist closed over it and I pushed myself up, dry-eyed.

And all of a sudden I knew something else. I wasn't alone in here.

Someone spoke from the hall beyond the foyer. It was a boy's voice, more tenor-sweet than Graves's and harsher than Christophe's, with the same queer space between words and sounds as the *djamphir*'s.

"Come into my parlor, said the spider." A light, happy giggle, as if someone was having a hell of a good time. "And obediently, she walks in and picks up the bait."

I raised my head. Strings of damp curling hair fell in my face.

There was a shape in the door to the hallway, a cloak of more-than-physical darkness clinging to it. I suddenly knew who had been on my front porch that night. He hadn't had an invitation, so my threshold was a barrier to him. But here I was, and here he was, and why had Christophe sent me *here*?

A cool bath of dread slid down my back.

"Sergej." I sounded normal, not terrified. As a matter of fact, I sounded pretty good.

He stepped into the wash of gold from the chandelier, and I understood why it was so cold. The cold was coming from him, breathing out from his poreless skin with its faint tint of swarthiness. And here was another shock.

He looked about eighteen—a little older than Graves, a little older than me. Broad-shouldered as if he worked out, and with a face chipped from an old coin—a long narrow nose, a chiseled mouth, a mess of artfully disheveled honey-brown curls. But his dark eyes were wrong. They were dusty, and far more adult than they should be. The closest I'd ever seen to eyes like that was on some city streets, where kids melted out of the shadows as cars cruised slowly past, their bodies young but something ancient shining from their faces. Kids who had seen a lot of things no kid should have to see, kids I shivered when I thought about always making me scoot closer to Dad on the truck's seat.

Only they were still human, those kids. And this thing wasn't. It looked young, and I suppose if you weren't in the habit of looking closely at things you'd just think he was lucky to have such great skin and killer lips.

If you looked any closer, the thing looking out of those dark sparkling eyes would leer at you. Right before it ate you alive.

He wore a thin black sweater and jeans, like Christophe. A pair of high-end black Nikes and a gold wristwatch too huge and ostentatious to be anything but real. Probably a Rolex. He looked like the Rolex type.

I stood there staring at him, my mouth fallen open a little. I heard something through the ringing in my head. A steady thumping, like a clock ticking against the head of a giant drum, echoing. Faster and faster, a sound that made me think of a small dark space, stuffed animals, and my own stale breathing as I listened before falling asleep. I'd been so tired.

I love you, baby. I love you so much. . . . We're going to play a game.

The knowledge rammed through me like a baseball bat swung by a player coming all the way up from his heels. That ticking beat was the sound of his heart. I was here in a huge pile of fake adobe with a snowstorm and Graves outside, and I was facing down a sucker all by my lonesome. A sucker who had turned my father into a zombie—and murdered my mother, back Before.

My left hand was still a fist around the locket. The pumping, thumping sound was very close, and the boy smiled at me. A very sweet smile, if you didn't mind looking at the needle-sharp fangs, much sharper and more grotesque than Christophe's. But white, so blinding white. And those eyes, like pools of mud just waiting to drag you down and fill your mouth and nose with cold, cold dirt Jell-O.

I heard something else, too. The muffled beating of wings.

He took a step forward. "Ripe," he said, the word contorted because of the way his teeth were now shaped. A trickle of something black slid down his chin, right below where the tip of one of his fangs scraped the perfect matte skin. "And coming so willingly to the slaughter. I've drunk from the veins of a thousand *djamphir*, but the sweetest are always the little birds, just before they flower." A low chuckle, like gas burping and bubbling up from oozing slime.

I raised the gun and his dark winged eyebrows flew up in mock astonishment. He looked just like a psychotic clown, and a red spark lit in the back of his weirdly shaped pupils. They were hourglass-shaped, darker slits against the black velvet of his irises, thin threads of black in the whites turning them gray. He looked almost blind.

The owl hooted nearby, the sound slicing sharp through a sudden howling outside, the door rattling behind me, and the sucker's eyes widened just a fraction before I squeezed the trigger and a neat half-dollar sized hole opened up in his forehead.

It was a perfect shot.

Good girl, Dru! I heard Dad cry, and a gout of thin blackness gushed down the sucker's face, his head snapping back like he'd just been kicked in the teeth. I heard someone screaming, thinly, and knew it was me.

Because his head jerked back down again, sharply, and he grinned at me through the mask of rotting black ichor, his teeth saw-edged except for the fangs. His entire body coiled, compressing itself. I knew he was going to jump me and knew I had no hope of getting out of the way. The blackness ate his eyes, turning them into singularity holes under the scrim of foulness, and he leaped, hanging in the air for a long moment as everything slowed down around me and the ringing in my ears turned to an agonized shriek.

The world stopped again, but only for a bare second. I dropped, one knee giving way and the gun fighting its way up through air gone clear and hard as a diamond. Pale feathers puffed as the owl swooped, razor claws raking the sucker's back, and it banked away, black goo dripping from its feet—and I knew it had missed, it hadn't hit where it wanted to, and as soon as the world snapped back up to speed the sucker was going to fall on me and bury its fangs in my neck, and I wouldn't feel a thing until it was too late.

Time popped hard, like a rubber band pulled back and let loose, careening across a classroom. A burst of warm air traveled across my skin, and there was a hideous wrenching sound.

The front door exploded inward. A streak of black and denim-blue leaped off the truck's hood, flung with sharp lances of broken, splintered wood. He flew like Superman and they collided like planets flung into each other.

Get out of the way! Dad's voice yelled in my ear, and I rolled, one fist full of the locket, the other weighted down with a loaded gun. Snow flew into the hole in the side of the house, the shattered door falling in bits and pieces. The headlights were on, and through the cracked windshield I could see Graves, his nose bleeding and his eyes running with green flame, clutching at the wheel like a life preserver. He must have bonked himself a good one when they hit.

Around the truck, flowing like a creek in spring, the lean long forms of werwulfen leaped. My gaze snapped back toward the roaring bloodlust, and I saw Christophe go down, red blood flying in a perfect arc before splashing onto a blank white wall.

That's what's wrong in here, I thought hazily. *No pictures. No furniture. Nothing living. It's an empty house.*

The sound was hideous. The wulfen were making that chilling glass-at-midnight noise again, and they flung themselves at the sucker like water running over rocks. The sucker was making a low inhuman growling, and Christophe . . .

He twisted to the side, avoiding Sergej's hand, suddenly freighted with claws that looked sharp enough to rip air. Two quick steps, Christophe's feet blurring, and he leaped, one boot cracking across the sucker's terrible-beautiful face. The kick was used to propel him *up* and *over*; it looked like he was on wires, landing lightly as a butterfly. His entire face was covered with blood, his sweater was sopping, but his eyes blazed winter-freeze blue and his lip lifted, snarling back at Sergej even as the wulfen descended.

It was the funniest thing. He *did* look like an angel, back from the dead. I choked on a sob, stared in wonderment.

The truck whined, chain-clad tires clattering, and heaved back. Thin light fell through the hole in the door, the walls on either side busted too. The engine died and Graves was scrabbling out of the truck. I was only barely aware of this, because the fight was still going on, and I was beginning to get the idea that it was more than a little one-sided.

And our side wasn't the winning one.

Sergej knocked down the wulfen like they were bowling pins and Christophe moved in again. He was shouting, but my ears were ringing too badly to hear it. He feinted, reversing to claw at the sucker's face as they closed, and I suddenly knew how the next few moments were going to play out. Christophe was slow and wounded, even though he was moving faster than anything human had a right to, and Sergej . . . He jerked a hand in a careless sweep and a wulf went flying, hitting the wall with a crunch of bones snapping and sliding down.

Cold air swarmed across my face, full of the smell of snow and coppery blood. Sergej spread his arms, inhaling as I did, a cloud of darkness crawling down from his eyes to bleed into his mouth, sliding down his throat in thin rivulets. The air popped and prickled with ice; the world slowed down again as Graves's hand closed around my arm and what he was shouting roared into my ears.

"*Come on, Dru, let's go!*"

My chest expanded, ribs popping as I took in the deepest breath of my life. Christophe crouched, fingers tented on the blood-slick floor, and his sides heaved. He looked very tired, and the blood coating him dripped, droplets hanging in the air as he gathered himself.

The wulfen didn't pause. They were still circling the sucker, clawing at him, but something invisible parried their strikes. The one who had hit the wall was just lying there, the fur running off him and the face—a young boy's face—rising out from under its sliding textures.

The ringing came again as I shook free of Graves's clutching fingers. My hands snapped out, hard, as if I was throwing a dodgeball, and something flinty and hot hit me in the stomach, boiling like water just after you throw macaroni in. The locket burned against my palm, silver scorching.

Gran's owl, glittering snowy white, arrowed over my head like a bullet, a streak of feathers and a cruel curved beak. Black claws extended, and this time it didn't miss. It caught Sergej right in the face, raking hard and sharp as the second hex I'd ever thrown in my life smashed into him with a sound like a huge Chinese gong I'd seen on a game show once. Glass broke, tinkling, the chandelier overhead veering drunkenly, lightbulbs popping. Christophe hit him at the same time, a leaping roundhouse kick that came all the way up from the floor and cracked against the sucker's jaw as the owl sheared away, its wings snapping once as it turned on a dime and shot away like a pinball.

"Come *on*!" Graves yelled, hauling me as the sucker flew backward. The wulfen followed, and the one knocked into the wall shook himself and leaped to his feet, the fur flowing back down over him, bones crackling as he changed once again.

I stared, my mouth hanging open like I was some sort of idiot.

"Get her *out* of here!" Christophe roared, and Graves pulled me along as a massive sound—like a pipe organ being smacked with the world's biggest feedback squeal and pumped through every amplifier, from every crappy garage band ever put together—tore the air into shivering bits.

I didn't resist as Graves dragged me. The gun was still in my hand, dangling, and I had locked my fingers outside the trigger guard the way Dad always told me to. Crashing sounds deeper in the house and high yapping howls from outside told me we weren't alone. Shadows filled the door, and Graves had to put up his arm, elbow out, like the prow of a ship. I crowded behind him, clinging to his waist with my free arm as the wulfen poured past. Their eyes flamed with yellow and their fur touched me, sandpaper-rasping, thin iron-gray winter light falling around us as the wulfen somehow twisted and ran like ink on wet paper. They poured past us, unlikely saviors, and I began to think we might have a chance.

It ended, my arm fell away from him, and Graves dragged me down the steps, his fingers digging into my arm right where I had a bruise. The pain jolted up through my neck, exploding in my head, and I found out my cheeks were wet. I was making little hitching sounds and my throat burned. Snow whirled down, blanketing the world. The wide expanse of driveway was starred with paw prints fast blurring under the onslaught. There would be no proof of them in a few minutes.

They didn't even touch us. And Christophe . . .

He was right. Dad and I were amateurs. There was no way we could have fought something like that.

And my mother . . .

Graves was swearing steadily, in a high breathy voice. He opened the driver's door and shoved me in, hopped up after me. It was still warm, and I collapsed against the passenger window, glass cold against my fevered forehead. I stuffed Mom's locket in my pocket, shoving it deep like a secret. My fingers were numb, and my palm burned.

"Jesus Christ," Graves said. "Are you okay?"

No. No way was I okay. I licked my lips with a dry tongue. "Christophe?" I whispered.

"Scared the hell out of me," he whispered back. "Showed up with those wulfen things; guess they're on his side after all. Told me to drive right through the wall, that you'd die if I didn't. Got up on the fucking hood and flew. Far out." His arm snaked over my shoulder. "Far fucking out. Dru?"

I peeled myself away from the nice cold glass and collapsed against him, burying my nose in the soft warm spot between his shoulder and his throat. He hugged me, resting his chin on my wet hair, and this time it was okay that we were both crying. We clung together like shipwreck survivors, and snow covered the cracked windshield with soft, deadly kisses.

CHAPTER 28

I had my face in Graves's narrow chest, and I was okay with that. He smelled good, and he was warm. The tears had trickled away, and his chin still rested on the top of my head. The windows were screened with breath-fog and with snow clinging to every surface it could find.

I could hear Graves's heart, too, ticking away. Just like a clock, but without the eerie meanness of the sucker's pulse. It was a clean sound, and it meant I wasn't alone. I hadn't been this close to anyone in a while.

Except him.

The door opened and a blast of chilly air scoured the inside of the truck cab. Someone climbed into the driver's side. It was a bit of a crowd, but the truck was big and the bench seat was long.

There was a long silence, a jingling sound as someone touched the keys in the ignition. Graves said nothing, so I figured it was okay.

And really, I didn't care. The whole world could have gone up in flames at that point and I wouldn't have given a rat's patootie.

A breath of apples touched the cold stillness. "Please tell me she's all right," Christophe finally said.

"She's okay." Graves didn't move. His chin settled more firmly atop my head and his arms tightened a fraction, that was all. "A bit beat up, but still breathing. She seems okay."

"Thank God." The *djamphir* let out a long, shaky breath. There was a scraping sound, and the engine turned over. The truck settled into running again, and the heater came on. Cool air poured through the vents. "Thank God again."

"What happens now?" Graves wanted to know. I did too, but I didn't feel like picking my head up and looking at either of them.

A slight sound of wet material as Christophe shrugged. "I take you out in the field and you get extracted. She'll go to the Schola. I'm going to vanish."

"Because there's a traitor," Graves supplied, and I was glad he was talking so I didn't have to.

"Yes." Christophe laughed, another bitter little sound. "This was my safe zone. There was no way Sergej could have known about this place, or that she would be coming here, unless someone in the Order told him. And someone in the Order sent the directive to set the wulfen on me back at her house. They didn't realize I wasn't *him*." He sighed. "If I *had* been him, you two would have been dead by the time they got there. Juan—the yellow-eyed wulf you met—is fit to be tied. He was just following orders, but the directive's disappeared. Someone's covering their tracks." He shifted a little on the seat. I wondered if he was still bleeding. "We've got to get her out of here."

"So you're sending us somewhere you know there's a traitor." Graves's chin dipped even further, resting harder on the top of my head.

I thought about all this, felt nothing but a faint weary surprise.

"I've got friends at the Schola; they'll watch over her just as I would. She'll be perfectly safe. And while she's there, she can help me find whoever's feeding information to Sergej. She's been drafted."

Graves tensed. "What if she doesn't want to?"

"Then you won't last a week out there on your own. If Ash doesn't find you, someone else will. The secret's out. If Sergej knows, *other* suckers know there's another *svetocha*. They'll hunt her down and rip her heart out." The windshield wipers flicked on. "Dru? Do you hear me? I'm sending you somewhere safe, and I'll be in touch."

"I think she hears you." Graves sighed. "What about her truck? And all her stuff?"

"I'll make sure they get to the Schola too. The important thing is to get her out of here before the sun goes down and Sergej can rise renewed. He's not dead, just driven into a dark hole and *very* angry."

"How are we going to—"

"Shut up." He didn't say it harshly or unkindly, but Graves did shut up. "Dru? You're listening."

Oh, God, leave me alone. But I raised my head, looked at the dash. There really was no option. Hair fell in my face, the curls slicked down with damp, behaving for once. "Yeah." It sounded like I had something caught in my throat. The word was just a husk of itself. "I heard."

"You were lucky. You ever put yourself in danger like that again and I'll make you regret it. Clear?"

He sounded just like Dad. The familiarity was a ragged spike in my chest. "Clear," I managed around it. My entire body ached, even my hair. I was wet and cold and the memory of the sucker's dead eyes and oddly wrong, melodious voice burrowed into my brain. It wouldn't let go.

That thing killed my father. Turned him into a zombie. And Mom . . . "My mother." The same flat, husky tone. Shock. Maybe I was in shock. I'd heard a lot about shock from Dad.

Silence crackled, but then Christophe took pity on me. Maybe. Or maybe he figured I had a right to know, and that I'd listen to him now.

When he spoke, his voice was husky too, whether with pain or with the cold I couldn't guess. "She was *svetocha*. Decided to give it all up, stop hunting, married a nice jarhead from the sticks and had a kid. But the *nosferatu* don't forget, and they don't stop playing the game because we pick up our marbles and go home. She got rusty and she got caught away from sanctuary, drawing a *nosferat* away from her home and her baby." He put the truck in gear. The windshield was clearing rapidly. "I'm . . . sorry."

"What else do you know?" I pulled away from Graves, his arm falling back down to his side. He slumped, looking acutely uncomfortable, a raccoon-mask of bruising beginning to puff up around his eyes. His nose was definitely broken.

"Go to the Schola and find out. They'll train you, show you how to do things you've only dreamed of. God knows you're so close to fully blooming, and once you do . . ." Christophe stared out the windshield, his profile as clean and severe as ever. His eyes were bright enough to glow even through the gray daylight. Drying blood coated his face, a trickle of fresh red sliding from a cut along his hairline. He was absolutely soaked in the stuff, but it didn't seem to matter to him. "And when you hear from me, I'll set you a challenge worthy of your talents. Like finding out who almost got you killed here."

The truck was still running like a dream. Good old American steel. Dad's billfold sat in my jacket pocket, a heavy, accusing lump.

Christophe measured off a space on the wheel between two

fingertips, looked intently at it. "So what about it, Dru? Be a good girl and go back to school?"

Why was he even asking? Like I had anywhere else to go. But there was another question. "What about Graves?"

The kid in question glanced at me. I couldn't tell if he was grateful or not. But I meant it. I wasn't going anywhere without him.

He really was all I had. That and a locket, and Dad's billfold, and a truck full of stuff.

A shadow crossed Christophe's face. The pause was just long enough for me to figure out what he thought of me even asking that question, and how hard he was weighing the likelihood that I might be difficult. Or just letting me know I didn't have anywhere else to go. "He can go with you. There are wulfen there, one or two other *loup-garou*. He'll be an aristocrat. They'll teach him too."

That's all right then. I nodded. My neck ached with the movement. "Then I'll go."

"Good." Christophe took his foot off the brake. "And for the record, next time I ask for the keys, hand them over."

I didn't think that merited a response. Graves scooched a little closer to me, and I didn't even think about it. I put my arms around him and hugged. I didn't care if it hurt my arm and my ribs and my neck and pretty much every other part of me, my heart most of all.

When you're wrecked, that's the only thing to do, right? Hold on to whatever you can.

Hold on *hard*.

* * *

We bounced out through the gingerbread gates, which were knocked inward, the wrought iron curling like it had been in a fire. Christophe turned left, tapped the gas, and we bumped out onto the road. The stone wall continued to our left, snow falling thick and fast. The sky, however, was brighter. You could finally tell there was sunlight up there, instead of just a flat pan of aluminum.

"It looks different now," I said, stupidly.

"Sergej." It was all Christophe needed to say, and I shut my mouth. What else could a sucker do?

Had Dad been chasing him all along? Because he'd killed Mom?

What else was I going to find out at this Schola? How to walk on snow without leaving a track, how to float while I fought?

Too bad I wouldn't learn what I really wanted to know. I had a sneaking feeling I wouldn't *ever* learn what I really wanted to know.

As soon as the stone wall ended to our left, he cut the wheel. I braced myself—there were ditches out here, and *deep* ones, running alongside the roads—but the truck merely bumped a little, up and over, and we were swimming through a wheel-deep sea of snow. The truck jounced and whined, and the cracked windshield was still a little foggy with all of us breathing hard.

We jolted and swam for a long time; then Christophe made a quick inquiring movement with his head. The blond highlights had slid back through his hair, little bits of them visible through clotted, drying blood. He didn't seem too bruised, though. "Ah." He let off the gas, and the truck rolled to a stop. "That should be transport now. Get out and wait for them."

"Here?" Graves didn't think much of the idea. "You're going to leave us in the middle of a snowstorm?"

Oh God, don't argue. I pulled at his coat. "Yeah. Sure." I reached for the door handle, pulled it. The door swung open with a protesting creak, and snow puffed in on an arctic breath. The temperature was dropping. My nose was full, but I didn't want to think of *what*. "Whatever you say, Christophe."

I didn't mean it to sound snarky. Really, I didn't.

And besides, I could hear what Christophe could. A thwopping, thudding sound I've heard on a lot of TV shows late at night.

"Dru." Christophe leaned over the seat, his mouth twisting down. I couldn't smell apple pie now, and part of me was vaguely glad about that. "I'm sorry. I—"

I didn't want to hear it. He hadn't told me everything, but I'd left him for dead. I guess we were about even, especially after he took on something so old and so powerful. Something that wanted to kill me.

Something that *would* have killed me.

What do you say when someone takes on a really badass, murdering sucker for you? There just aren't words for that.

"See you around, Chris." I pulled at Graves; he slid out behind me without protesting. It was like agony to stand upright again, my hamstrings and glutes singing in pain, my neck like a solid bar of crying steel. I grabbed my bag, too. Half my body groaned in protest when our feet sank into knee-high snow, and I slammed the truck door on whatever Christophe wanted to say next.

The truck idled, and the thopping sound got closer. It hovered into view—a red-and-white helicopter, the only blot of color in the wasteland around us. The stone wall was in the distance, swallowed up in white, and the snow was coming down so heavily even the city in the distance, or the houses a few blocks away, wasn't visible. Fierce cold swallowed my sneakers and stung my calves.

White spray fumed up as the helicopter hovered for about twenty seconds, its downdraft scraping snow away before it touched down. I gingerly ducked through my bag's strap, held up an arm to shield my eyes, and almost missed it when a hatch opened on the side and a figure leaped down, bent over, and scuttled for us.

The truck pulled away. I still had the gun in one hand. For the life of me I couldn't remember if I'd clicked the safety on. I looked down to check, found it *was* on, and the scuttling figure reached us.

It was a brown-eyed kid in an orange parka, a thatch of curly brown hair filling up with snow because he'd shoved the fleecy hood back. "Holy shit!" he yelled over the sound of the 'copter. "You'd better give me that."

Whatever you say. I handed the gun over. He checked it expertly and made it vanish under his parka. "Don't worry, I'll give it back. Come on, we don't have much time." He waved, way up over his head, at the retreating truck, and then reached out to grab my arm.

I twitched, Graves stiffened, and Orange Parka's hand stopped in midair. He turned it into a beckoning motion, like a mama duck trying to pull recalcitrant ducklings along.

"Sorry about that. We just got scrambled half an hour ago; I'm all excited. Come on." His voice broke, reedy against the onslaught of the helicopter's noise, and we trudged through the snow after him, bending almost double when he did. My hair tried to lift up and strangle me in the downdraft, and the hatch on the side of the 'copter opened again. There was a step. I put my foot on it, grabbed the handles, and Graves boosted me. I almost creamed my head a good one against the top of the hatch, and wondered if the rotor blades would grab my hair.

The space was cramped and full of weird angles, but it was warmer than outside. I wedged myself in a part-bench seat that looked like it was made for a third-grader, and Graves piled in, wedging his taller frame beside me. The pilot didn't even look at us, and the hands on the controls were bigger and thicker than mine, though they looked young and smooth-skinned.

Jesus, how many teenagers are doing this sort of thing? I strangled a tired, half-hysterical snort-giggle—my nose was still full. Graves reached over and grabbed my hand, and the curly-headed kid hopped in and closed the hatch. The noise dropped, but not by much. He reached up and whapped the pilot twice on the shoulder, and the helicopter immediately lifted, whining.

My stomach turned over, hard.

"Hi," the curly-headed kid called, dropping into the little jump seat behind the pilot's chair. His hands moved with ease and familiarity, buckling himself in like it was the most natural thing in the world. He had a snub nose, freckles, and a wide innocent grin. "I'm Cory. Welcome to the Order. You must be Dru Anderson. We're really excited to meet you."

I closed my eyes, collapsed against a porthole showing the white earth receding like a bad dream, and cried. Graves clutched at my hand, his palm sweating, and he didn't let go.

finis

Acknowledgements

If not for Richelle Mead (who talked to Jessica) and Jessica Rothenberg (who talked to Miriam) and Miriam Kriss (who talked to me), this book would have never grown past a small snippet that someday I'd maybe, probably, sort of get around to. Thanks to them, Dru's story got to come out.

Thanks are also due to Gates, who was my first and best reader. If this story rings true at all, it's because of his suggestions and not-so-gentle shoves.

There are also the usual suspects to thank: Mel Sanders, the other half of my writing brain, who listens to me obsess over every story; Christa Hickey and Sixten Zeiss for all the love and coffee; Maddy and Nicky for being my strength.

I could go on and on with the thanks, but I will content myself with thanking you, gentle Reader. Without you I am just muttering at the wind. Let me thank you the way we both like best, by telling you a story. . .

Read on for an extract from Book Two in the series,

BETRAYALS:

A STRANGE ANGEL NOVEL

published in November 2009 by Quercus

CHAPTER 1

A week later I was already in trouble.

The thing with a school full of boys being taught to kill suckers is that sparring gets to be a group event. It's like a fight in a regular school, only here the teachers don't intervene—or at least, they hadn't in any of the other four fights I'd seen since I arrived. You get a mob of onlookers, all shouting, and it can turn into a melee easily enough. Things don't stop until someone's bleeding. Or worse. Being able to heal just makes the boys more likely to hurt themselves.

I couldn't heal like they could yet, because I hadn't "bloomed." So much for being special. Here I was just as fragile as a civilian. But when you've spent most of your spare time learning how to make the best of what you have against things that go bump in the night, you don't give up easy.

I came up from the floor with a punch, getting my feet under me, and Irving grabbed my wrist. He used my momentum to whip me past him, but I'd expected that, hooked my other fingers, and got a handful of his face. That's what Dad would have called "dirty fightin'," something he approved of in a girl.

Hey, there are no rules in a *fight*. Thinking there are "rules" can get you killed. Dad drilled it into my head over and over again—you fight to win, to survive. Not to look good or give the other guy a chance.

Stop thinking about Dad, Dru. I had other problems.

Irving had bet he could best me in under two minutes. We were at ninety seconds and counting, and I was winning.

A bet like that doesn't go unchallenged. Not when your former Marine dad's been teaching you how to kick ass for years. Not when there's a hot boiling bubble of acid right behind your breastbone all the time. Not when you're practically alone in a school full of teenage boys.

Not just any teenage boys, either. Boys who can turn into fur rugs with bad attitudes at the drop of a hat. *Djamphir* boys who were born with the eerie stuttering speed of suckers, blurring through the slow stupid daytime world like a cheesy special effect at the drop of a hat. Boy *djamphir* don't have to wait to "bloom," oh no. They're stronger and faster from the start, and they only get better once their voices break and they "hit the drift" in puberty. Some of them hit it later, in their mid-twenties. But even before they hit the drift they're more than a match for any human.

I twisted, my sneakers digging into the frayed mats, and kicked back. That caught him in the knee, and I heard bones popping and loud growling. I hit the dirt, the mats scraping against my elbow because I was only in a tank top and jeans.

I'm not stupid. When you hear the distinctive noise of werwulfen changing into the furry shape that makes them almost impossible to kill, that's the reasonable thing to do.

Except Irving wasn't wulf. He was *djamphir*, and he was already committed to his leap. So where was the sound coming from?

I rolled over just in time to see Irving hanging in the air over me, pale face alight, golden highlights slipping through his chestnut curls as the aspect took him. The world slowed down, moving through syrup just long enough for me to scramble, the clear heavy weight of physicality straining against every muscle in my body. The *snap!* like a rubber band popped off expert fingers rang through my head as time speeded back up again and he rammed down into the mats a good three feet away from where I was now but exactly where I'd been. His knee hit too hard—without my face to cushion it—and he let out a short, sharp cry. The lines across his cheek from my fingernails flushed an angry red, and his hair stood up, writhing.

Now he wasn't just a teenage boy needing to save face in front of the crowd. Now he was *serious*. And we were at twenty seconds left.

Good.

I gained my feet in a rush and skipped back twice. The mass of onlookers exploded away, giving us enough room to move. Irving bounced up like he was full of helium, his curls moving just like in a shampoo commercial, and he threw himself across the intervening space with the weird blurring speed I wasn't even close to getting accustomed to.

The speed I couldn't use—yet.

So instinct took over. It wasn't precisely a bad instinct—brace yourself and punch the guy straight in the face. But Dad would have yelled at me for being stupid, since Irving was so ungodly fast, and straight-on force, like in karate, doesn't work so much for me. I'm built too thin and rangy. I don't even have moderately big breasticles. They just look like—well, never mind what they look like. At least they stay strapped down when I worm into a sports bra.

It doesn't quite suck being a girl, but sometimes it's close.

I *should* have grabbed Irving's arm, twisted, and slid him past me, using his own momentum to help him right into the stone wall across the room. Instead, I hit him. There was a crunch as my fist met his nose, and he collided with me like a freight train. We were heading for the wall, and the thought *this is going to hurt* flashed through me like electricity popping through a lightbulb filament.

And it would have, too, if something hadn't hit us both from the side, roaring. I got an elbow in the face and went tumbling, slapping the frayed, stained mats and wrenching my back a good one. I just lay there for a second, bells ringing inside my skull and the entire world seeming very far away.

It took a long time for me to blink, looking up at the arched, ribbed vault of the ceiling. This part of the complex had been a chapel, but now it was the armory and a sparring space unfolding with mats that had seen better days and the smell of healthy young boysweat. Underneath was the ghost of incense, and if it was daytime shafts of weak sunlight might slip between the bars and pierce dusty dimness.

During the day, though, the Schola sleeps. Right now it was just past midnight, and I was in deep shit.

"Dru?" Someone was bending over, shaking me. I tried to push them off, but my hands wouldn't quite work right. A dreamy sort of panic slid through me then, and I heaved back into my body with another elastic *snap*!

I was doing a lot of that lately. The air was full of rumbling and muttering, and there was a lot of shouting going on.

Oh God. This might've been a bad idea. I grabbed at a waiting pair of hands and hauled myself up. My head was ringing and my back hurt something awful.

"What the bloody blue *hell* is going on here?" The words sliced through the hubbub, except for that deep thrumming growl. I shook my head, a sliver of warm wetness threading down from my nose, and pushed between two *djamphir* boys—Clarence, his straight black bowl-cut damp with sweat and excitement, and Tor, his aspect on and thick streaks of buttery yellow sliding through his hair. Both of them were taller than me, but I shouldered them aside and found myself in the front row.

Graves had Irving down, his long, tanned-looking fingers closed on the *djamphir*'s throat. His eyes were chips of green flame, and the growl was so thick it blurred the air around him, the sound of a very pissed-off skinchanger. He probably couldn't talk, either—his jaw was subtly modified, accommodating fiercer, longer teeth. The crackle of bone had been *him*. He wouldn't get furry—he was *loup-garou*, not wulfen, only half-imprinted with the thing that made them able to shift—but he was pretty motivated to do some serious harm, and angry enough not to care about hurting someone.

It had happened three or four times by now. Twice back in the Dakotas, each time when we were in danger—or when he *thought* we were in danger, since Christophe had turned out to be on our side after all. And on the first evening I'd woken up at the Schola, I'd almost walked right into a shoving match between him and a *djamphir* in the cafeteria. From what I heard, the *djamphir* had asked him something about me, and Graves had turned on him. The result was shove, shove, growl, shove some more, yell, and me wading in to make them cut it out.

I didn't think I'd gotten the whole story, but Graves wouldn't talk about it. And now there was this.

"What the—" Dylan said again, elbowing his way through the throng.

I tuned him out and stepped forward. My right leg felt funny, and something dripped onto my upper lip. Three steps, four, my boots dragging a little against the mats. When I laid my hand on Graves's shoulder, the buzzing going through him felt like I was resting my hand on a juiced-up power transformer.

He actually snarled, his dyed-black hair curling, all but standing up and snapping with vitality. The sharp, strong bone structure of his face was subtly off-kilter now, nose less proud and cheekbones taking on the higher wolflike arc instead of the broadness of "human." Rich color flooded through his skin, making his perpetual tan deeper.

"Calm *down*," I managed. Only I sounded like Elmer Fudd, because I had a stuffed-up nose. My eyes were smarting and watering, too. "Jesus." It came out like *Jebus*, and I could have laughed. Except it wasn't funny.

"Everyone *shut up*." Dylan folded his arms, his leather jacket creaking. The noise went down. Here at the Schola, when a teacher talks, you *listen*. "And back up. Back up!"

Graves growled again, and Irving choked. He was turning an awfully deep shade of crimson. His fingers plucked weakly at Graves's hand, but with his arm twisted underneath him and an angry skinchanger on top of him, he couldn't get any leverage.

I hauled back on Graves's shoulder. A bolt of pain went down either side of my spine. "Come *on*, asshole. Calm down. This is getting ridiculous."

"Why didn't you wait for me?" Dylan addressed the air over my head. "I'm getting a little tired of—good God, girl, you're *bleeding*."

Graves let go of Irving and flowed to his feet, shaking me off. His lips were pulled back, teeth gleaming, his eyes awash with feral phosphorescence. I realized the wulfen had settled into a bloc behind him, and the tension running through them was palpable.

A few of them had gotten a little hairier, too. The tension made the wulf boys bulk up as well, shoulders straining at shirt seams. They don't take on werwulf form unless they really have to, but you can tell them from the *djamphir*. It's in the way they move—like they're shouldering fluidly through sunlit grass, instead of with the sharp hurtful grace of the half-*nosferat*.

The *djamphir* don't change, but the aspect ran through all of them—their hair moving and rippling with color changes, eyes glowing, and one or two of them showing little dimples of fangs touching their lower lips.

Boys. Jeez.

Dad had always taught me that wulfen and suckers didn't get along. I was beginning to think it was genetic. As far as I could figure, *djamphir* and wulfen were on the same side against the suckers. That was what the Order was about. But they sure as hell didn't seem to like each other much.

I pulled Graves back, and we only had a bit of a problem when I stepped in front of him and he tried to shove past me. I grabbed him by his used-to-be-bony shoulders and shook him. My fingers sank into muscle, and I didn't worry about hurting him. His head bobbled, but his gaze snapped down to mine and the snarl petered out.

I held his eyes for what seemed like a very long time. He blinked, and his shoulders relaxed a little. That's when I turned and found Dylan, arms crossed, standing over Irving with one winged black eyebrow raised and the rest of the *djamphir* utterly still behind them both. The *djamphir's* eyes gleamed and their fangs were out.

Oh, the testosterone. You could have cut it with a cafeteria spoon.

"We were sparring. I got stupid." I took another two steps, my heels landing harder than they should have and pain jarring up through my entire spine. "You all right?" This was directed at Irving, who was coughing, a deep rasping sound. But he didn't look almost purple now.

He glared at me, and I felt sorry. It had just been a little friendly workout, nothing big. I should have just rolled my eyes and let his posturing pass.

But instead, I'd gone off on him. And I was supposed to be so much more mature than boys at this age.

"Sorry, Irving." My back seized up again, and I breathed out through my mouth. The muttering growl behind me receded a little, and I put my hand down to help him up. "I should have grabbed you and helped you into that wall instead of trying to punch you in the nose. Go figure." It was really hard to sound conciliatory with something dripping and dribbling off my top lip. I was hoping it wasn't snot. That would be gross.

I sniffed, and the rest of the nosebleed let loose in a pattering gush.

Irving froze, staring up at me. His pupils shrank. A spatter of bright-red blood hung in the air, then splashed—

—right on his clothes, starring the mat next to him too.

"Shit," Dylan said, and leapt on him. "*Get her out of here!*"

Hands grabbed me, hot against the bare skin of my upper arms. I was dragged backward, and the world threatened to turn over without me attached to it. The ringing inside my head got worse, the sound of owl wings brushing the inside of my skull in frantic bursts. The wulfen hauled me out, and I heard Irving screaming as Dylan held him down, the bloodhunger turning his voice into a harpy's shriek.

Yeah. Just another night at the Schōla. The fight doesn't stop until there's blood on the floor.

But when the blood is mine, it can send the boy *djamphir* a little crazy. It's something about me being *svetocha*. Super-happy stuff in my blood even before I "bloom," something that reaches down and wakes up the crazy in anyone with a touch of *nosferat*.

After the blooming hit, I'd have my own superhuman strength and speed. And that super-happy stuff in my blood would make me toxic to suckers just like Raid is toxic to insects.

But now it just made me vulnerable. I smelled like a really nice snack.

Dylan had been drilling it into my head for the whole week now, on and on, that I couldn't spar with the *djamphir* students. They couldn't control the bloodhunger very well, I could get seriously hurt, yadda yadda.

Christophe had never told me about that.

There were a lot of things he hadn't told me.

The wulfen dragged me out into the hall, and the rushing noise inside my head got bigger. I think I probably passed out. At least, the world got really faraway and dim, and the only thing that mattered was hearing Graves. He could talk now that the rage had passed, and he was saying the same thing over and over again, a catch in his voice right before my name.

"It's okay, Dru. I promise it's okay."

He didn't sound like he believed it either.